Gabriel McKenna is living the dream. A rising country music star he's no stranger to fame, money, or beautiful women. Despite his bad boy image, he's also got a heart of gold, and when his ten-year-old brother is orphaned, he wants to take him under his wing. But the judge on the case is less than impressed by Gabe's reputation and awards custody to the grandfather Gabe knows firsthand is abusive.

Michaela Finn is no stranger to heartache. Years ago she was engaged to Gabe McKenna, but two days before their wedding he ran off to Nashville with a female talent scout. Now Gabe is back in her life with an insane plan. Marry him, so he can get custody of his younger brother. Michaela can't bear to think of any child being hurt, but she's just not sure her heart can carry a happy tune when Gabe is playing lead…

# Books by Sara Walter Ellwood

*Colton Gamblers Series*
Gambling On A Secret, Book One
Gambling On A Heart, Book Two
Gambling On A Dream, Book Three

*Singing to the Heart*
Heartstrings
Heartsong

Published by Kensington Publishing Corporation

# Heartsong

*A Singing to the Heart Novel*

## Sara Walter Ellwood

**LYRICAL PRESS**
Kensington Publishing Corp.
www.kensingtonbooks.com

Lyrical Press books are published by
Kensington Publishing Corp. 119 West 40th Street New York, NY 10018

Special book excerpts or customized printings can also be created to fit specific needs. For details, write or phone the office of the Kensington Special Sales Manager:
Kensington Publishing Corp.
119 West 40th Street
New York, NY 10018
Attn. Special Sales Department. Phone: 1-800-221-2647.

Kensington and the K logo Reg. U.S. Pat. & TM Off.
Lyrical Press and the L logo are trademarks of Kensington Publishing Corp.

First Electronic Edition: January 2016
eISBN-13: 978-1-60183-492-8
eISBN-10: 1-60183-492-6

First Print Edition: January 2016
ISBN-13: 978-1-60183-493-5
ISBN-10: 1-60183-493-4

Printed in the United States of America

*To my readers…*

# Chapter 1

Before Gabe's stage crew set off the final pyrotechnics, the crowd was cheering. The energy from sixty thousand fans hit Gabe McKenna, lifting him higher than any drug or drink ever could. Hell, this might've been better than sex.

Almost.

Gabe belted out the last words of his first number-one song and finished with a flourish on his electric guitar.

He bowed low, winked, and grinned at the hyperventilating, screaming girls in the front row. A redhead tossed him her panties. They landed on the stage by his feet along with other intimate garments, teddy bears, flowers, and scraps of paper with everything from *Will you marry me?* to phone numbers on them. He bounced back from the edge of the stage, his arm held high as he waved his tan Stetson in a farewell to another sold-out sports arena.

The tabloids called him "Country's Rock Star," and on nights like this, he believed it.

With one more look at his adoring fans, Gabe headed backstage. He handed his guitar to a crew member, while another, walking beside him, removed his wireless microphone and sound transmitter. After taking out his earpieces, he also handed them to the guy. His road band came off the stage behind him, and several of the members slapped him on his back, encouraging him to hurry. The party couldn't begin until he got there.

His manager, Gary Russell, rushed over to him with a huge grin on his pointed, bony face. "By God, Gabe, if you keep up this momentum, you'll own the *CMAs* in November."

Gabe took the bottle of water and towel the older man offered him. He wiped the sweat from his face and chugged half of the water. Performing in the Midwest was hot business in early September.

"That's the plan. I really want to be the next Entertainer of the Year." He grinned at the lanky man in poor-fitting jeans and a black T-shirt. "Male Vocalist"--Gabe slanted his glance toward his manager--"and Song, Single, and Video of the Year wouldn't upset me either."

Gary laughed and took the towel from Gabe. "Hell, you might just be the darling of them all: the *CMT*s, *CMA*s, and *ACM*s. Maybe even the Grammys."

"Wouldn't mind having another one of those golden record players in my trophy cabinet." But the competition for the Grammys was tough; beating his best friend, Seth Kendall, would be hard.

"I have to admit, it's been a good year for me too." Gary laughed again.

Gabe didn't doubt the statement. Gary not only managed him but also Seth Kendall and his teenage daughter. Emily Kendall was burning up both the country and pop charts with her first few singles.

They turned down another hall. The noise from the crowd disbanding wasn't as deafening down here. "You get the Billboard ranking of my album yet?"

Several fans and winners of local radio station contests gathered in the green room for a chance to meet him. He and Gary paused at the door. Two security guards waited to ensure no problems at the meet-and-greet.

Gary's smile broadened, splitting his narrow face and nearly taking in his ears. "*One Night Rodeo* landed squarely in the top spot on the country and number two on the pop charts with over three hundred thousand copies sold the first week out. If you would've sold a few hundred more you would've unseated Emily Kendall's reign on the pop chart."

"Yes!" Gabe punched the air. He would have liked to hit number one on the pop chart, but he wasn't a pop singer. His fans were as country as his Stetson and cowboy boots. It amazed him he crossed over at all, but as Gary kept telling him the genres were blending and blurring.

Hitting number one on the country chart was what mattered to him. This was the first time he had hit the top spot during release week. He hoped the feat proved to the doubters his career was anything but dead.

Gary's management of him deserved all the credit. "Thanks, Gary."

"Yeah, well, just don't party too hard tonight. We have to be in Omaha at seven AM to do that radio interview."

"We'll behave." Gabe flashed another grin.

Hard to believe that only seven years ago his day job was punching cattle on a ranch in central Texas and he was spending his weekend nights singing in honky-tonks.

Back then Michaela Finn had been the most important thing in his life.

Would he ever forget the way her blue eyes darkened to sapphire when they made love?

Gary cuffed him on the shoulder, dislodging her memory and the ache thinking about her always brought. They headed into the green room to meet his fans.

This was what he lived for now, had dreamed about doing since he first saw a Garth Brooks concert as a kid, and he wouldn't ever want another life.

Then why did he look for her in every crowd, hoping she'd be there?

\* \* \* \*

Micki Finn hated crowds almost as much as she despised Gabriel McKenna. She looked at the woman next to her, obviously a groupie, as were the rest of the frenzied females. All waiting outside the backdoor of the sports center along a cordoned-off path to Gabe's tour buses.

The redhead beside her was trying for that naturally tussled look with her hair, but the spray glue holding it in place ruined the effect. Compared to some of the other women and girls gathered, Red was overdressed in her skintight, barely there tank dress. Micki's faded jeans and T-shirt made her regular nun material.

Security held the throng back and the crowd became louder when the doors of the arena opened. Red bounced, her extremely large breasts nearly dislodged from the flimsy constraints of the tank top. She pushed past a pair of women old enough to be Gabe's mother. The yellow ribbon appeared ahead of the redhead, and Micki followed her, shoving her way around Red to get to the line. Women yelled obscenities and scowled, but Micki ignored them and focused on the man heading toward the waiting bus.

She hated the way her heart skipped a beat before it galloped off like a horse out of the pen after a pistol shot. He was surrounded by men, but he outshined them all. His smile was cowboy handsome as he winked and tipped his hat at the groping women.

Gabe stopped along the line and signed autographs, but when some of the groupies became too daring and grabbed at his black T-shirt or lower, he withdrew to the center of the security guards.

A tan Stetson sat over a shock of raven hair that brushed his collar. Micki wasn't ready for the sudden desire to run her fingers through the black silk. She fisted her hands until her nails bit into her palms.

The entourage drew closer under the harsh lights, which brightened the area to almost daylight intensity. Micki ducked under the yellow ribbon.

"Hey!" called the security guards and the women behind her at the same time.

She ignored both and got the response she wanted. Gabe stopped and pushed the Stetson back over his high forehead. He peered at her for a beat before dark brows rose over golden-brown eyes, set in a broad, angular face suggesting some Native American genetics. His full lips twisted into a smirk. "I'll be damned. Never figured you'd become one of my groupies." When a security guard grabbed her upper arm, Gabe said, "It's okay, Chuck. I don't think Miz Finn means me any harm."

Micki shook off the big man's grasp then adjusted her own hat. Gabe's blatant gaze traveled over her scuffed cowboy boots all the way to the Stetson on her head. When he met her gaze again, the heat flowing over her had nothing to do with the temperature of the early September night, her hatred of him, or her anger. She shouldn't have been affected at all, considering the reasons she'd driven half the night and all day to confront him.

Taking a deep breath to steady the nest of hornets in her stomach, she squared her shoulders. "We need to talk."

A minute later, Gabe and a lanky man holding an incensed conversation on a Bluetooth ushered her onto the first bus. They left the security folks to deal with the crowd of jealous women jeering behind them. When they entered the common area of the bus, the seven members of Gabe's band looked up from the couch and restaurant-like booth. They all held longneck bottles of beer and two of them held cigarettes, the smoke of which clung to the cool, conditioned air and made her throat burn.

A burly man she recognized as Gabe's lead guitarist stood and smiled at her. He went to the refrigerator, pulled out a beer, and raised a brow at Gabe. "Not your usual type. I like."

After he returned to the couch, Gabe reached into the fridge then pulled out two Budweisers. He handed her one of the longnecks. "This is Michaela Finn." Using his unopened bottle, he pointed to the men and the lone woman, going clockwise. The lead guitarist was first. "Brian, Chris, Jessica, her husband Caleb, Joel, Robby, Kenny. My band. And the man on the phone is my manager, Gary Russell."

Gary nodded his head once and grunted, then turned away and sat beside Robby at the table. He booted up a laptop as he lit a cigarette. Gabe got another beer out and set it on the table beside Gary. No word of thanks, no acknowledgment came from the man now tapping on keys and talking on the phone at the same time. No doubt, Gary would be dead from a coronary by the time he was seventy.

At least he was here and not *that* woman. Before Micki could let Gabe's betrayal bog her down any farther, she tipped her hat at the motley men and the woman of the band.

"Hello. Most people call me Micki. Gabe's the only one who's ever really called me Michaela." Her smile was stiff as she grasped the beer bottle with a death grip and tried to not stare at the man taking up more than his share of space beside her. She shouldn't drink, she had a long drive back to Bluebonnet Creek, Texas, but she needed it more now than ever.

Joel, Gabe's bassist, pushed his long black hair from his face and looked her up and down from where he lounged on the couch. "You're not a groupie. You're the ex."

Taken aback, Micki glanced at Gabe, who took a big swig of his beer. They hadn't been together since Gabe decided he was tired of cowboying and singing in honky-tonks and then hightailed it to Nashville only two days before their wedding seven years ago.

With another woman.

"You were married? How'd you keep that secret?" The bright light over the table turned Robby's spiked bleached blond hair white. A cigarette dangled between the fingers of the drummer's left hand. "I'm surprised Andrea didn't let the world know you were married before her when you broke up."

"Never quite made it to the altar." Gabe took another pull on the bottle before he sat it on the counter of what passed for a kitchen of sorts. He peered at Micki with narrowed eyes. "What did you want to talk about?"

Micki downed a quarter of the beer, trying to get her bearings. It was impossible. She'd already had the eleven-hour drive to Kansas City to figure out how she was going to tell Gabe the news. She sat her bottle beside his. "Can we..."--she glanced at the men and woman watching her with amusement and curiosity--"go somewhere..."

Gabe nodded and led her though a door at the end of a narrow passage. A burst of panic zinged through her at the sight of the bed taking up most of the space. How many women had he had sex with in this room? Had Andrea been one of them? Of course she'd been. When the door clicked closed, she jumped and turned to him. She didn't care about his private life. Couldn't care.

"What's going on, Michaela?"

She wrung her hands together. "I've come to--to tell you Sam and... and Frankie..."

"If this is about Dad and your sister, I don't care."

She sniffed back the sudden burn of fresh tears. "Oh, Gabe..."

When she wobbled on her feet, he was there in a heartbeat and guided her to sit on the edge of the bed. He quickly withdrew his arm, but sat next to her. Their thighs touched. Her heart leapt and her breath caught. How could she want him to wrap her up in his strong arms? She never wanted him to touch her again, did she? Mustering all of her strength, she pulled her shoulders up, breathing air scented with leather, sandalwood, and Gabe.

No amount of pretending she was strong would stave off her overwhelming grief. How could she have any more tears left to cry? The last thing she wanted to do was bawl in front of him, but she detested the news she was about to break. Even if he didn't care.

"What's going on?"

His face was a blur through a watery haze. She used her hands to wipe away the tears and sniffed again. "Sam and Frankie were flying from Dallas to Brownwood and Sam's plane crashed. They're gone, Gabe. That's all I know."

\* \* \* \*

Gabe let the news sink in. When it did, the shock quickly gave way to... nothing. He wanted to feel grief for the man who'd given him life, but in the end only numbness and hatred penetrated his heart.

His hand fisted against his thigh. Micki reached out, and after a brief hesitation laid her hand over his fist. He sucked in a breath at the buzz of awareness zipping through him at her gentle touch. All too fast, and yet not soon enough, she withdrew and folded her hands together in her lap.

Gabe despised his father for cheating on his dying mother with Micki's older sister. She was half his age, but Sam married her three months after Gabe's mother died from breast cancer. Frankie had been five months pregnant.

As Gabe met Micki's shimmery blue eyes again, fear twisted his gut. "Where's Jesse?"

"He's with Momma, and Mary Nelson is looking in on them."

Her words eased the fear a little. He wanted nothing to do with his father or his father's wife, but he didn't hate the product of their union. Somehow, their ten-year-old son had stolen his heart. His baby brother was safe.

"Momma and me are..." She hiccupped and shook her head. "We were watching him while Sam and Frankie went to Dallas for one of her art shows." From her back pocket, she pulled a red and white handkerchief to wipe her eyes and nose. "I knew you'd want to know."

He stared at her. Despite everything that went wrong between them, she'd brought him the news instead of him hearing it through other channels.

*Don't read too much into it.* Michaela never cared about him before, or she'd not have broken their engagement two days before the wedding. She'd have believed in him when Andrea took him to Nashville, and she would have trusted him.

"Thanks for telling me." Gabe stood and leaned on the doorframe. His father was gone. What did it all mean for him? Loud music sounded from the main room, drawing his attention. The drivers of the two busses would be anxious to get moving; the production crew would follow with their semi-trucks and another two busses. They had another show in Omaha tomorrow night. Jesse's being alone was all that mattered now.

Gabe jerked when a knock sounded on the door. As he straightened, the panel cracked open and Gary said, "Gabe, we need to get rolling."

"I've got to go. I have to get back home. Momma is taking all of this hard." Micki stood by his side. "And I can't leave Jesse with her too long."

He focused on her red-rimmed cornflower eyes. She'd been crying for a while. "Michaela, I'm sorry."

She sniffed, close to tears again, and nodded stiffly. "I loved my sister. Despite all of her bad behavior and her marriage to your daddy, I loved her."

"I know." He wanted to touch her wet cheek and take away the tears.

Gary shattered the impulse. "Is the girl staying or going? We've got to move."

"I'm leaving." Micki headed out the door as Gary moved to the side in the narrow passage. She glanced over her shoulder. "I'll take care of the arrangements. If I can have your number, I'll call you with the time of the service. That is, if you're interested."

"Yeah. Call me." Gabe dug in his wallet for a personal business card. "My cell number's the last one listed."

Micki nodded again and took the card with a shaky hand.

"What's going on?" Gary asked after looking from Micki to Gabe.

Gabe stopped at the door of the second bedroom, drawing the attention of the guys in the common area. "My father and his wife were killed in a plane crash."

"Oh, man. I'm sorry, Gabe."

Gabe caught up with Micki before she exited the bus. Someone turned down the music and the band waited in silence. He never talked about his nonexistent family or much about his personal life, so this was all news to them. The world only knew about the messy split between exciting new star Gabe McKenna and his wife and manager Andrea Rose less than a year after they'd eloped, but even the guys didn't know all the facts. He wanted to keep it that way.

"Michaela, wait." She paused and turned to him with fresh tears drowning her eyes. "Do you know if they ever made any kind of arrangements for Jesse?"

"I don't know." The quiver in Micki's soft Texas drawl gave away her fear. She shuffled her keys in her hand and looked down at them. "What will happen to him if they didn't? He's just a little boy."

"The state will give custody to your mom. She's his grandmother."

"But Momma's not Frankie's real mother and besides, she isn't healthy enough to take care of Jesse. What will happen to the ranch? Do you know if Sam left it to you?"

Gabe snorted and looked past her into the night and the glaring lights of the parking lot. "You have to be kidding. Dad told me he'd never leave the ranch or the business to me. It's supposed to go to your sister in the event..." He stopped and met Micki's searching gaze. "I guess it will depend on what Dad's will says about such things. My guess is it will be sold and the money will go into a trust fund for Jesse."

He didn't miss the shiver that quaked through Micki's athletic body or the rounding of her eyes. She and her mother lived on the Lazy M Ranch. If the place were sold, they'd have nowhere to go.

But before she could comment, Gary broke in. "I'm sorry, but we have to go." He looked at Micki. "Gabe will give you a call when he gets the chance."

With a tip of her hat brim, she exited the bus, crossed the empty parking lot to an old pickup truck, and climbed in. There had been a time he'd loved Michaela Finn, but she hadn't loved him enough to believe in his dreams.

The guys passed by him, patting him on his shoulder and offering their condolences as they headed to their own bus for the night. Jessica hugged him and tears brimmed in her eyes. The party was over.

He stepped down to where the driver and Gary were talking. "I'm not going to Omaha."

Gary turned to face him. "What are you going to do?"

The last thing he'd ever wanted to. He didn't care what happened to his father or the ranch, but Jesse was his responsibility. "I'm going back to Texas to take care of my little brother."

# Chapter 2

Micki stopped on the county road and stared at the wood arch over the entrance of the driveway. *Lazy M Cattle Ranch* was painted in black. The five-hundred acres in Brown County were the only home she had ever known, and soon she and her mother would have to leave. Her sister and her sister's husband--her employers--her family--were dead, and seeing Gabe McKenna last night hadn't helped her poor, battered heart.

The day was too beautiful for all this angst, but she couldn't stop the tightening in her chest or the desire to curl up in a ball somewhere.

Sucking in a hot, dry breath of the air blowing through the open windows, she hit the gas and turned onto the gravel driveway. A few of the colts in the pasture noticed and kept pace with her for a few hundred feet until they came to the rail fence dividing the pasture.

At the fork, about halfway down, she took a right. To the left was the main house. Without looking at the white clapboard two-story where Sam and Frankie had lived, she sped away, leaving the house in a cloud of dust.

Micki stopped the pickup in front of the cottage where she and her mother lived. The barn and training arena were set off to the left of the cottage, the bunkhouse and her office to the right. Three of the ranch hands stood on the porch of the bunkhouse. She got out of the truck and shut the door. With a lift of her hand, she returned their waves, but ignored their questioning gazes.

Birds chirped in the pecan trees surrounding the house, and knobby red apples hung on the snarled trees in the old orchard between the cottage and the main house. In the pasture, horses grazed on the breeze-swept grass. Although she couldn't see them, two hundred cattle grazed on the grassland beyond the horse pasture.

All so normal.

When her gelding, Beau, trotted to the corral rails, she almost gave into the temptation to climb over the fence, hop on the bay's bare back, and take off for parts unknown.

The sound of the screen door opening and the soft whirl of an electric motor wrenched a sigh from her. She headed around the Silverado. A sad smile tugged on her lips at Jesse standing beside her mother's wheelchair.

"Aunt Micki!"

She bypassed the wheelchair ramp and took the steps two at a time. "Hey, squirt." She ruffled the boy's dark hair and avoided looking in his deep blue eyes.

"Did you see him?"

With a nod, she hugged him close. "Yeah, I found him in Kansas City."

He swallowed, stepped back, and glanced at his feet. "He ain't coming home, is he?"

She fought the urge to correct his bad grammar and tugged him to her again, holding his head to her chest. God, she'd do anything to take away his pain. "He'll be here, Jesse."

"Gabe never liked me."

His quiet words stabbed at her heart. They weren't true, but Gabe's no-showing until the funeral would hurt Jesse. Gabe never came home much, but from what Frankie had told her, he called and Skyped Jesse often, and he never forgot his birthday or Christmas. Pulling back, she held him and met his gaze. "That's not true, and you know it. But Gabe also has commitments."

"Our dad's dead. That should mean somethin'." He stepped out of her embrace and ran down the stairs.

"Jesse…"

But he was already past her truck and headed for the orchard where he'd discovered Gabe's old clubhouse. She took a step to follow him, but her mother's voice stopped her.

"Let him go, Micki. He's in a world of hurt."

She met her mother's puffy, bloodshot eyes. The constant pain Momma was in and the ravages of disease had etched deep lines on a face that had once been beautiful. "You okay, Momma?"

Loretta Finn folded hands as crooked as the apple trees in the lap of her useless legs. She nodded, her chin-length gray hair brushing the collar of her plaid housedress. "I'm fine. So, what did Gabe have to say?"

"I'm to call when the arrangements are done."

Her mother sighed. "Sam and Frankie hurt him a lot, but I hope he remembers Jesse needs him."

Micki shifted into a chair on the porch and changed the subject. "Did Cash take care of the horses?"

Momma turned her chair around to face Micki and a shadow of a smile twisted her pale lips. "Of course he did. Cash is sweet on you."

"He's also almost ten years younger than me." Micki looked out past the potted geraniums and the blooming peace roses to the orchard. She didn't want to talk about the crush twenty-two-year-old Cash Nelson had on her.

"It's only eight years. Cash comes from a good family and just got a teaching job. Besides, he's still working on the ranch. He'd make--"

"Momma, stop right there. I'm not getting married, and I'm definitely not marrying Cash Nelson. I'm not a cougar."

Her mother flattened her mouth into a fine line. "Why would you say such a thing? My mother was ten years older than my father and they were happily married. It's all because of that woman."

That woman being the talent scout-turned-manager, Andrea Rose. The woman for whom Gabe had left Micki.

"Now that's just ridiculous. Gabe's marriage to an older woman has nothing to do with my aversion to following in my grandparents' footsteps. I won't chase after a younger man for the same reason I'd never go for a much older one. I'm not..."

"I know you aren't Frankie."

She'd gone too far. Frankie may not have been her mother's biological daughter, but Loretta had been the only mother Frankie had ever known, and Momma loved her as if she'd been her flesh and blood. "I'm sorry, Momma. I didn't mean..." She shook her head and swallowed. "I like Cash--as a friend. Nothing more." She bent and picked up a baseball lying on the floor by her chair leg.

The sound of a vehicle crunching on the gravel of the drive had her turning toward it. She stood and leaned on the railing as the nondescript sedan stopped beside her truck. When a middle-aged woman exited the car, fear snaked around Micki's gut, and she gripped the white rail. By the look of the woman's high heels and pinstriped suit, she didn't get out of her Brownwood office much.

Jesse came out of the orchard and rounded the car. The woman smiled at him, but he only hurried up the steps to move in close to Micki. Her need to protect him was strong and undeniable as she wrapped her arm around his slender shoulders and pulled him close.

Momma must have felt the same compulsion because she positioned her wheelchair at the edge of the porch steps between the pillars. "What can we do for you?"

The woman stopped on the concrete walkway at the bottom of the stairs and glanced at Jesse. He snaked his arm around Micki's waist and held on.

The woman smiled and held out an envelope along with a badge.

"It'll be okay," Micki said to Jesse with a gentle squeeze. He didn't look convinced as she let go of him and made herself descend the three steps. Stopping in front of the woman, she read the identification the lady was holding out.

With a smile the Department of Family Protective Services agent put her badge away. "Allison Fennel. Are you Michaela or Loretta Finn?" She handed Micki an envelope with the seal of Texas in the corner and her and her mother's names in the middle of it.

Micki numbly nodded and met the woman's eyes. "I'm Michaela. My mother is Loretta. Why are you here?"

She already knew--Jesse.

"Jesse, be a good boy and go inside please," her mother said.

"I'm not going anywhere." Jesse stomped down the steps to stop beside Micki. "What do you want, lady?"

Fennel's smile dripped sugar as she leaned forward. "I bet you're Jesse."

"So?"

"Jesse, please go inside--now." Micki ruffled his hair.

He squared his shoulders and ran up the stairs. The screen door slammed behind him.

"I'm his grandmother. What do you want?" Loretta's voice was as hard as concrete.

The woman's eyes shifted from Micki to Loretta. "DFPS was contacted this morning by Judge Lemont Finn regarding the deaths of Samuel and Frances McKenna. It's my office's responsibility to make certain the child is taken care of."

Son of a bitch. Figured her father would get involved. Micki stuck her hands into her back pockets to keep them from forming fists. "My sister and her husband left him in our care while they were on a business trip. We aren't stopping now. We're his only family."

Micki's throat froze shut at Fennel's slight, lopsided grin. "I'm here at the request of the child's grandfather. Mrs. Finn, it's my understanding you were Frances's stepmother. Lemont Finn's first wife died in a car accident when she was a year old."

"Yes, that's correct. Before I could adopt her proper, Lemont and I divorced. But Frankie was as much mine as Micki is." Her mother's voice quivered. "I loved her as my own child."

Dear God, they weren't seriously thinking of giving Jesse to her father, were they? Neither Frankie nor Sam would have ever wanted that. They despised him as much as she and her mother did.

Micki heard another vehicle on the drive, but she was too focused on Allison Fennel and her thoughts to heed the sound. A car door slammed.

"Is it also true you do not own this house? You lived and worked on the ranch, Miss Finn?"

"Yes, I'm the manager."

"You aren't taking that child anywhere. I'm Jesse's brother."

Fennel turned at the sound of Gabe's voice. If the situation weren't so dire, Micki would have smiled at the way her eyes bugged out of her head. She opened her mouth and closed it again. Finally, she sputtered, "Gabe McKenna?"

The hardness of Gabe's face never softened.

"Gabe!" Jesse bounded down the stairs and leapt into his older brother's arms. "You came!"

"Of course I'd be here." Gabe held his brother and kissed the top of his dark head. "I'm so sorry, buddy."

At the tenderness in his voice, Micki's heart did a fast little flutter.

Gabe set Jesse back on his feet and placed his trademark tan Stetson on the boy's curls, completely covering the top half of his face.

"I'm glad you're here, Gabe. This lady wants to take me away to live with Grandpa Lemont." The flash of fear in his dark blue eyes filled Micki with a need to keep him away from her father.

Gabe knelt in front of his baby brother and rested his hands on Jesse's small shoulders. "That's not going to happen. So, don't you worry about it, okay?"

Jesse gazed at Gabe with hero worship causing Micki's heart to swell. He'd always been good with Jesse and never held their father's affair with Frankie against him. A fierce longing for what could have been hit her hard enough to knock the breath out of her. A lot of years had passed since she had thought of Gabe as father material, but even then she'd never considered he'd be so patient and attentive. So loving.

Gabe tugged the brim of his hat down over Jesse's forehead. "Now you go inside with your grandma while your aunt Michaela and I talk to the lady. Okay?" He glanced over Jesse's head to her mother and she nodded. He winked at Micki and shooed Jesse up the steps.

Momma held out her hand for Jesse to take, and together they entered the house.

Gabe stood beside Micki and faced the agent. "I think you can leave now. Despite Loretta's relationship to Frankie or Jesse, Michaela is his aunt by blood and I'm his brother."

The woman looked flustered as beads of sweat formed on her brow and upper lip. "I have to deliver the boy into the care of Judge Finn."

Gabe put his left hand into the pocket of his faded jeans. "You can explain to Judge Finn he isn't taking Jesse away from his home at a time as painful as this. The boy doesn't even know the man."

Micki jumped when he put his other arm around her shoulders. The touch was light and more show than anything else, but it sent a zing through her.

"Now if you will excuse us, we have funeral arrangements to make. Loretta and Micki have been taking care of Jesse for the past week while my father and Michaela's sister were in Dallas. Our lawyer will be in contact with DFPS as soon as possible."

Gabe turned Micki around and headed up the steps to the screen door as if he'd done it a thousand times. At the open door, Loretta gave him an appreciative look as she backed away.

Fennel followed them up the stairs. "I'll have to inspect the home, at the very least. Judge Finn wouldn't want his grandson subjected to an unsafe environment."

Micki held Gabe's narrowing gaze. Fennel might work for DFPS, but she was also on Lemont Finn's payroll. She'd find something wrong no matter how insignificant. When had she last picked up Jesse's toys from the small living room? She also hoped her mother had put the dirty dishes from the past two days in the dishwasher. Micki swallowed and looked over her shoulder. "Yes, of course. Follow me."

She glanced around the cool interior as they entered. In the small eat-in kitchen, a few plastic cups sat on the counter, but the sink was free of dishes. An old Monopoly game lay out on the small round table. In the living room to the left, two Tonka trucks that were probably old enough to have been Gabe's were parked next to the couch. Jesse, still wearing Gabe's hat, sat on the braided rug in front of the couch playing with his iPad. He peeked over the screen with worry etching his forehead when they entered the house with Fennel hot on their tails.

Gabe stopped and turned in the space dividing the kitchen and living room. Crossing his arms, he stood like a barrier in front of the social worker. "You have two minutes, Miss Fennel. I suggest you start your inspection because your time is already ticking."

His hard jaw line and the amber stones of his eyes let Micki know he wasn't here for her or her mother but for Jesse.

The sudden wave of begrudging relief for his taking over the situation with the social worker turned into dread of another kind.

What if he wanted to take Jesse away from her?

# Chapter 3

Typical for an early September day in Central Texas, the day of the funeral dawned warm and bright. In the graveyard behind Bluebonnet Creek's nondenominational church, Gabe stood by the side of the graves, suffocating in his new suit, which was much too warm for the hot day. He'd bought it yesterday in Brownwood, since he hadn't brought anything suitable for the double funeral with him.

Bluebonnet Creek's citizens, along with the ranchers and farmers in the surrounding area, turned out for the funeral. Beyond the white picket fence, Gabe spotted several local reporters; a few from as far away as Dallas were mixed with them. His father had been a respected businessman and rancher while Frankie had been an emerging artist, not to mention the estranged daughter of a local billionaire. Legitimate news agencies stayed back, recording their pieces for their eleven o'clock shows. The paparazzi weren't as respectful of the mourners. He'd hired security to keep them back, but many were still trying to get pictures of them.

Normally, he didn't mind the attention the media gave him, but today the jerks were pissing him off big time. They didn't just want his photo; they were after his never-seen-before little brother and the woman Gabe had once been engaged to.

Jesse sniffled beside him and tightened his grip on Gabe's hand. His little brother was doing his honest best not to cry, but the wet tracks running down his cheeks betrayed Jesse's pain. Gabe's heart broke for his brother's loss, despite his confusion over his own emotions. He held nothing but numbness in his heart for the man they shared blood with and for his wife--a woman Gabe had once considered his best friend.

Gabe glanced at Michaela. She had her arm wrapped around the shoulders of the boy between them. They'd put their past aside for a few days while they worked together to arrange the funerals.

Grief had taken a toll on Michaela. Her once vibrant blue eyes were dull and red rimmed. She'd used makeup to conceal the smudges of dark circles under her eyes, which only made her fatigue more noticeable.

The black dress and low heels were also anomaliesy. She never wore anything but jeans and boots. Considering the circumstances, he shouldn't have noticed how the jersey fabric fit over her breasts and hips and stopped just above her knee. Despite her pantyhose, the fabric showed off her long, toned legs in a way he hadn't seen in a long time.

He looked back at the burnished bronzed caskets. Although he didn't feel shame for his attraction to Michaela during this moment, Gabe reminded himself of the pain she'd caused him.

The narrowed gaze of the man standing on the other side of the grave drew his attention. If Lemont Finn mourned his eldest daughter's untimely and tragic death, he hid the emotion well. Gabe squared his shoulders and met the man's steady gaze with one of his own. Finn may be the richest man in the county, but Gabe's bank account wasn't as empty as it had been when he had lived here. He was never getting Jesse, who he wanted to bend and mold into the ruthless heir his daughters never could be.

Jesse sniffled again and Gabe glanced at his brother. Gabe's heart bruised a little more every time he thought about the loss of Sam and Frankie in Jesse's young life.

When the preacher tossed a handful of dirt onto each of the caskets, Michaela let out a loud sob. She'd held it together fairly well until then. She hugged Jesse and her back curved in with the weight of her grief. Before he thought his actions through, Gabe wrapped his arm around her shoulders, pulling her to him with Jesse between them. She stiffened and stepped away when Jesse wrapped his arms around Gabe's waist. Shaking from her tears, she turned to her mother. Michaela and Loretta held on to each other and sobbed.

Gabe held the boy as the preacher finished the final prayer.

Jesse pressed his face into Gabe's chest and murmured too low for anyone else to hear, "I will always love you, Momma and Daddy."

Gabe looked down at Jesse as he held him close. Emotion crashed over him so fierce and blinding, Gabe fell to his knees. Memories of his own childhood with his father hammered at the shell he'd built around his heart. Gabe had once loved Sam McKenna as much as this sobbing boy in his arms did.

The first tear Gabe had shed in public since his mother's death dropped off his lash. "They know."

Jesse met his gaze and hiccupped. "We're orphans now, aren't we?"

Gabe stroked his brother's unruly black curls. He looked so much like Gabe had as a boy, except Jesse had inherited his mother's blue eyes. "Yeah." He swallowed the lump in his throat. "We are, buddy. But you will always have me."

Michaela rested her hand on Jesse's shoulder, and he turned to look up at her. "And you've got me and Grandma. We won't let anything ever happen to you."

As Gabe stood, he glanced at Lemont. The man's challenging glare sent a shiver down his spine. Lemont put his hands into his pockets, turned away from the grave, and headed toward the social center where a meal had been set up by the church ladies.

Jesse watched his grandfather walk away, and a tremble ran through the boy's lean body.

"C'mon." Gabe squeezed Jesse's shoulders and turned toward the church. "Let's go."

Micki followed with her mother into the cool interior of the social hall. In her motorized wheelchair, Loretta stopped beside Gabe and Jesse. Gabe glanced at the older woman's tear-streaked face as a grimace pinched her lips. Micki had told him yesterday that Loretta was in constant pain. A symptom of her multiple sclerosis.

"You okay, Loretta?" Gabe lightly touched her shoulder.

"I'll be fine. Stop fussing over me." Loretta's speech was slightly slurred and slow. She closed her eyes and sniffed before moving away from him.

Michaela shook her head and held back the moisture he saw in her eyes. "Jesse, please help Grandma."

He nodded and quickly caught up with her as an older couple stopped to offer their condolences. Jesse held Loretta's hand and nodded at something Mrs. Owens said to him.

Michaela cleared her throat and folded her arms in front of her. "I hate all of this."

"Yeah." The tension tightened around Gabe like a belt binding his chest. "It's got to be hard on you, seeing your momma like this all the time."

She took a deep breath raising her shoulders; then she met Gabe's eyes. "Usually she has a sensation of pins and needles, but recently her trigeminal neuralgia has been worse."

He raised a brow. "What's that?"

"Facial pain."

"Can't something be done about it?" They moved farther into the room. Although people observed them, quietly sending their sympathy, they kept their distance. They seemed to understand Gabe and Michaela's need to be alone.

"There's a surgery, but it's expensive and Momma's Medicare would only pay a very small part of it." She glanced toward her mother. "I'll get something worked out."

Near a table set up for drinks, Loretta talked to an older woman he recognized as Mary Nelson. The woman poured Loretta a plastic cup of Seven Up, which she took with shaky hands. Jesse helped her hold the drink to her lips.

Before he had a chance to say anything on the matter, Michaela squared her shoulders and stared at him. "When are you leaving?"

Michaela had never been anything but direct.

Gabe shrugged and shoved his hands into his pants pockets. "I'll be leaving tomorrow after the will reading. I have meetings with my record company and a show in Cheyenne next week." He nodded an acknowledgement to a guy he'd gone to high school with. "I haven't told Jesse yet."

"He knows you live in Nashville. He'll be okay with Momma and me."

"About that…" He met her eyes again, the sparkling blue hauntingly deep and inviting. And scared. She'd had the same frightened look the day she'd given him the ultimatum--either he chased his dream or he stayed and married her, but he couldn't have both.

"You can't take him with you." She stepped closer and dropped her arms to her sides, fisting her hands. "Gabe, dear God, he just lost his parents. You can't rip him from everything he knows."

"I know." A terrible pain twisted his gut. The road wasn't the place for a kid. There was only one thing to do. He took a deep breath and glanced at Loretta and Jesse. "If you need anything, Michaela, let me know. I could help you out."

Her face became a storm cloud ready to burst as she stiffened her back. "We're fine. And I most certainly don't need your money to take care of my family. Excuse me."

She spun away and shifted through the crowd and around the long tables filling with people. A younger man approached her and sat down beside her at the table in the back. He looked to be in his early twenties and was dressed in a dark Western-cut blazer and slacks. Something about him seemed familiar; then he recognized him. He was Mary and

JP Nelson's youngest son, Cash. He worked part-time on the Lazy M. Hadn't he become a high school history teacher or something?

Michaela bit her lip and nodded to whatever he said. Cash pulled her into a one-armed embrace, and she laid her head on his shoulder.

Gabe wasn't ready for the sudden jolt of jealousy zipping through him when she snaked her arm around Cash's waist. Why did he care if they were an item?

"Aren't they a handsome pair?"

Gabe turned to face the man behind him. Lemont watched him with calculating blue eyes, reminding Gabe of a rattlesnake before the strike. Gabe didn't justify his question with an answer. Straightening his shoulders, he unlocked his back teeth. "I'm sure you aren't here to offer your condolences. So, what do you want?"

Lemont's grin never reached his cold eyes. "You know what I want."

"Jesse is not living with you. I believe DFPS made that clear."

Lemont chuckled and rested his hand on Gabe's shoulder. "My dear boy, hadn't your daddy told you anything about me?"

Gabe glanced at the big, age-spotted hand on his shoulder. "He told me plenty, and so have Michaela, Frankie, and Loretta."

Slowly nodding with a smirk Gabe wanted to knock off the bastard's face, Lemont said, "Then you should know I usually get what I want." He patted Gabe's shoulder. "See you around."

He moved away, leaving fear and anger tangling in Gabe's belly. Lemont wasn't an enemy anyone wanted. He'd destroyed more than one adversary, including stealing his father's partnership in Finn Energy, his oil company. Lemont's ranch was one of the biggest in west central Texas, and his wealth came from a variety of business interests he'd acquired along the way like a person might collect coins. Not to mention, he'd somehow gotten himself elected county judge twenty years back. Despite being out of office, he still held power in the county.

"Gabe, I'm so sorry for your loss."

He took a deep breath and focused on Mary Nelson's concerned brown eyes and friendly face. With her dyed-blond hair teased high, she reminded him of Dolly Parton, but that's where the comparison ended. Mary was rail thin. She pulled him into a tight hug.

"Thanks." He let her go and glanced over her head to her son and Michaela. "Cash still working at the Lazy M?"

She smiled and nodded. "When he's not teaching." He met her gaze, and she squeezed his upper arm. "You don't have anything to worry about."

"I'm not worried about Lemont Finn," he lied. He'd be foolish not to be concerned over what the man potentially had planned for Jesse. Lemont was heartless and brutal. While he'd been judge, he swindled his daughters out of their trust funds and doctored evidence to prove Loretta had cheated on him before their divorce; therefore her alimony payments ceased. Not to mention all of the other crooked things he'd done while judge. Even the state attorney general investigated his office. After the AG's investigator had been found dead in the woods behind the hotel he'd been staying in and the death ruled a suicide, the government never pursued the issue. Lemont walked away without so much as a wrinkle in his Armani suit and a pat on the back by the same Attorney General who'd been gunning for him. Gabe's father suspected Lemont had something on the state's top lawyer and had the investigator *taken care of.*

She patted his arm. "Micki and Cash are just friends. Oh, my son has been crushing on her since he was a boy, but she doesn't feel the same."

"What?" Her statement caused mental whiplash. She wasn't talking about Lemont but Cash and Michaela. He didn't care about what went on between her son and his ex. "I think you're misreading whatever you think you saw." The hard edge in his voice surprised him. "Micki and I have a common interest--Jesse."

Mary nodded and smiled as if she knew he was talking bullshit, but she didn't push the issue. "I bought your newest CD. I must say, I think it's my favorite."

He glanced down at the floor. "Thanks. I'm proud of the record."

"At the grocery store, I saw you on the cover of *Country Music Magazine.*" Shaking her head, she snorted. "What were they calling you? The sexiest man in country music. Hard to believe I remember when you were born. Heck, I even changed your diaper a time or two." She blushed and patted his arm.

He laughed for the first time in days. "And to think, women now would pay good money to see what you have."

"Oh, you devil!" Her blush only got redder as she fanned herself with an old-fashioned lace fan. "So, is the movie actress shown in one of the photos with you--what's her name? Tiffany Wills--is she your girlfriend?"

He looked past her shoulder. Cash left Michaela and brought back a Styrofoam cup of steaming coffee and a plate with a slice of chocolate cake on it. He sat beside her and wrapped his arm around her shoulders again.

Gabe wanted to be with Michaela. To be the one comforting her and taking care of her, which irritated him to no end. Since when did he want to spend time with Michaela?

He would have paid for Loretta's surgery if it helped her, but Michaela wouldn't want to owe him anything. She'd never acknowledge he'd been right to leave when Andrea Rose offered him the chance of a lifetime after he'd performed at a honky-tonk in Brownwood. If he'd listened to Michaela and stayed in Texas, he wouldn't have been able to afford the suit on his back.

Instead, he was a superstar with another set of problems--money being the least of them.

"No. She's a friend." No way was he telling his mother's friend the actress was nothing more than a fling. The photo was taken as part of the red carpet procession for some Hollywood shindig and used as part of the photo spread he'd recently done for the magazine.

"Better watch out. If she's a smart gal, she'll want to be more than friends."

He grinned and shook his head. "She's enjoying her new single status. I think she views marriage as I do. Once is enough."

"Ah, I guess I understand that. Your divorce sounded awful."

"It was." He looked around, wishing he could escape. The last person he wanted to talk about was Andrea. Despite his dislike for his former wife, Andrea had turned him into a sex symbol. She'd transformed country bumpkin Gabe McKenna into a country music bad-boy. As long as he'd kept the reports of womanizing and wild partying on the magazine and tabloid pages and never lived the lie, she was happy. When he'd decided he was tired of her made-up life and wanted to live it, she went all kickass crazy on him and nearly destroyed his career. "But I'm better off without her."

Mary grinned again and nodded; then she lost the smile. He followed her line of sight to Lemont speaking with Loretta and Jesse. Loretta openly scowled at her ex-husband and Jesse cowered behind her wheelchair like a scared puppy.

"That man has gall," Mary said. "If he feels an ounce of grief over Frankie's death, he sure hasn't shown it. I better rescue poor Loretta before he agitates her more than she already is."

Michaela got there before he and Mary did. She stood with her feet apart and rested her hands on Jesse's shoulders. "Leave us alone, Lemont."

Lemont frowned as if hurt, but the cold blue eyes bespoke of his true feelings. "Now, is that anyway to speak to your daddy?"

"Maybe if I considered you my daddy, I'd be more generous." She moved around Jesse and her mother and glared up at her father. "What are you really doing here? Everyone knows you despised Sam and disowned Frankie long ago--just as you did me. Then you stole the trust funds your father set up for us."

He squared his shoulders. "Maybe if you and your sister hadn't turned your backs on me, I would've been a little more generous." Glancing at Loretta, he smirked before looking at Michaela again. "But you chose your course in life. I won't let that happen again. You both know you can't provide for Jesse. I'm his grandfather, and I have every intention of curing the boy of the poison y'all have filled him with." He stepped around her and smiled at Jesse. "I'm not as terrible as they all make me out to be, son."

A peculiar glimmer in Lemont's eyes as he looked at Jesse sent cold fear through Gabe. He'd do everything possible to keep Jesse out of Lemont's clutches. Resting his hands on his little brother's shoulders, Gabe pulled him snug to his side. "Jesse will be taken care of. Now leave before I call in my security."

Lemont chuckled and put his hat on his head. As he walked to the door, the other people in the hall stared after him. Jesse looked up at Gabe and shivered.

* * * *

Samuel McKenna had been a fool and his wife an idiot.

Gabe ran both hands through his hair in frustration. The will reading turned out to be a disappointment. Everything Sam owned had been bequeathed to Frankie or to her estate in the event she passed on before him.

However, Frankie had never written a will, which meant probate court would appoint an executor to handle the estate. Fortunately, Jesse, by the simple fact that he was Frankie's son, would inherit the funds from her estate. But Jesse was still a child, and now he was thrust into the system, too. How could Gabe's so-called stepmother be so negligent?

"What do you mean she never kept the appointments?" Gabe stood by a bookcase full of old, leather-bound law books in the Brownwood law office of his father's lawyer and friend Tom Fleming.

With a sigh, Tom shook his head full of thick, graying dark hair and leaned over his rich rosewood desk. "I think Frankie was afraid to make a will. A lot of younger people these days are. Or they don't think they need to do it now and that they can wait until they're older."

"So, what happens to Jesse?" Micki held Jesse in her lap. He was too big for her to hold, but he clung to her and quietly cried against her shoulder.

Gabe's heart broke at the sight. How could his father be so callous as to involve a ten-year-old boy in this mockery? Sam had given the boy an inheritance and some old junk, but he shouldn't have been here to be subjected to all the rest.

"Loretta, would you take Jesse out into the reception area, please?" Gabe leaned down in front of Micki and Jesse. Loretta nodded, and he rubbed over Jesse's quivering back. Swallowing hard, Gabe met Micki's imploring gaze before taking Jesse into his arms. "Hey, buddy, go out with Grandma for a little while, okay?"

Jesse sobbed and wiped his nose on the back of his hand. "What's gonna happen to me, Gabe? Will I have to go with--with Momma's daddy? Why can't I stay with Grandma and Micki or with you?"

"We'll figure it out."

With a hopeful gaze at Gabe, Loretta rolled her chair over to take Jesse's hand. "C'mon, sweetheart. Let's go outside."

As they exited the office, Jesse glanced over his shoulder at Gabe. "Don't send me away to live with that mean man."

"We won't let that happen." Micki stood and gave him a weak smile. When the door closed, she turned to the lawyer. "Now what?"

"As the family's lawyer, I'm going to suggest to the court to appoint me executor of Frankie's estate." He shrugged and leaned back in his leather chair. "Unless either of you have someone else in mind."

Micki shrugged and sat in her chair again. "Sounds good to me. I'd rather have a lawyer I trust take care of things than me trying to figure it out. Lemont's less likely to take over with you handling things."

Gabe paced before the bookcase. "I agree. Besides, I have to go on tour." For the first time in his career, he hated the thought of being on the road. Stopping at the end of the case, he turned and rubbed the back of his neck. "What will happen to the ranch?"

"Since Frankie doesn't have a will and Jesse is too young to inherit it, the Lazy M will be sold and the funds set in a trust fund for him as her sole heir. Same goes for the businesses."

Micki gasped and ran her hand through her long hair. She'd worn it unbound and Gabe's fingers itched to touch it. He fisted his hands and stomped on the treacherous thought.

"That means Momma and I will have to move."

"Yes. However, I'll ask probate court to allow you to stay as long as there's stock to be taken care of on the ranch."

Micki nodded, but the worry etching a frown on her forehead wasn't eased by the news.

"You haven't answered our question about Jesse." Gabe's heart raced. He'd known Tom his entire life, and the one thing he'd always admired about him was his honesty.

Fleming cleared his throat and leaned over his desk. "I think you both know what will happen. In most cases like this where a child is orphaned, he is given into the care of a grandparent, which means he'll go with Lemont since Loretta wasn't Frankie's mother."

"He doesn't even know the man." Micki shook her head. "He's cruel and hated both Sam and Frankie. All Lemont Finn ever wanted was a son. Why the hell do you think he named his daughters Frances and Michaela? We're named for his grandfathers, Francis Finn and Michael Harper. He'll twist Jesse into a ruthless man like he is. And considering the world of hurt Jesse is in right now, that might not be a hard thing to do." She looked at Gabe, her eyes pleading him. "Please, isn't there something you can do?"

Gabe swallowed hard. He wanted his little brother taken care of, but he had no room in his life for a ten-year-old. "I'm his brother. Doesn't that hold some kind of clout with the court?"

Tom sighed and his brown eyes bore into Gabe. "I've represented your family for years and I considered Sam a good friend, so I won't lie to you, Gabe. Your being Jesse's brother normally would have some sway. However, your lifestyle is questionable. Especially for the current batch of conservative judges in the county. Maybe if you would take a break from touring, things would be different."

"You know I can't do that." He fisted both hands and shoved them into the pockets of his sports jacket as another possibility came to him. Was he crazy to suggest this? "What if Michaela and I fought for Jesse?"

Micki turned in her seat and gaped at him. "What do you mean?"

He shrugged and sat down beside her. "Think about it. If we had joint custody of him, that would get him away from Lemont and give him a stable home with you and Loretta. I can provide for him and even help you find a place to live. Then we can adopt him."

"I don't need your help."

"Actually, that's not a bad idea." Tom smiled and stood. "I think right now it's your best option if you want to keep Jesse away from Lemont."

# Chapter 4

Two nights after the will reading, Micki awoke from a restless sleep to the sound of her mother's cries. Glancing at the three a.m. hour on her alarm clock, she sighed. She'd been asleep for a whopping twenty-seven minutes.

With a groan, she threw the covers off and dragged herself out of bed. On her way to her mother's room, she peeked in on Jesse, who sprawled over the twin-sized bed and slept as soundly as only a kid could.

The thoughts that had kept her up for the past few nights pounded in her head. How was she going to afford a three-bedroom apartment, even if she did find one in Bluebonnet? She had to find another job besides managing the ranch, but how was that going to work?

Her mother cried out again. She closed Jesse's door and trudged on to her mother's room.

Micki sat down on the edge of the full-sized bed. Her mother had pulled herself into a fetal position with her hands curled in under her as she moaned in pain.

Taking a deep breath, Micki touched her mother's shoulder and spoke softly. "Momma? I'm gonna give you some pain medicine. Do you think you can sit up?"

Her mother shuddered and let out another wail. "It hurts!"

"Shhh…" Micki rubbed Momma's thin shoulder. "I'll be right back." She went out to the cottage's only bathroom and returned to her mother with a glass of water and a painkiller.

Momma protested the jostling to get her up into a sitting position, but she cooperated and swallowed the pill with water.

"Hopefully it kicks in soon." Micki sat the plastic cup on the table and tucked her mother under the quilt.

Momma's face was drawn and pale as she reached out and took one of Micki's hands. "I'm sorry, Micki."

"Don't be. You can't help the pain you feel." She sat on the edge of the bed again and held her mother's cold hand. "It's getting worse, isn't it?"

Momma glanced at their joined hands. "I'll be fine."

Micki swallowed. Her mother was lying. Momma hated being dependent on anyone, including her. The doctor had explained what was happening. As her mother's MS progressed, she'd feel pain along certain nerve roots, the most common being in the face. "We need to make an appointment with Dr. Meyers. He might be able to explain more about that surgery for the trigeminal pain."

Momma slowly shook her head. "No. No surgery."

"But it can help. You're in--"

Her mother's blue eyes grew stern as they narrowed. "And how are we going to pay for this fancy nerve surgery?"

"I have some savings, and maybe I could go back out on the rodeo circuit. Beau's still in good shape, and with a little training, we could win enough points to get into the NFR--" She'd given up barrel racing two years ago when her mother had become wheelchair bound and began needing almost constant care. She couldn't ask Frankie to take on all the responsibility, so she retired after winning the Nationals Final Rodeo for the third time and asked Sam for a job. To her surprise, he'd made her his manager, saying he'd wanted more time for his family.

"I can't afford it. No, I won't take your money. But if you really want to go back to racing, I won't stop you. I know you miss it, and I'm so sorry you quit because of me." Momma sniffed and slowly shook her head but didn't meet Micki's gaze.

Damn, why hadn't she kept her mouth shut about the rodeo? She took a deep breath, but before she could tell Momma how wrong she was, her mother's hoarse, slurred speech resumed.

"As soon as this place sells, we'll have to move. My Social Security isn't much, and we need a place big enough for Jesse." Momma weakly squeezed Micki's hand. "Mary told me she heard that Lemont is considering putting a bid on the ranch when it goes on the market Monday. You know if he does that we'll have to leave sooner rather than later."

Micki's heart fell out of the bottom of her gut and landed at her feet. "That son of a bitch." Sam and Frankie would turn over in their graves if they knew Lemont bought their ranch. No way could they stay much longer. Bluebonnet Creek was a small community, and apartments or houses for rent were nearly nonexistent--especially one that was handicap accessible and affordable. She also had her horse and tack to consider. "I wish I could put a bid in."

Momma sighed and closed her eyes, as defeated as Micki. "You know around here a ranch this size would go for at least five million dollars."

She had a few thousand bucks, but not enough to buy the ranch. To keep the sob from escaping, she bit her lip. Crying in front of her mother wasn't going to help. Micki had to be strong for all of them. Like she'd had to be when Momma's illness started to affect her by stealing her strength. She'd been diagnosed with MS only two years after she and Lemont married.

He divorced her because of it and took three-year-old Frankie and year-old Micki away from her. When he divorced her, Lemont trumped up a claim that Momma had cheated on him with a rodeo cowboy she'd grown up with. The accusation had been enough for the judge to deny her any alimony payments. She was homeless, sick, and penniless, until Gabe's mother offered her the job of running the horse-training program on the Lazy M with her. They'd been friends from the days they'd been champion barrel racers.

With the McKennas' help, Momma fought him and gained custody of Micki when she was four. When Frankie turned twelve, she ran away from their father and Loretta took her in. Again with the McKennas' help, they fought Lemont and the courts allowed Frankie to decide whom she wanted to live with. Life had never been easy for them as Loretta's health deteriorated, but they'd had each other and they'd had love. Something Micki wasn't sure her father was capable of.

Squaring her shoulders, she stood, then kissed her mother's forehead and gently squeezed her hand one more time. "We'll think of something, Momma. We've been in rough spots before and we've made it through."

Her mother's attempted smile fell flat. "I keep telling myself that, too. Now, you go back to sleep. Jesse's an early riser."

Micki went back to her room as if she were walking through wet cement. She stopped to look again at the sweet boy in the room across the hall from hers and let the tears slip past the dam she'd constructed to keep them back.

Gabe had said he'd help her, but she'd never ask him for it. How could she? He'd left her when she'd needed him the most and never looked back. Just like her father had left her and Momma.

*God, what will I do?*

\* \* \* \*

Gabe lifted the bottle of water to his lips and stared out the French doors of the kitchen in his Nashville home. The late Wednesday morning sun sparkled on the pool in the center of his enclosed, professionally landscaped backyard. For a brief moment, he considered completing his morning workout by taking a dive into the heated, crystalline water. When was the last time he'd swam in the pool?

He'd returned to Nashville four days ago and had gone to a meeting with several bigwigs from his record company. They were confident he would sweep the Country Music Awards in early November. His album was sitting on top of the charts, with the first three singles blasting to the top of the country charts within weeks of their releases. Sales of his first and third records were climbing into the double-platinum range. Even profits from his disastrous, self-produced second album were on the rise. His concerts were all sold out, and his agent was booking bigger venues next year.

The executives wanted to put together a live version of his current album. Recording was to happen at his last two shows of the tour-- Cheyenne, Wyoming, on Friday night and Dallas, Texas, in early October. Tomorrow morning he was flying out to Cheyenne.

He lifted the bottle to his lips to drink again and made his way toward the front of his home into the great room. Why wasn't he more excited? Just a couple of weeks ago this was what he worked and sweated for. Now all he could think about was the cornflower-blue eyes of a woman who'd broken his heart and the little brother he loved with all of his heart.

He wanted to go west, but Wyoming wasn't the place. Jesse was safe and happy with Michaela and her mother, but he was worried about him. Tom Fleming had secured temporary guardianship of Jesse for Michaela and him, but for how long wasn't specified. Lemont hadn't given up; that he was sure of. Leaving the little boy behind had been hard, but he couldn't stay any longer.

When his cell phone rang, he set his empty bottle on a marble-topped table next to a black leather couch and picked up the iPhone. He glanced at the ID, frowned, and connected the call. "Michaela?"

"Gabe! They took him." Micki's voice was borderline hysterical.

"Who took whom? Jesse?"

"Yes! That witch in heels and pinstripes came here ten minutes ago and served me papers that said our guardianship of Jesse was revoked. Lemont petitioned the court and is going to adopt him."

"Fuck!" He stood straighter and tightened his hold on his phone. He had to work at unlocking his jaw to bite out, "Has Tom contacted you?"

"Yes! He said DFPS sent you a letter."

He glanced at the pile of mail he'd put on the large table in the center of the dining area. The sleek chrome and glass table with its eight black

*Sara Walter Ellwood*

leather captain chairs had never been used, except to be a place for the mail he collected every morning he arrived home after his five-mile run.

He bounded up the step past a stone pillar supporting the loft above. When he reached the pile on the table, he started flipping through the junk and bills he'd brought in that morning. His assistant stopped by and collected the bills to pay every couple days and threw away the junk mail.

"Gabe, are you still there?"

"Yes. I'm checking to see if they sent me a letter." His stomach ached when he finally found the letter from the Texas Department of Family Protective Services. "I have it."

"What's it say? Don't you know? How long have you had it?"

He stiffened his spine and squared his shoulders at the accusation in her rapid-fire questions. Annoyed at himself more than he was at her, he glanced at the postmark. "It just came in this morning." Thank God he hadn't had it for longer. He ripped open the envelope and read the letter inside. "It's from Judge Bentley Anderson and basically informs me and you of the rescinding of our guardianship of Jesse. That he will be put into the care of his maternal grandfather until a hearing on October eighth to determine temporary custody of Jesse. The official adoption proceedings are scheduled for early next year."

"It's the same letter I got served this morning."

He heard the disappointment. Had she hoped he'd gotten a different letter?

"Gabe, what are we going to do?" Micki sniffed and let out a shuttering breath that tugged uncomfortably at his heart. "I don't want to lose him."

Moving back into the living room, he dropped into the supple leather of his couch and let out a deep breath. "I don't know, but I'll think of something. I've got to fly out in the morning for Cheyenne, but I'll try to swing by Bluebonnet Creek before I'm due in Dallas. I'll call Tom and set up an appointment for us. I also know a lawyer who might help, too. The more legal muscle we have, the better."

"Good. Rumor is Lemont put a bid in on the ranch." The fear and worry ripped at his heart. He hated that she was caught up in the middle of all this.

Closing his eyes, he leaned his head against the back of the couch. The thought of Lemont getting his hands on the Lazy M bothered him as much as the man gaining custody of Jesse. He gripped his phone until his hand hurt. "Damn. I won't let you go homeless, Micki."

"And I told you I don't want or need your help. We're working together for Jesse and that's all. I'll take care of him and Momma."

Sighing, he agreed only because he was too tired to argue with her. "Okay."

Before he had a chance to say more, she said a quick "Goodbye" and hung up.

He dialed Tom Fleming's number. After finding out nothing more than what Micki had told him, he called his good friend and the best family law lawyer in Tennessee. Lucky for Gabe, he also had an office in Dallas. Maybe Reese could help them get Jesse back.

* * * *

Two hours later, Gabe entered the office of his friend and shook the man's hand. Reese Goodwin smiled and led Gabe to the tan suede couches facing each other next to a refreshment bar. Everything about Goodwin oozed success, from the large executive office to his charcoal Armani suit and red and gray silk power tie. Gabe sat on the couch facing the bright midday skyline of Nashville while Reese went to the bar.

"Coffee? Or would you like something stronger?" Reese lifted a carafe into the air.

"Coffee's fine. Black. Thanks."

Reese poured two mugs full, then added cream and sugar to his own. He handed Gabe a mug and sat on the couch facing him. They'd met six years ago when he'd hired Reese as his divorce lawyer. He'd managed to save Gabe from owing Andrea more than a year and a half of his life, which he'd paid in spades while married to the witch.

The lawyer studied him for a moment over his cup as he sipped. "Okay, tell me what's on your mind."

Gabe looked into his mug contemplating where to start. He pulled the letter from the judge in Texas out of the back pocket of his Levis and handed it to his friend.

Reese read it, then refolded it and handed it back. "That's tough. I've heard of Lemont Finn. But I don't know him."

Gabe glanced at the letter in his hand. "He's a hard man. My father wasn't a saint. Far from it, but Lemont is the devil. His family made a fortune in cattle and oil, and he's expanded it at the expense of anyone who stands in his way. His first wife was killed in a car accident, which has always been suspected of being a suicide. He divorced his second wife after she discovered she had MS. Then he disowned his daughters when they decided to stay with Loretta rather than him after they were old enough to decide. I may not have liked Frankie, but I know she wouldn't have wanted Lemont to have Jesse. And I damn well know my father didn't. Not after Lemont stole most of my family's fortune when he swindled Dad out of his partnership in Finn Energy. Michaela Finn is good with Jesse, and it's logical she should raise him. She and Frankie were close, and if she'd made a will, that's who she would've wanted him to live with."

Reese sat forward. "What about Miss Finn? Is there anything you haven't told me about her?"

Gabe ran his free hand through his hair. "She and I were engaged seven years ago. A couple of days before our wedding, I played a honky-tonk gig in Brownwood. I had no idea Andrea Rose was in the audience." He signed and leaned his head back on the couch, suddenly exhausted. "Michaela broke my heart when she handed my ring back and telling me if I left we were done. All I wanted was to go to Nashville and see if Andrea was as good as her word. If she made me as famous as she promised, Michaela and I could start a new life away from all the shit we had to live with on the ranch." With a shake of his head, he rid himself of the painful memories. He sipped more of his coffee. "Michaela didn't believe in my dreams. I refused to be stuck punching cattle in Bluebonnet Creek, Texas, for the rest of my life."

"She sounds a little unreasonable." Reese leaned over his legs. "You really believe she'll be a better parent for Jesse than you?"

"I love that boy, but of the two of us, she's the stable one. She was unreasonable when she left me, but that was a long time ago. She loves Jesse and can give him what he needs." He stood and moved to look out over the city he called home. "My life is no place for a kid."

Reese stood and headed for the coffee pot. After offering more of the strong brew to Gabe, who shook his head, Reese refilled his cup. "She lives on the ranch, correct? Isn't it to be sold?"

Gabe sighed and set his empty mug on the windowsill. "Yeah, on both accounts. Lemont supposedly wants to put a bid on the place."

"Emm... interesting..."

Looking over his shoulder, Gabe frowned. "You know I hate when you do that."

"Most people do." Reese retook his seat on the couch. "Think about it. If Finn buys the ranch, the funds would go to Jesse, correct?"

"Yes. In a trust fund." Gabe rubbed the back of his neck as he paced in front of the windows. He'd no doubt find a way to steal Jesse's trust fund, especially if the boy ever broke away from him as his daughters had. "Damn. Lemont won't just get the ranch and Jesse, but his money, too. He'll get my family's ranch for nothing."

"That's what I'm thinking. I'm assuming the money can't be touched until Jesse's adopted?"

"That's how I understand it." Gabe fisted his hands by his sides as another thought came to him. "Goddamn it. Finn has wanted to put the screws to my dad for over thirty years for various reasons. Lemont's been biding his time until he can destroy everything my family's worked for. And what better revenge than to turn my father's young son against his family."

Reese watched him for a few passes. "But aren't you afraid Miss Finn would take Jesse's money? I mean, from what you've told me, it sounds like she doesn't have much."

With a scowl, Gabe stopped and faced the lawyer. "No. I'll provide for Jesse. But I doubt she'll take my money. She hates my guts and believes I somehow cheated on her."

Reese stood next to him at the window with a skeptical expression. "All the more reason for her to take Jesse's."

Gabe sighed and looked back out over music city. "She would never touch the money. She's too proud to. But life would be hard, even with any survivor benefits he would receive." He tapped the plate glass with his knuckles and turned to Reese. "Thing is, Michaela will be homeless after the sale of the ranch. She will also be out of a job since she manages it. Her mother's MS is bad, and Michaela takes care of her, too."

"A court will never grant her custody of a child. Why don't you sue for him yourself?" Reese sipped his coffee and pinned Gabe with a probing gaze.

"I already told you why." He stared out the window at the city without really seeing it and shifted his feet. His chuckle was short-lived and without mirth. "I'm a rock star in cowboy boots and a Stetson. I can't take on a ten-year-old."

The lawyer shrugged. "Then your options are pretty clear. Lemont Finn will adopt him. You send an occasional birthday gift and life goes on." He set his cup on a low table. "No need for you to feel guilty."

"He's my brother, Reese." A hard lump formed in his chest. Was he out of options? "I love him."

"I know, buddy." Reese patted Gabe's shoulder. "I'm leaving for my Dallas office in the morning. I might be able to get the court to extend the joint guardianship, but with the situation with Miss Finn and Lemont, it will be a long shot."

Gabe didn't like the twist in his heart. "Michaela's good with him."

"You would be, too." Reese lifted his hand to forestall any protest. "Look, there are a lot of single parents out there in the business, Gabe. They take their kids with them on the road with a good nanny. Schedule their tours around their kids' schedules, and they're fine because of it. My father is a lawyer. Mother was a singer. They split when I was three and each of them married a half dozen times after that. I spent summers with my mom and whatever husband she was with while she toured. The winters were spent with my dad and my latest, and increasingly younger, stepmother." He smiled and spread his hands. "I think I turned out just fine."

Gabe turned his back on the view of the city and laughed. "That's debatable. You've been divorced twice. Besides, you're a freakin' divorce lawyer."

"I already had tons of experience with divorce by the time I graduated law school. I figured it was the perfect career path."

Chuckling, Gabe shook his head. "Hey, I'll be in Dallas on the fourth of October. You bringing your kids to the concert?"

"Wouldn't miss it." Reese spent October through May in Dallas with his kids from his second marriage. The summer months he spent in Nashville with his daughter from his first wife. He checked his watch. "I hate to cut this short, but I'm due in court in less than an hour. I have to make sure the bank accounts of a certain cheating husband are cleaned out by the mother of his three kids." Gabe smiled. "I'm so glad you're my friend."

Reese laughed. "Representing you was fun, but if Andrea had hired me..." He shrugged and cuffed Gabe on the shoulder. "I'm sorry, buddy, you'd definitely be singing the blues."

"Ouch." Gabe winced at the thought. She'd sabotaged his career by dropping him from Rose and Thorn Records and castrating him in the tabloids. "I don't want to imagine what damage she would have done if she'd had a better lawyer."

After a moment, Reese asked, "So, what do you want me to do about Jesse?"

Gabe picked up his hat from the couch and turned it in his hands a few times before putting it on his head. When he looked up at Reese again, he knew what he had to do. "I can't let Lemont Finn poison Jesse. If you really think Michaela and I don't stand a chance at adopting him together, then I want to do it on my own." He pulled his keys from his pocket and looked at them. "And, Reese, there's something else I need you to do."

"Why am I not surprised?"

# Chapter 5

Micki came out of the turn around the third barrel and leaned over Beau's neck as they raced back to the starting point, but she knew they weren't fast enough. Despite retiring from barrel racing two years ago, she had kept Beau in shape and hoped that someday she might return to the sport she loved. Besides, racing had always been a great stress reliever.

She brought the gelding around and stopped before Cash. Standing near the high rail fence, he waved and smiled. "You looked pretty impressive. Thinking about going back on the circuit?"

"No. I just needed to think about something other than what's happening around here."

Cash stroked the neck of the bay. The horse's black-tipped chestnut hair and dark mane glowed in the morning light. Beau pranced under her, wanting to run again, but the horse hadn't been worked this hard since Sam and Frankie's death over two weeks ago. He needed to rest.

"I can understand that. I figured you could use some help around this place." Cash squinted up at her from under the brim of his old felt hat. "Sorry for not being around much, but I had some school stuff I needed to take care of." He'd helped out around the ranch as much as he could, but she hadn't seen him in about three days.

She'd encouraged the ranch hands to look for other jobs, and the last one was leaving today. The men and women employed by the Lazy M didn't want to go, but they refused to work for the corporation buying the place. She couldn't ask them to stay. "Thanks for coming today. I can really use the help."

"So, what's going on?" Cash entered through the gate, closing it behind him. She dismounted and led the horse around the corral. Cash walked along with her. "I heard about the sale. Is your daddy going to let you stay?" Cash lifted his hat and ran his hand through his short red hair. A few strands stuck to the sweat on his forehead. He resettled the hat.

"Lemont wasn't the buyer."

Cash stopped, his wide eyes making his round face more boyish than normal. "Who bought it?"

"No idea. Tom Fleming said a feedlot corporation bought it." She led Beau around the corral one last time to cool down. Glancing over her shoulder at Cash, she sighed. "Apparently, they out-bid Lemont and he let it go. Probably because he figured if he couldn't have it, one of those damned feedlot corps would be just as perfect to destroy the place."

"Damn…" He let out a long breath and looked around. "What about the animals?"

"They bought all the stock and the horses, too. Hell, even Frankie's stupid chickens and her prized peacocks were sold to these people." She looked away and blinked her eyes, fighting the burn in her sinuses. "I imagine they'll resell them or have them slaughtered. I don't know who'd want to eat a scrawny peacock, but I suppose there's folks out there that do."

"What happens to you?" He set his hand on Beau's lead rein to stop him.

"I'm trying to decide if I want to stay or leave." She shoved her hands into her pockets and leaned her back on the top rail of the fence, suddenly too tired to move. "I've been offered a job by the corporation, but honestly I hate that so many ranches are being bought and turned into feedlots."

"I can't even imagine that happening to the Lazy M." His voice deepened with a malice she'd never thought him capable of.

She envisioned what the ranch could look like in a few months. When too many cattle were crammed into fenced areas and fattened up on subpar grain rather than allowed to graze as natured intended. All the horses sold or sent to Mexico for slaughter, as had happened to a ranch over in Coleman County. The thought not only made her angry, it sickened her.

With a mental shake to get the horrible images out of her head of her beautiful Angus cattle dirty and living in mud and their own excrement, she nodded. "I tried to call the head of the company to find out what they have planned for the place, but I got nowhere. I've left at least five messages since the sale and haven't gotten a single call back. What would you do if it were you?"

He shook his head and watched as Beau reached under the bottom rail with his tongue to capture a few blades of grass growing around the fence post. "I wouldn't do it, but I don't have the responsibility you do."

No statement was ever truer, but she wasn't signing any contracts yet. The idea of leaving the ranch scared her to death. Would the judge think she was stupid for not taking a good-paying job on the ranch? Or could she prove that she can make it on her own merit?

"I haven't decided, but I can't wait until I do. If I leave, I have to have a job." She'd cashed out the retirement fund Sam had set up for her. It wasn't much and wouldn't last her more than two months if she decided to leave the ranch, but it added a bit of padding to her bank account.

As she reached for Beau's reins, a wave of sorrow hit her. There wouldn't be anything left of the ranch she loved in a few months. She'd seen too many beautiful spreads destroyed by the corporations buying them up and turning them into nothing more than cattle factories.

"These people even bought Jesse's Bobo." She swallowed at the lump in her throat.

"That goofy duck you gave him for Easter a few years back?"

"Yep." When Jesse was five years old, he'd gotten the biggest thrill from the duckling following him around the yard as he looked for the eggs Frankie had hidden. For the past several years, the duck had seemed more content to stay on the small lake in the pasture closest to the house rather than waiting to waddle after Jesse, but Jesse still loved it and letting it go would be just one more hurtful thing. "I'm so glad your sister took Frankie's cats and you took Sam's dogs. I would've loved having them if Momma wasn't so allergic..."

"You know we'll love them, Micki."

She knew, but it seemed like she was giving away everything her sister and husband loved. Looking toward the big white house through the orchard, she sighed. She wasn't ready for starting over. "The household goods are going to auction on October first."

"I saw the sign at the gate. I'm sorry, Micki."

Not wanting the sympathy she heard in his voice and wishing she'd kept the sorrow she felt to herself, she glanced back at him and headed toward the barn with Beau trotting beside her. "C'mon. I'm done here."

Once they were in the breezeway, he began to remove the bridle and saddle. She led Beau into his stall. Cash filled the trough with water, then the feed bucket with grain. While she used a currycomb to groom Beau, Cash took the horse's protective boots and bridle into the tack room. He had been unusually quiet for the past few moments. For as long as she could remember, which had been most of his life, Cash was a chatterer.

Hoping she hadn't hurt his feelings, she leaned against a stall door and crossed her arms over her chest. When he returned from the tack room, she said, "What's on your mind?"

He glanced down at his boots and kicked the straw covering the concrete floor. "I wish I could've bought this place--stock and all."

She pushed away from the stall and dropped her arms. "Why?"

He looked at her, and she wished she could see his brown eyes, but the brim of his hat hid them in a shadow. "Then you wouldn't need to worry about anything."

She swallowed so hard it hurt. Cash was one of her closest friends. "Cash, I..."

He let out a sigh loud enough she'd heard it from across the space of the breezeway. "I know you think I'm a kid. I love this place, too, Micki. I've been working here since I was thirteen." He cleared his throat and closed the distance between them. When he was standing before her, boot to boot, he pushed back her hat and met her eyes. "I hate seeing you like this. You worry about everyone, but you don't think about yourself."

Glancing away, she bit her bottom lip. "I'm okay."

But she wasn't okay. Ever since Gabe had walked back into her life, she couldn't stop thinking about him. He'd promised to help her with Jesse, but he went back to his high life, leaving her to work everything out again.

Her heart ached over losing Jesse to her father, and the loss of her family in the crash. Helping the women from church pack away Sam and Frankie's life had been one of the hardest things she'd ever done. She was also scared her mother wasn't being truthful about her level of pain. Momma had become withdrawn, her speech more slurred, and her appetite was nearly nonexistent.

Closing the stall door, she met his skeptical expression and reiterated a little more forcefully, "Cash, I'm okay."

They left the barn together, and he looked around. "What do you have in mind for today?"

"We need to get some hay out to the cattle across the creek. With this drought, they're burning through that piss-ass poor grass over there."

He rubbed his hand over the back of his sunburned neck. "How much hay do we have?"

Micki shoved her hands into the back pockets of her jeans. They were so faded that the blue was washed almost white in places. "Enough for two weeks. After September thirtieth, feeding the stock will be the problem of the corporation." She swallowed and looked toward the bunkhouse.

Eddie Rodrigues loaded a warn La-Z-Boy onto the back of a pickup. He was the last of the full-time hands to move.

"Where's Eddie going?"

She kicked at a clump of dry dirt with her boot. "He got a job on a ranch somewhere south of Dallas with his cousin."

He shook his head. "Eddie's been here forever."

"Yeah, I know. He didn't want to go but didn't really have a choice. Even though the new owners offered jobs, none of the hands applied for them. We all hate these faceless corporations that are buying up ranches and farms and destroying them."

"Damn." He cleared his throat and wiped sweat from his forehead with the back of his gloved hand. "Do we still have to vaccinate the cows?"

God, why couldn't things have stayed as they were? "The cattle have to be counted and vaccinated by Wednesday. Eddie and I did about a hundred fifty of them yesterday."

"That gives you less than a week to do the rest." He paused and faced her. "We can start with those cows across the creek today."

She kicked at the dusty gravel in the driveway with the toe of her worn boot and slapped him on the shoulder. "C'mon. Let's go get something to eat first." At the steps of the cottage, she turned to him, squinting into the bright morning sun to look up into his face. "I'm glad you're here. I don't know how I would've survived if I would've had to take care of this place on my own."

Pink flared to life in the cheeks of his baby face, and his earlobes turned red. He looked at the ground and shrugged. "What are friends for if we don't help each other out?"

* * * *

"Hello." The soft and sleepy word sounded through Gabe's cell and did all sorts of things to parts of him that had no business responding to anything Michaela Finn said.

"Hi, Michaela." He shifted in the leather seat of the BMW convertible and cleared his throat of the gruffness. He must have strained his voice singing the last song during the concert tonight.

"About damned time you call me," she snapped without preamble, and he smiled. Michaela always was a straight shooter.

When the light changed, he flipped on his turn signal and maneuvered into the driveway of the hotel. The streets of downtown Cheyenne were virtually deserted.

She yawned and didn't bother hiding it from him. "It's one thirty in the morning."

He winced and slowed the rental car as he pulled into the parking garage of the luxury hotel where he and the band were staying. "Sorry it's so late. I just listened to my messages."

"Nice to see I rate in importance to you. I called at ten a.m. this morning."

"I'm sorry. I was busy all day. My concert was tonight."

He may have been busy, but that didn't stop him from thinking about her. About the way she took care of Jesse and how right it all looked.

Or how much it would hurt her to lose him.

She sighed and her voice softened. "Actually, I probably would've missed your call anyway. I helped move cows all day." He wanted to tell her not to worry so much about the cattle, but before he could speak, she asked, "Have you found out anything? How can we get Jesse back?"

He sucked in a breath and pulled the BMW into his parking space. "I have a plan, but it involves me adopting Jesse. Alone."

A rustling and the soft creaking of bedsprings sounded over the line. From the buried past, an exhumed memory hit him as hard as a fist when the image of Micki in her bed and dressed in one of his T-shirts jumped to the front of his mind. How many times had he peeled the soft cotton from her body and kissed the tanned skin, tasting, teasing, until she'd begged him to take her? His groin jumped to life, and he had to concentrate on his plan.

Before he could tell her he'd bought the ranch and she wouldn't have to move, she seethed, "How can you do this to me? I thought you believed the road wasn't any place for a kid. Damn you, Gabe! You know I love him. Frankie would've wanted me to have him. You're doing this to spite me, is that it?"

Why did she always have to assume he was trying to hurt her? Maybe he shouldn't even try to keep her involved. Gritting his teeth and gripping the steering wheel so hard his knuckles turned white, he decided to stop trying. Even if he told her his plan, she'd refuse to be a part of it. She'd never take anything from him, and damn it, he was tired of being punished for leaving her. "My decision has nothing to do with you. He's my brother, and I want to do what's best for him."

"That never mattered before! You hated my sister and your own father."

In his mind, he saw her sitting in bed and clutching her cell phone. Looking sexy as hell with her long blond hair tumbling wild over her shoulders and her blue eyes fiery with anger.

He squeezed his eyes shut, hoping to stop the erotic images. She'd never be his again, if she ever had been. The only person who mattered was Jesse. "Damn it, Michaela, I love him and I'll do anything for him."

"What kind of life can you give him, Gabe?"

Now, *that* was a million-dollar question. He turned the engine off and sat under the spotlights of the garage. As he stared at the concrete wall, he got his body under control but not the seething anger boiling his blood at her lack of faith in him. Reese was right. He didn't need her to raise Jesse. Gabe loved him. He had a home and enough money to provide for him. What else did he need? Considering Michaela's feelings had done nothing but cause him a shitload of grief, it was about time he started thinking about what was best for his brother. "A home. A good education. He'll never want for anything."

"I can give him those things as easily as you."

"How? You refused to take me up on my offer to support him. Do you plan to use his inheritance?" He crossed the line with the accusation, but he didn't give a goddamn. He'd had enough of her playing the martyr.

"I can't believe you think I'd touch his money." She was quiet for a moment, and he figured she was squaring her stubborn shoulders to blast him with some other crap. "I'm not going to deny things will be tough, but a lot of kids are raised in tough situations and do just fine. At least if he's with me, I'd be the one raising him. Have you hired his nanny for when you're partying with the latest slut? Or will you just pawn him off to the next bimbo you marry for advancement of your career?"

He'd wondered how long it would be before she brought up his ex-wife. Too wound up to hear Michaela's thoughts about her, Gabe set his back teeth and hit the disconnect button.

With a frustrated push, the door opened and he climbed out of the sports car. Why had he told Michaela his plan to adopt Jesse? He should have known how the conversation was going to go to hell.

All she'd ever done was find fault in everything he did. Michaela thought he slept his way to the top. Hell, a lot of people thought that, especially after the release of the stink bomb that was his second album. So, why did her belief that he did cause a sharp pain in the middle of his forehead like someone was poking him with a penknife from the inside of his skull?

He made his way to the bank of elevators and pushed the *up* button.

The vision of moonlight shining through the window next to their bed in the bunkhouse and turning her skin silvery flashed before his eyes. In the pale light, he'd kissed his way from her firm breasts down her belly to the hot, wet, sweet place between her legs.

"Shit," he hissed through his teeth and tapped the *up* key again. He dragged in a breath, glad no one was around to see the bulge he sported in his tight jeans. How could he have a hard-on for a woman who irritated the hell out of him?

Maybe he should find a woman and get himself laid. But he knew a meaningless fuck with just anyone he wanted wouldn't help. Hadn't for a long time, if ever. He wanted one particular woman.

As the door slid open, he scowled and stepped in.

Hell would be enjoying snowball fights and the devil would be ice fishing on the River Styx before he'd ever touch Michaela Finn again.

Music blaring over a sound system greeted Gabe when he stepped off the elevator. Gritting his teeth, he rushed to the door of his luxury suite. He dug his key card out of his jeans pocket and opened the door, dreading what he'd find on the other side.

Scantily dressed women danced provocatively with his band members and the men of Gabe's production crew in the living room. Alcohol freely flowed and cigarette smoke hung at the ceiling of his non-smoking room like a low ominous storm cloud.

"Isn't this great?" Joel Horner, the bass guitar player in Gabe's band, rushed over and flung an arm around Gabe's shoulders. His long dark hair hung around his face, reminding Gabe of a hair band member from the eighties. Joel flashed a cocky grin. "You've been way too glum lately. So, we planned a little pick-you-up party."

"Fuck." Gabe gritted through clenched teeth and moved away from the one-time hard rock-turned-country musician. "What the hell?"

The last thing he wanted was a party in his posh hotel suite. His flight to Texas was scheduled to leave at six in the morning. All he wanted to do right now was crash for a few hours and try not to think about the woman he couldn't have.

Or the little boy Gabe loved with all of his heart.

Joel straightened, affronted. "A party, man. Remember? You used to have 'em all the time. What the hell's going on with you? You might have lost someone you're close to. But, damn, man, tonight's show was downright painful. You were like a robot out there. But this goes beyond that. You haven't been yourself for months. The guys and me decided to remind you of the good old days. Ever since Gary came on the scene, you've changed."

"I think you should remember where we were headed before Gary took us on." Gabe shook his head and forced his hands to stay relaxed at his sides. He owed his best friend, Seth Kendall, for talking Gary into taking him on. Gary's rules were strict, but under his management, Gabe's career was bigger than even he'd ever dreamed. "I can't afford to trash hotel rooms anymore." What was wrong with him? He wasn't a wet blanket, but he sure was acting and feeling like one. Why didn't everyone go the hell home?

Two of his other band members watched the confrontation happening in the entry of Gabe's suite. A woman approached wearing a short, shimmery tank dress. The top plunged deep to show off her ample cleavage and the hem stopped short to show off her muscular legs from her ankle to just an inch or two below her pussy. Her long blond hair hung to her waist in sexy curls, and her blue eyes were smoky and mysterious. If the sexy black dress and red fuck-me heels weren't enough to let him know she hoped for more than an autograph from him, the pouty smile was seductive enough to assure there was no mistaking what she desired.

"Hello, Gabe." The blonde held out a bottle of Corona and sidled up closer to him.

"We met in Vegas a little over a year ago?" Gabe asked. He took the beer and forced a smile as he lifted the Corona and drank.

"I think we did more than just meet. Three days of the best sex of my life is what I remember." Her pouty smile turned purely seductive and her eyes burned with open lust as she ran her hand over his chest.

He shivered, but it had nothing to do with desire and everything to do with revulsion.

"I loved your show tonight." Her husky voice dripped sex.

Gabe lowered the beer as recognition hit him. "Lydia?"

She raised a brow and shifted a shoulder in a half shrug. "My favorite song is 'One Night Rodeo.' The video is so hot."

Which was code for *I'd like to star in the X-rated version.*

He had to get out of here. The last thing he needed was to get tangled up with Lydia Greenhow. He'd picked up the stripper after a show in Vegas. At the time, he'd thought she was a showgirl, which was bad but didn't have quite the stigma a stripper had. Something the tabloids had reminded him of.

But hadn't he been wishing for a willing woman? With her blond hair and blue eyes, he could almost pretend she was Michaela. Hell, wasn't that what attracted him to her the last time they'd met? Maybe if he was drunk enough, he wouldn't notice she could never match Michaela's natural beauty. He would never be seen outside his hotel room with the woman, so the chance of the tabloids ever finding out was nonexistent.

He slipped his arm around the girl and moved her toward the couch. Leaning close, he sang the chorus of his latest single in her ear,

*"The party's over, you don't have to go,*

*This cowboy's not ready to go down,*

*So why don't you stick around,*

*We'll have ourselves a one night rodeo."*

She smiled and her hand slid down to cup his ass. "Hell, yeah."

A member of his crew sat on the couch with a woman in his lap, but he got up and gave it up to his boss. Gabe winked his thanks and pulled Lydia across his lap. When she giggled, the shrillness went right through him, nearly ruining his determination to have fun--no matter how painful.

She put her hands on his shoulders, and his free hand landed on the curve of her hip. He turned his head and finished off the beer, watching her. "What are you doing in Cheyenne?"

"I grew up in a small town north of here."

He lowered the empty bottle, remembering his last encounter with the woman. "Not working in Vegas anymore?"

She sipped her beer and her eyes slipped from his. "I had a baby six months ago. My mother wanted me to come home so she could help out with it. I plan to go back soon."

A warning bell sounded in his head. "I take it the father isn't in the picture."

She met his gaze again and shrugged. "He doesn't know and I want to keep it that way." She straddled his thighs and leaned in. After nipping his ear, she whispered, "I'm ready anytime you are for that rodeo, cowboy."

He couldn't remember much of those three days with her, only Gary's outrage afterward when Gabe's picture with the stripper hit the tabloids. "I can think of plenty to do with a woman as pretty as you."

She ran her fingernail over his jaw line, then slid her hand down his chest and over his abs. When she settled her palm over his groin, she stroked him through his tight jeans. Leaning in, she nipped his earlobe, her breath warm on the side of his face. "I'm so hot for you. I have a sudden urge to play cowgirl."

He tried to find desire in her caress, but the sensation wasn't arousing. "In a minute. Let's have another drink."

Her long, fake lashes veiled her eyes but not her disappointment. "Sure, whatever you want."

Gabe shifted her hand from his groin. Despite his original intentions when bringing her to the couch, he suddenly hoped she'd get bored and leave him alone, but he couldn't bring himself to make her go. "Let's have a drink."

Someone handed her a margarita and Gabe another Corona. He took a long draw on the beer before setting it on the table beside his empty bottle.

A hard rock song blasted from the speakers, and she moved to the beat in his lap, sloshing her drink all over the silk couch and him in the process. After tossing back what was left of it, she wrapped her arms around his neck and the lap dance got a lot more provocative. Her dress slipped up to reveal a red lace thong. As she pressed herself into him, he found it perplexing that just a memory of Michaela had him so hard his cock ached, but this woman did nothing for him.

"I want to fuck you all night long," she whispered in his ear, then kissed him square on the mouth, surprising him. Before he could push her away, someone opened the door. Hotel security rushed in.

# Chapter 6

The large white sign painted with black and red lettering situated by the gate of the Lazy M caused Gabe to stop the rental car and stare at it. *Auction of Household Goods, October 1, everything must go.*

A sold plaque over the realtor sign gave him another pause. He'd decided to buy the ranch on a whim. Now, he wasn't so sure the way he'd gone about it had been a good decision. Michaela and Loretta, hell, even Tom Fleming should have been told of his ideas. Reese had convinced him total anonymity was the best way. Reese discovered through his contacts in Texas that Lemont only wanted the land to keep it out of Gabe's hands, then hoped to sell it to a development company. To prevent him from going after the ranch more seriously, Reese created a dummy feedlot corporation to buy it for Gabe. He outbid Lemont by nearly two million dollars. When the old man didn't counter the bid, Gabe knew he'd been right about Lemont's intentions. He planned to buy the place, but instead of the money going to Jesse, it would end up back in Lemont's pockets. The retired judge and oilman lived like a wealthy man, but was he as rich as he pretended to be?

He intended to hire Michaela as the manager and leave Jesse in her care while he was on the road after the adoption. She'd have guardianship of Jesse and together they'd raise him. But first, he had to tell her what his ideas were, before she did something like move off the ranch. Reese had neglected to tell him until that morning about Micki's repeated phone calls asking for the head of the corporation to contact her.

He hated that Reese had to come up with such a ruse to trick Lemont Finn into thinking he'd won even if he lost the ranch. Gabe's father may have been an SOB at times, but he loved his land and animals. The last thing he'd ever want was the Lazy M in the hands of a feedlot corporation. Michaela would never work for a feedlot. They went against everything she believed in.

But would she stay if she knew he'd bought the ranch? She'd been furious with him when he'd announced his decision to go after Jesse himself. Closing his eyes, he sucked in a deep breath. For any of his ideas to work, she had to stay on the ranch. He should have told her about that part of his plan first, then brought up his hope of adopting Jesse. The little boy was her hot button, and he pushed it last night.

Bracing for the confrontation with Michaela, he shifted the rental Mercedes back into drive and turned down the gravel lane.

This morning he'd landed at the airport, then dropped his things off at the hotel in Brownwood; however, as he'd paced his room, the walls started closing in on him. He had to see Michaela and hoped she would hear him out before she jumped to conclusions that weren't true.

Gabe knocked on the screen door and peered into the cottage. No doubt his antics from two nights ago would be a hot topic on the gossip show blaring from the living room TV.

He'd missed his flight yesterday morning. After spending hours talking to the hotel manager, he finally convinced the guy not to press charges for the damages done to the suite by writing him a whopping check to cover the cost of fixing the room and another for the manger to add to his bank account.

Then he'd spent the afternoon begging Gary not to dump him and the band. Gary Russell had taken a chance on Gabe when he'd signed him, but his conditions were straightforward and strict--no hotel trashing. Gary didn't care about the women Gabe paraded in and out of his bedroom as long as he didn't do something stupid--like getting caught kissing a stripper. Again.

Although Gabe was furious over the damage done and at his band for arranging the party Saturday night, he was more concerned about how the tabloid media would spin Lydia Greenhow's lip lock on him. Gary had seen a picture someone had taken of the kiss on the Internet, and soon after that the connection was made to a photo taken of him with the same Vegas stripper fifteen months ago.

Reese was more than ten kinds of mad at Gabe. But, then, he was as disappointed in himself. None of this was going to help his custody battle with Lemont.

He rapped on the rickety old door again. This time Loretta heard him and called out a slurred, "C'mon in."

Gabe opened the door and entered the darkened living room just as the picture of the stripper kissing him flashed on the TV.

Loretta hit a button on the remote, mercifully muting the report about his rock star antics. She didn't turn to look at him when she said, "Looks like you had quite a Saturday night."

He removed his hat and glanced at it before hanging it on a peg by the door beside a few other old hats. "You could say that."

"Was that before or after you called and upset Micki?"

"After. I'm sorry about that. I didn't mean to anger her. But she drives me crazy." He moved into the living room and sat on the couch. The brown corduroy was worn smooth on the arms and fronts of the cushions, but it was clean. His mother had made the mauve and sage-green crocheted afghan folded in the corner of the sofa. He took a deep breath and brushed his fingers over the soft wool before leaning over his legs and clasping his hands together, unable to meet the older woman's eyes. The need to tell her about his purchase of the ranch caused his heart to pound. But first he needed to speak to Michaela.

Loretta let out a strangled chuckle. "She always did."

He chose to let that particular bit of truth slip by without commenting. "How're things going around here?"

"As good as can be expected all things considered. We miss Jesse."

"Have you talked to him?"

"No. Have you?"

He nodded, remembering the brief call from a week ago. "Yeah. But Lemont caught him and forced him to hang up."

She hissed and shook her head. "The jerk."

Not wanting to trouble her further, he peered around the small room, hoping to think of something else to talk about. Knickknacks crowded the top of the TV cabinet. On the shelves between the windows were the buckles and trophies Michaela--and before her, Loretta--had won as barrel racers. Empty cardboard boxes sat in the corner, and his heart sank. "You're moving?"

Loretta looked down at her crooked fingers splayed out over her faded housedress. She curled them into loose fists and nodded. "I don't know. Micki's trying to find a place in town."

"Why would she do that?" Damn, now what did he say? He needed to find Michaela. Standing, he went to the front window and looked out over the driveway toward the barn. A cloudy haze muted the late morning sun.

Michaela was coming out of the second turn around a barrel she had set up in the corral. She headed for the third and leaned sharply in the saddle as the horse took the turn at a full gallop, horse and rider working together as one beautiful, connected being.

He glanced over his shoulder. "Michaela's training?"

Loretta whirled her wheelchair over to sit beside him. He dropped the lace curtain and met her troubled blue eyes.

"She says she rides to keep her horse in shape, in case she decides to sell him. I know she'd never part with Beau. I think she's got it in her head to go back out on the circuit. She wants to use any of the winnings she might get to pay for some fancy surgery the doc thinks will stop the pain in my face." She averted her eyes to her knobby hands. "I wish she'd not worry so much about me. She should've never quit racing to begin with. I could've gone to a nursing home, then she wouldn't have to be burdened with me."

"Michaela loves you, Loretta. She would never consider you a burden." Gabe was no shrink, but he recognized depression when he saw it. But, then, if he'd lived the life Loretta had before the onset of her MS, he'd be disgruntled, too. She'd been a champion barrel racer in her younger days and as much a cowgirl as her daughter. Now, she couldn't walk and lived in constant pain.

When he and Michaela had dated, he'd become close to her mother and wished he could do something now to make things better for her. He forced a smile and gently touched her shoulder. "She only wants what's best for you."

"She's too stubborn for her own good sometimes."

He snorted and watched as Michaela put the horse through another cloverleaf pattern. "She is definitely that." Resting a hand on Loretta's frail shoulder, he said, "I have a plan. Can you trust me?"

Loretta stared out the window through the lace curtain, then shook her head as if physically shaking off a thought. She looked up at him with narrowed eyes. "I don't know. Are you gonna tell me why you are all geared up to take Jesse from Micki? You know damn well Sam and Frankie would've wanted you to share him."

"I don't want to take Jesse from her or you." He looked back out the window. In the corral, Micki led her horse toward the barn. "I need to talk to Michaela." Leaning down, he kissed the older woman on the cheek, then headed out to the barn.

* * * *

No one else but Gabe would be parked out front of her home in some fancy luxury car. Was he here to gloat over his desire to adopt Jesse?

The echo of footsteps filled the breezeway of the barn, and Micki sucked in a breath. The image of him and that stripper she'd seen on the computer last night flashed before her closed eyes. Why did it bother her so much? She didn't care what Gabriel McKenna did. Nor should she have expected more from him.

Gabe stopped on the other side of her horse, but she didn't look at him. She continued stroking Beau's neck with a currycomb as he slurped water. "What the hell are you doing here?"

He stroked the other side of Beau's neck. "I'm here because we need to talk about the ranch. Loretta said the owner offered you a management position."

"They did and I'm thinking I'll tell them to go to hell."

With a sharp look, he said, "I wish you'd take the job. There's something about this whole thing you don't know."

She tossed the comb onto a shelf. "What isn't there to know? One of those sleazy out-of-state agglomerates wants to destroy the ranch I love, and the man I should have known better than to trust is stabbing me in the back."

Gabe stiffened his stance and glared at her. "Damn it, Michaela, I'm not trying to take Jesse away from you. I want to keep him out of Lemont's hands. I still want you to have guardianship of him."

She stepped away from the horse. "I thought only you were good enough to raise him."

"I never said that." He stepped away from Beau and put his hands in his jeans pockets. "We're in this together. All my lawyer thinks is that it would be easier for us if I petition the court for adoption than for us to try to adopt him together."

"That doesn't explain your appearance here at the ranch."

He shifted his feet, his hat hiding his face. "I consider the Lazy M my home as you do, Michaela. I..." His Adam's apple bobbed as he swallowed and met her gaze.

Before he had a chance to tell her more pretty words that were nothing but lies, she said, "We aren't friends. If your father and my sister hadn't died, we wouldn't even be talking to each other. Now you want to take Jesse away from me."

Micki spun away from Gabe. Beau shifted his feet, bumping into her, probably sensing her frustration. The last person she wanted to talk to was Gabe.

She led the horse into his stall. Micki hoped Gabe would have gotten the hint and left. Her luck wasn't that good. He leaned against a door of the stall next to Beau's.

Micki dragged her gaze up his body. Over his polished snakeskin boots, his long, muscular legs encased in faded denim, the T-shirt that covered a flat belly she knew was washboard solid. She'd seen enough pictures of his bare torso on the Internet to know--as if her memory didn't already provide enough X-rated images on its own. With his arms crossed over his broad chest, his biceps bulged. A tattoo of his mother's first name, scripted over a breast cancer ribbon and surrounded by an intricate border, peeked out from under the edge of the black cotton of his sleeve.

She wasn't prepared for the burst of heat shooting through her as fast as a brushfire in dry grass at high noon. The flash melted her insides into a wet, achy pool in her low belly.

Not wanting him to know how he affected her, at least not in that way, she turned toward the wall. She grabbed a rake and opened the stall door farthest away from him. As she busied herself with cleaning out the empty stall, she said, "You know, I'm glad you're such a jerk."

"Michaela, I have a plan that--"

"You honestly think a conservative judge like Anderson will let you have Jesse?" she cut in, glancing up to find him standing by the door of the stall she was working in. With more force than required, she raked the manure and straw on the floor. Pausing, she fixed him with a glare and let him have the full weight of her frustration and anger. "You're fucking delusional! You showed the world, and more importantly Judge Anderson, what kind of life Jesse would be exposed to if you were to adopt him." She stopped and smiled. "Makes my small town life not so damn bad. Tom Fleming thinks I have a pretty good chance of beating you at your own game."

"What the hell is that supposed to mean?"

She came out of the stall and closed the door as if she had all the time in the world, which she didn't. The animals needed to be taken care of; then she had to make an appointment for the neurologist in Brownwood for her mother. Later that afternoon, she had a job interview at The Lasso Café and Bakery. The job had opened up, and she couldn't let it pass her up. Work in Bluebonnet Creek was hard to find, and she hadn't decided whether she would stay at the ranch or not.

But she'd be damned if she'd let him know any of it. When she faced him, she leaned on the rake. "Everyone in the county knows Anderson almost always sides with women in custody battles." She paused and forced a confident grin she didn't feel. "Besides, Anderson is no friend of Lemont's, so that's in my favor, too. Jesse will be better off with me. He'll live here in his hometown, and I'll be the one raising him. That's more important than what you can offer: a revolving door of nannies, starlet flings, and groupie hookups."

His jaw ticked as he clenched his teeth and his dark eyes flashed golden-brown fire. He stood with his feet apart, his arms tense at his sides. "As always, you blew this whole damned thing out of proportion. My only concern is my baby brother."

Micki had waited too long to have it out with him to stop now. She set the rake against the wall and crossed her arms. "Oh, you might want Jesse now, just like you wanted to get married. But the moment something you want more comes up, you'll leave Jesse flapping in the breeze."

The muscle in his jaw quivered again, and he took a step toward her. "This isn't about Jesse at all. This is about *you* breaking up with *me*."

"You're the one who left with that woman and never came home."

The fire of a moment ago turned as cold as burnished bronze in his eyes, and his hands fisted at his sides. "You broke our engagement when you handed back my ring and told me I had no damned business coming back."

"I wasn't myself then! I'd just lost our baby. I saw the way Andrea touched you and you ate it all up at the bar that night she saw you sing." She shook her head, hating that she bared so much of her pain to him, but she couldn't stop. "If you loved me, you would've come back regardless of what I said. You sure has hell wouldn't have fallen into bed with Andrea Rose! Or was that the only way you could get the recording contract?"

His nostrils flared and his shoulders moved as he sucked in a breath. "At least Andrea believed in my dreams. If you'd loved *me*, you would've, too." His hard, low voice raked over her and abraded the raw places in her heart. "Yes, you had lost our baby. A baby I didn't even know about until I found you bleeding in the bathroom, so don't even go there."

"I planned to tell you on our wedding night." The burn in her eyes was almost too much. But she wouldn't cry in front of him. "I wanted it to be a gift. I know it was stupid not to tell you I was pregnant, but..." She swallowed the lump and shut up before she started bawling. Pain from the memories of the night she lost the baby, less than two weeks before their wedding date, stabbed at her heart. She'd discovered she was pregnant only a week before she miscarried, but she'd loved the tiny child they'd created.

"None of this changes the fact that you--the most important person in my life then--didn't believe in me." He sniffed and his hard jaw ticked again. "I never once said anything about your damned rodeo obsession, but you hated my singing. Why, Michaela?"

His singing had nothing to do with it and she had believed in him, but she wasn't about to reveal that much of her soul. She pulled herself up to her full five feet four and fought the crumbling of her defenses. Refusing to show any more emotion to him, she opened another stall door. "I have things to do. Goodbye, Gabriel."

"See you in court, sweetheart." He turned and strolled toward the door.

As she watched him leave the barn and speed away in the flashy car, she lost the battle with her pride and a tear rolled down her cheek. She was a damned fool for letting him get under her skin again.

# Chapter 7

"After deliberating the case, I've determined neither Miss Michaela Finn nor Mr. Gabriel McKenna are suitable caregivers for the ward of this court, Jesse McKenna. The child will remain in the temporary custody of his maternal grandfather, Lemont Finn, until formal adoption proceedings on January sixth, at which time this court will reconsider the case."

Gabe jerked as if punched in the gut when the meaning of the judge's words sunk in. He looked at Reese, who sat beside him. The other man looked as perplexed as Gabe. Reese Goodwin wasn't used to losing.

The past few weeks had been a roller coaster of concert dates, recording the live album, and attending appointments arranged by Judge Anderson. A few meetings had been with Allison Fennel, who supervised Gabe's visits with Jesse in Lemont's home. Jesse clearly wasn't happy, but he hadn't said so to Gabe in Fennel's presence. After the second meeting with the social worker and Jesse, Gabe became more determined that Fennel was on Lemont's payroll and Jesse was scared to death of his grandfather.

As the judge shuffled papers on his desk, Reese stood. "Your Honor, may I ask for an explanation as to why my client is considered unsuitable? You have reports from Ms. Fennel and from my office to substantiate the special relationship Mr. McKenna has with the child."

Reese had figured Bentley Anderson's conservatism would give Michaela an advantage; however, after the case started, Lemont's million-dollar female lawyer made sure Micki didn't have a chance at winning on her own. And both Tom Fleming, who represented Michaela, and Reese, representing Gabe, blasted Lemont's custody of Jesse.

Gabe swallowed and looked at the woman beside him at the table. She held her head high as she stared straight ahead. He hated that Lemont dragged her through the dirt. Although he hoped to adopt Jesse, Gabe knew Micki loved the boy as much as he did.

She turned, her gaze cutting through him. Her long blond hair, which she normally pulled back into a ponytail, was styled into a demure bun at the back of her head. He wished he could take the pins out and run his hands through all the softness. The same black dress she'd worn to the funeral stretched over her subtle curves. The sight never failed to make his mouth go dry.

Lemont's lawyer glanced across Michaela's table to glare at Gabe. Amy Johnson, Esquire, had worked hard to make both Gabe and Michaela look as bad as yesterday's news.

The judge's words brought his attention back to the matter at hand. "I am concerned with Mr. McKenna's behavior. Only last month he was caught in a provocative photograph with a woman of questionable morals. I cannot take the chance of allowing him to care for the child, no matter how strong their relationship appears to be."

Tom Fleming stood and cleared his throat. "Your Honor, I'm unclear as to why my client wasn't given custody. Despite Mr. Finn's claims, Miss Finn has a steady income and can provide a home for the child."

Anderson's shoulders shifted as he took a deep breath before leaning over his beefy arms on the large oak desk, which served as the judgment bench. "I beg to differ, Mr. Fleming. Miss Finn has her plate full with taking care of a disabled mother, as Miss Johnson pointed out," he said, referring to Lemont's lawyer.

Lemont shifted in his seat, a smug, satisfied smile curling his lips. Michaela scowled at him, then looked at Gabe as the judge went on, "This decision wasn't an easy one to make. I can see how much both Mr. McKenna and Miss Finn love Jesse and that he loves them. He also confided his dislike for Mr. Finn." The statement wiped the smugness off Lemont's lined face.

"Despite these observations, I can't bring myself to put this child in such an unsteady home. I admire Mr. McKenna and Miss Finn's desire to share custody until the adoption hearing, but I do not believe they can provide a secure home; however, I'm not completely convinced Mr. Finn can meet Jesse's needs, either." He leaned back and shook his head. "A strong, loving family is what the boy should have now. Not all this squabbling."

Gabe stood, gaining a grumble from Reese, which he ignored. "So, what you're saying is that if either Michaela or I were married, your decision would have been different?"

Anderson shrugged his massive shoulders under his black robe. "It would have been if I could ensure Jesse would have a good home." He lifted his gavel and hit the block on the bench. "Court adjourned."

They all stood when the judge left the small chamber. Lemont shook his lawyer's hand. "Great job, Amy." He looked over at Gabe and Micki with an arrogant grin and nodded. "It was a good fight, y'all. But I told you I'd win. Now, I have to fetch my grandson. I promised him we'd go to Disney World if Anderson had any sense and ruled in my favor."

Gabe glared at him and took a step toward him. "You can't buy his love, Lemont."

The oilman paused and shrugged. "Jesse's young. He'll learn I can provide the better home for him."

"Like you did for your own daughters?" Michaela shoved up beside Gabe.

She might not like that he wanted to adopt Jesse, but they both had a common goal--keeping him away from his grandfather.

Lemont shrugged and put his hat on his head. "Have you ever considered the problem isn't me at all?" He smiled and patted Gabe on the shoulder. "Sorry about your little indiscretion on the road. Have a good day."

Gabe and Micki watched Finn and his lawyer walk to the door.

"God, I hate that man," Micki said.

"Yeah." Gabe glanced over at Michaela.

Could he really be considering the idea forming in his head? She met his gaze for a beat. Was she thinking the same thing?

* * * *

Micki pinned the order slip on the wheel and spun it back to the cook behind the counter. She grabbed the coffee pot and turned to refill the cups of the two truck drivers eating the lunch special at the bar. After making sure her other customers enjoying the Lasso Café's chicken-fried steak and cornbread were fine, she returned to wrapping flatware in paper napkins behind the counter. The lunch rush was winding down; now she had to get ready for the supper rush.

Since the court decision Monday, she couldn't keep the crazy idea from her mind. If she got married, she'd have a better chance of getting Jesse. Therein lay the problem: she wasn't even dating anyone. The only prospect she had was a man eight years younger than she was.

At the thought of Cash Nelson, Micki shook her head. He would jump at the suggestion of them getting married, even if she explained it was only for convenience. Despite his crushing on her since he was thirteen, she never considered him more than a friend. As much as she wanted to raise Jesse, she couldn't imagine being married to Cash. He'd expect more from her than she could give him, and she valued his friendship too much to hurt him.

The bell above the door gave a friendly tinkle, singling another customer for the Friday lunch special. When gasps from the table full of college-aged girls echoed through the suddenly quiet space, she knew who had walked in. The energy changed in the room, and the short hairs on the back of her neck stood up.

She slowly finished wrapping the service of flatware in her hand. Sucking in a deep breath, she turned around. Gabe slid onto a stool at the bar, and she caught him looking at her jeans-covered backside. The heat she saw in his dark eyes made her blood rush through her and tightened the skin over her breasts.

"Hello, Michaela."

Did she imagine the gruffness of his voice? It reminded her of the way he sounded when he'd made love to her and said dirty things in her ear.

She immediately pushed the memories back into the dungeon of her brain and locked the door.

"I figured you went back to Nashville." Micki handed Gabe a menu, aware that every eye in the place was on her and the country star.

He looked at the fare and shrugged. "I actually just got back in town. I flew out Monday after the hearing and drove back yesterday."

"Drove?"

Gabe grinned at her. "I figured it made more sense than renting a car. I intend to spend a few months in Texas."

*Months?*

With a squeak, the swinging door connecting the kitchen to the dining room opened, and Darla Tillman carried three heaping plates of her special out to the table whose order Micki had placed last. The rotund woman smiled at Micki and Gabe as she passed by, heading back into the kitchen where she supervised the cook.

From the times Micki had eaten here, she couldn't remember the woman ever serving a meal. She rarely left her steamy domain behind the swinging door. Which threw Micki off as much as the man smiling at her with amusement twinkling in his golden-brown eyes.

He closed the menu and laid it aside. "I think I'll have a piece of Miz Darla's famous coconut cream pie and a cup of black coffee. Please."

For a second, Micki just stared at him. "What do you mean you intend to spend a few months here?"

He leaned over the counter. Micki tried not to look at the way his muscular arms bulged in all of the right places. His white T-shirt stretched over his shoulders and chest.

She turned around, poured him a cup of coffee, and plated a piece of Darla's sky-high coconut cream and meringue pie. Her hands shook, which she was glad no one could see. After she placed the cup and plate on the counter in front of Gabe, she crossed her arms under her breasts and glared at him.

Gabe picked up the fork beside his pie and took a bite. "Mmm. Fantastic. Miz Darla, c'mon out here."

When Darla peeked out from around the door, her face was bright red. "You like?"

He motioned for her to come out of the kitchen. Darla touched her tight gray bun at the back of her skull and moved forward. She stood beside Micki and wrung her hands in her starched white apron.

While Gabe swallowed another bite, Darla's plump, ruddy face took on the look of someone waiting for the final judgment from God himself. "Darla, you know darned well you make the best pie in the whole state of Texas. Tennessee, too. Heck, maybe the whole country." He took another bite. "I've missed this."

He flicked a glance at Micki, and something hot and wet settled deep within the pit of her center.

"Aw, Gabriel." Darla's face broke into a large grin. "You always were a charmer. But thank you."

"I'm glad someone finds me charming." He picked up his coffee cup and again grinned at Micki.

She turned away and headed with a pitcher of sweet tea for the table of goggling girls. As she refilled their glasses, a pretty brunette with big brown eyes and freckles scattered over her nose gushed, "Oh my God, is that Gabe McKenna?"

With a sigh, she set the pitcher on the table and stacked empty plates into a pile at the edge. Four pairs of eyes stared back at her waiting for an answer. None of the girls looked old enough to drive, let alone be college students. She pasted on a smile. "Yes."

The blonde with metal frames and thick lenses covering gray-green eyes sipped her tea. "Do you know him?"

Time to go. She picked up the half-empty pitcher and stack of dirty dishes. "A little. Can I get y'all anything else?"

"No, I think we're good," said another blonde sitting beside the girl with glasses. "When you get a chance, may we have our checks?"

Micki nodded. "Sure. I'll be right back."

Once she deposited the dishes in the dishpan by the kitchen door, Micki headed for the table Darla had served.

The old woman paid her a decent wage, but the bulk of her income came from tips. She couldn't neglect her customers just because Gabe thought the world turned on his time.

To her surprise, waitressing had come to her easily. After her initial two weeks, she'd become a natural. Although she'd decided to sign on with the corporation, she'd also taken a part time job at the café, working Friday and Saturday evenings. She hated her mother being alone that much, but with Mary Nelson's gracious help, Micki was making it work. The extra money would help her get some leverage on Gabe. With the men who'd started last week, the ranch was more manageable. Although the cowboys were good workers, she didn't know much about them and found it odd that neither of them seemed to know anymore about their employer than she did.

She checked out the truck drivers and a few other folks, including the college girls, before she made it back to where Gabe and Darla were chatting. After she cleaned the bar of the truckers' empty coffee cups and wiped the counter, Darla took another dishpan and headed for the recently vacated tables, surprising Micki again.

With nothing more to do, she stopped before Gabe on the service side of the bar. "Okay, what the hell is going on, Gabe?"

He swallowed the last of his coffee and pushed away his empty plate. Leaning over his arms, he met her gaze. "I'd like to take you to dinner tonight."

"You can go--"

"Before you tell me to go to hell," he said, in that low baritone which did funny things to her blood, "I think you may want to hear me out."

She squared her shoulders and crossed her arms over her chest. "What makes you think you have anything to say that I'd want to hear?"

Gabe laughed and shook his shaggy head of black hair. "You are the most stubborn woman. I have a plan. Let's just leave it at that." He threw down a hundred-dollar bill and stood.

She picked up the money and headed for the cash register on the opposite end of the counter. When she turned with his change, he was already at the door. "Wait. Here's your change."

Gabe winked at her as he placed his tan Stetson on his head. "You keep it, honey. I'll be by your place at six. Wear something sexy."

Every person in the diner turned to gape at Micki as Gabe exited, the bell ringing in her ears.

*What the hell is he up to?*

She wasn't so sure she wanted to know.

\* \* \* \*

Micki paced the small living room of the cottage. Looking at the antique clock on the wall, she sucked in a breath and tapped her right hand against her thigh in time with the ticktock. Gabe would be here in less than five minutes.

Her mother sat in front of the TV watching *Wheel of Fortune*. As Micki made another pass behind the electric wheelchair, Momma said, "You are as jumpy as a gun-shy coonhound during hunting season. You must have a really hot date."

"What have you heard?" Micki stopped and glanced at the back of her mother's head.

The grin when her mother turned the chair around to face her told Micki everything. "Only that Gabe McKenna stopped by the diner today, and it looked like y'all were seeing each other."

Letting out her breath, she shook her head. "You know better. I don't know what's going on. He said he had a plan, which is the only reason I'm going anywhere with the jerk."

She started pacing again. When the knock came at the door, she about jumped out of her skin.

Her mother chuckled. By the sounds of the whirl, she'd turned her chair around again and turned up the TV.

Micki moved to the entry and filled her lungs with air not polluted with Gabe's bewitching scent before she opened the door. Immediately she lost the breath when she looked at the man waiting on the other side. Gabe was dressed in black jeans that fit like a second skin and showed off his long, toned legs in amazing glory. A big silver buckle he'd won in a tie-down event at a local rodeo years ago gleamed low on his waist. When she comprehended the meaning for the not-so-subtle bulge, she jerked her eyes up over his white western shirt to his face.

Hot blood scalded her cheeks, and she wanted to shut the door on his wicked grin. Before she had the chance to act on the impulse, he stepped over the threshold and removed his hat. His eyes held a heat she didn't want to see, let alone respond to. But her body had other ideas. Her insides turned to hot mush, and she began aching in places she didn't want to for Gabriel McKenna.

"Hello, Michaela." He moved over to where Loretta sat, leaned down, and kissed her cheek. "How are you tonight, Loretta?"

Her mother peered up at Gabe with a mix of confusion and warning in her clear blue eyes. "I'm good. What's going on, Gabriel?"

\* \* \* \*

He glanced at Michaela and more blood drained to his groin. He'd told her to dress sexy, thinking she'd not take the challenge; however, she not only met his challenge, she surpassed it. Tonight would be torture. Michaela was never one to wear dresses, and tonight was no exception.

She wore tight faded jeans and a short-sleeved white blouse trimmed in eyelet lace. The scooped neck allowed him a peek at her cleavage. With her blond hair flowing around her tanned shoulders and a pair of bright red cowgirl boots upon her feet, she was a cowboy's dream. Michaela arched a brow and her lips turned upward as if she knew exactly how she was affecting him.

He swallowed and turned back to her mother. "I'll let Michaela explain when she gets home. Right now, I think we'd better get going before it gets any darker."

She kissed her mother on the cheek, then grabbed a white Stetson from the pegs by the door and led the way out. He came up beside her and guided her to his truck. Michaela let out a low whistle as they stopped beside the Ford 150 Raptor SVT parked in the drive.

He opened the passenger door of the cherry-red pickup and intended to help her in, but she had climbed in on her own before he had a chance to blink. "So, you like my truck?"

With a shrug, she looked over the dashboard. "It's nice, but I've never liked Fords." She flashed him a smile. "I'm a Chevy gal myself."

Chuckling, he closed the passenger door. After he climbed behind the wheel, she said, "My question is, what do you need an off-road truck for when you live in the city?"

The big engine roared to life when he turned the key. "I have plenty of friends who don't live right in Nashville. Don't worry. This thing's been in some places a Chevy would never have gotten me out of."

She laughed, and it settled somewhere in Gabe's low belly.

Michaela was quiet until he turned at the Y in the drive to head to the big white house. "What are you doing?"

He glanced at her and smiled. "We aren't headed for a restaurant. I cooked."

Her eyes rounded. "But where? The house is locked up…"

"You'll see soon enough."

When he stopped the truck in front of the garage, her eyes narrowed. "Okay, I've played your game. Now I demand to know what's going on."

"I bought the ranch."

"What the hell are you up to? Everyone knows some corporation bought it."

He shut the engine off and met her puzzled expression. "That's what I wanted everyone to think. It's a dummy corp Reese set up for me."

She gaped at him. "Why the hell didn't you tell me? Heck, it might have helped our custody case."

He fumbled with his keys. "I wanted to tell you that day in the barn, but things..." He didn't want to bring up the fight they'd had. "Reese wanted to use my buying the ranch, but I talked him out of it. I don't want Lemont to know until I'm good and ready for him to know. I paid two million more than it's worth, and the last thing I want is Lemont to get his hands on what is now Jesse's money."

"But it's in a trust fund. Lemont can't touch it... Can he?"

"It's Lemont. You know he's as crooked as the hind leg of a jackrabbit. He'd find a way to get to the money. After all, he stole yours and Frankie's."

She twisted away from him, only to swing around and glare at him with her hands fisted at her lap. "You've owned it all this time?"

"Look. Let's go inside and I'll explain. I told you I have a plan."

She didn't answer and shoved the door open. By the time he got out of the truck, she was waiting on the concrete in front of the double doors of the semi-detached garage with her arms crossed under her breasts and the toe of her cowboy boot drumming steadily on the pavement.

Did she have any idea how damned sexy she looked with the way her breasts pushed upward? He walked past her and headed up the back porch steps to the kitchen door. She followed him into the house and let out an exhalation of air as she looked around.

He turned on the oven and faced her. "I figured we could eat here. I'd prefer that none of what we discuss be overheard by someone."

She slowly met his eyes, pulling her attention from the heavy, antique oak table. "That's Frankie's table. You bought the furniture, too."

"Some of it. I had two different agents attend the auction." He rubbed the stubble on his jaw. "I knew this table had belonged to your grandma and thought it only right you and Loretta have it. I bought all of Jesse's bedroom furniture and the things that were Frankie's and Dad's I thought he'd like to have when he's older." He'd set the table with china that had belonged to his mother and a bunch of red roses and white daisies. "And

I bought everything that was my momma's they had in storage and didn't give to me in Dad's will."

She stared at him for a moment, then blinked, shaking her head. "What smells so good?"

"Lasagna. It should be ready in a few minutes."

"You made lasagna?"

The sudden sense of déjà that came over him wasn't comfortable. He pulled a bottle of Dom Perignon from a chiller on the counter and turned to her across the butcher block of the island in the big country kitchen. "Yeah."

Neither of them had to be reminded of the last time Gabe cooked lasagna for them. He saw her replaying the same memory in her mind in the way she bit her bottom lip. He'd made it for her the night he'd proposed to her almost ten years ago.

"I should have told you sooner, but the timing never seemed right, or you'd rip into me like a pitbull." He softened his words with a grin. Before she could react to his comment, he said, "That day after my Cheyenne date I'd come here to tell you I'd bought the ranch and that you didn't have to move, but then you..."

She narrowed her eyes on him. "I was upset. You told me you were going to adopt Jesse. What was I supposed to think?"

He swallowed and tossed his hat on the counter by the refrigerator. "I'm sorry. I never meant for you to think you'd never be part of his life. In fact, I wanted quite the opposite. But I screwed up and I was mad, at myself because of my antics in Cheyenne and because..." There was no way he was going to tell her his desire for her was driving him crazy. "Because I was afraid I'd never see Jesse again."

Her expression melted, and she hugged herself. "I'm afraid, too."

He positioned his thumbs on the cork, but then stopped short of opening the bottle, suddenly unsure. "I've been thinking. Judge Anderson said he would've given both of us, or at least one of us, custody of Jesse if we were married." She sucked in a breath and her eyes widened. He rushed on before she could shoot him down. "Just hear me out before you say anything. Okay?" She nodded; then he popped the cork and poured two fluted glasses full of the champagne. He handed her one, but neither of them took a drink. Her hand shook as she set her sparkling drink on the granite top of the island.

He set his glass beside hers and plowed on. "I know the judge liked you, and if your living and financial situations were different, you would've gotten custody. Reese mentioned that Anderson is a fan of mine. He also said the judge thought I was good with Jesse."

He paused to take a deep breath. "I don't blame him for not giving me custody. Hell, I even said the same thing. The road isn't a place for a kid. You're fantastic with Jesse, and we both love him. So, I was thinking that maybe if we were--uh--married, the judge might give us Jesse." He picked up the champagne, suddenly needing a drink.

"You want to get married?" Her voice shook, and he barely heard the quiet words.

He met her gaze and drained the glass. "It would be a business deal. After we adopt Jesse, we'll get divorced and have joint custody. I already have the pre-nup drafted. You'd get to stay here at the ranch with Jesse, but the place will go to him when he turns twenty-one. I'll pay child support and provide for him--and for you and your momma too, if you'll let me, at least until Jesse's older. He needs a full time momma now." Her lips flattened. She was about to argue. He had to get all of this out, or he was afraid he wouldn't be able to. "Anyway, I'll visit as much as possible. You and Loretta would live here at the main house, and I could stay in the cottage when I'm here. Basically, we'd have the custody deal we wanted." He shrugged, watching her for a reaction other than total disbelief and anger, amazed when only quiet resignation settled over her beautiful face.

"Okay." She breathed the word.

"You'll marry me?" He didn't bother hiding his surprise.

She drained her glass with a wince. "Damn, I've never liked champagne." Michaela headed for the fridge. "Do you have any beer in here?"

He was more uncertain now than he'd been before he started thinking about this crazy idea. "Yeah. Lone Star. Get me one, too." When she turned with the longneck bottles in hand, he chuckled. "A two hundred dollar bottle of fine French bubbly, but we'd rather drink Texas beer."

"I'm a country girl, Gabe. You've always known that." She handed him one of the bottles. "I've actually been thinking the same thing--that if I were married the judge would've given me Jesse. But the only man I can think of is Cash Nelson." She twisted the top off the beer and took a long draw. "But he would read too much into the agreement. I never considered you. Hell, the whole town knows I can't even stand you. How is this gonna work?"

Gabe didn't like the way his heart pinched at her words. He tossed the cap from his beer beside hers on the island top and took a drink. "We'll have to convince them otherwise. We have a history and we've been working together"--he grinned as he remembered the custody hearing-- "or against each other for weeks now. Everyone knows there's a fine line between love and hate."

# Chapter 8

Micki moved to the French doors that opened to the patio and pool at the back of the house. The sun had set, and darkness shrouded the yard. Was she seriously considering this madness? "How soon for the wedding?"

"The adoption hearing is set for January sixth," he said. "We'll have to be married long enough before then for the judge to see our marriage as legitimate and not a stunt."

She looked over her shoulder at him. "Which of course it is."

He shrugged and rubbed a hand over his chin. "Anyway, I don't want to wait more than a couple of weeks."

She faced him. "That doesn't seem very long to convince people I've totally lost my mind."

The corners of his lips twitched upward. "Oh, I don't know about that. Mary Nelson asked me today at the grocery store if we were together again. I think the folks around here are kinda expecting us to tie the knot, and my buying the ranch and you working for me will only reinforce that belief."

"So, as soon as we adopt Jesse, we get divorced?"He moved to the stove and turned it off. "Yes."

"What if I find someone else and want to get remarried?"

He pulled the lasagna from the oven to sit it on the stovetop. "No matter what you do, the ranch goes to Jesse when he's old enough."

"I wouldn't have it any other way."

She watched him pull two salads out of the refrigerator and set them on the table. Her heart pounded at his smooth and almost graceful movements. Being married to him would be pure torture, which had nothing to do with them getting along for appearances sake.

He looked at her and pulled out one of the carved oak chairs. "I think we should eat."

As if in a dream, Micki sat and let him move her chair in. She pushed the fresh salad greens around on her plate, her appetite replaced with a lump. Gabe wasn't eating his salad either. With a sigh, she looked around the kitchen. "I think living here in the house would be nice. I've always loved it. Remember how your momma would bake us all cookies when we were kids?"

Gabe picked up his beer and took a long swig. "Yeah."

She didn't miss the pain that flashed over his amber eyes. One thing she'd always admired about Gabe was his love for his mother. Her breast cancer and death had destroyed him. Gabe and his father weren't ever close. When news of Sam's affair with Frankie came to light while Annie was dying from cancer, Gabe swore he'd never have anything to do with him again. He'd moved out of the house and into the bunkhouse and couldn't wait to get off the ranch.

"I'm sorry, Gabe. Frankie had always been a little wild and she and your dad had been close long before they got together romantically. He was her best friend. As weird as that sounds, considering he was old enough to be her father."

He picked at his salad. "I know Frankie had a crush on Dad since she was about eighteen. And Dad never really loved my mother." Laying down his fork, he looked at her. "Though it would have hurt me, I could've accepted Dad and Frankie being together if they'd had the decency to wait until my mother was dead."

They ate in silence for a few moments, then she said, "I still think Sam and Frankie will walk through that door and tell us it's all been a mistake."

He picked up his beer, then downed the last of it. "I know."

Her fork clattered on her plate. "Gabe, I'll do anything to make sure Jesse is raised the way they would've wanted."

His eyes darkened, and he nodded. "I know you would. I feel the same way. That's why I'm asking you to do this."

"Will we have to petition the court to adopt him together?"

"Yes."

She looked down at the greens on her plate. "I suppose we'll have to pretend to be in love, too."

He cleared his throat. "This will be tricky since the picture of me with that groupie hit the tabloids, but we can come up with some kind of story."

She played with her salad, unsure if she liked the nonchalant way he spoke about the incident with the striper. He had no qualms regarding casual sex with women he didn't know. He'd cheated on her with a woman he had just met. Would he do the same thing to her again? *The marriage won't be real*, she reminded herself.

Micki picked up her beer. "I'm supposed to be stupidly in love with you, right? Maybe pining for you since you left me?"

His jaw twitched. "I guess."

She took a big swig of the Lone Star and grinned. "So, the story could be that you groveled at my feet, and like some lovesick idiot, I believed you."

Gabe snorted. "Hell, that actually sounds believable. However, you'd never let anyone grovel. You'd kick him in the balls and toss him out on his ass."

She leaned her head back and laughed. "When you cheat on me again, I'll do just that. Then I'll file for divorce--conveniently after the adoption."

Gabe narrowed his eyes on her. "I didn't cheat on you."

"You know, you hate your father for cheating on your momma, but you did the same things. To me, and then to Andrea." She lost the smile and pushed the uneaten salad away. "Did you love her?"

He shook his head. "No. I was her latest conquest." Setting his own plate away, he laughed, but there wasn't any humor in it. He left the table and came back with two more beers. "I never cheated on her."

"But the tabloids were filled with stories of you with other women." She took the bottle he handed her as he sat in his seat at the end of the table.

"Stories Andrea leaked herself." He twisted off the top and took a long draw on the bottle. "I was nothing but clay to her, Michaela. She took a singing cowboy and turned him into a sex symbol. Everything she did was calculated. Even our marriage. I didn't want to marry her--she proposed to me. She conned me into it, saying that a wholesome boy like me wouldn't ever live with an older woman unless we were married. Then she turned that wholesome boy into a party-happy rock star in a cowboy hat."

She couldn't believe him. Doing so would mean giving something of herself away. Hiding her conflicted thoughts, she shrugged and took a bite of salad. "How soon do we make the announcement?"

"Sunday at church. The wedding has to be something elaborate, so the sooner we let the world know, the better. We probably should start planning it tomorrow, in fact."

"Yuck." She wrinkled her nose.

He grinned and sipped his beer, guessing correctly her reaction had nothing to do with the bite of the spicy salad dressing. "I figured we'd make our official public appearance at the *CMAs* in November. I'll want to show off my new wife, of course. Are you planning to go to the NFR?"

She may be retired from the rodeo circuit, but the National Finals Rodeo was the place where anyone connected to the sport would meet and cheer their friends on. Going to the rodeo every year had become something she and Frankie did together. She picked at the salad with her fork as memories flooded her. "I have tickets. But I'm thinking of not going this year." She sighed and laid the fork on the plate. "Frankie and I planned to go, but without her it wouldn't be the same. Why do you ask?"

"Don't sell those tickets just yet. I have a concert date on December fourth at the MGM. We can spend the week together." He stood and took their uneaten salads to the sink. "We'll be in the public eye the whole time."

She groaned, bringing a full-blown smile to his handsome face.

As he dished out the lasagna, he said, "It's a lot to ask, I know. But if we can pull off acting like the loving couple at those two events, Anderson will have no doubt our marriage is real."

Closing her eyes, she groaned again. She hadn't even considered the very public aspect of being Gabe's wife, but neither of them had mentioned a more personal problem. "What are we going to tell Jesse? You know he'll be ecstatic that we're together. Same goes for Momma."

"We can't tell him the truth. He might tell Lemont what we're up to. As for Loretta, I think we can let her in on the game." He set a plate of lasagna before her, then took his seat again. "I've thought about hiring a housekeeper with nursing experience to help out with her care."

"I can't let you do that." She picked up her fork but had no appetite for the delicious-smelling pasta. "I'll take care of Momma."

"Michaela, if we want to convince the world--and more importantly, the judge--that we are committed to each other and to Jesse, we have to use all of our available resources." Gabe flashed that lethal grin of his. "I can afford a housekeeper and enough ranch hands to take care of things around the ranch. Besides, what better way to prove to Judge Anderson that you have plenty of time to devote to Jesse? I'm not saying you can't still help out. She'll be living here in the house. Hell, if you still want to manage the ranch, go for it, but you don't have to punch cattle and round up horses. When are you going to admit you're not Superwoman?"

"I never claimed to be Superwoman." It would be nice if she didn't have to worry so much about her mother. She considered his words and the reasons the judge hadn't given her Jesse to begin with. Depending on a man to take care of her wasn't what she wanted to do. Her father left her mother when she needed him, and Gabe walked away from her when she thought he'd loved her. What would stop him from doing it again?

She forked up a bite of the lasagna, but as the thoughts cascaded through her head, she couldn't eat it. Accepting his offer was dangerous to her heart, but for the short term, she had to do it for Jesse's sake. "I see your point. But I don't have to like it. I don't want to have to owe you anything."

"You don't owe me a thing. All I ask of you is to be a good aunt to Jesse. Which I already know you are, or I wouldn't be asking you to do this. I don't care about the money."

"You might not care, but I do." She met Gabe's eyes over the table. He held the biggest damn diamond ring she'd ever seen toward her. The forkful of lasagna hit the plate with a clang.

He raised a brow, and his lips twitched into a lopsided smile. "I bought this when I was in Nashville. Hopefully, I remembered your ring size. The love of my life has to have some serious bling to show off."

The diamond ring was at least seven carats and shimmered in the bright light of the kitchen. "Gabe..." The ring didn't mean anything. The proposal was a sham. His words of love weren't real. Micki didn't love the man holding the ring, but she had at one time, and for a moment, her heart remembered the first time he'd proposed to her. The first time he'd promised to take care of her. "I can't take--"

He took her shaking left hand from beside her plate and slid the ring onto her finger. A perfect fit. "Yes, you can. It's part of the act. Just as the wedding will be. As soon as we figure out when it is, I'll make sure the tabloids know that we're getting married."

Gabe's grin and the twinkling of his dark eyes snagged on something deep inside Micki and set her insides on fire.

"I have to make sure everyone knows I'm completely off the market." He hadn't let go of her hand and began to rub his thumb over the area behind the ring he'd put on her finger. The heat from his touch branded her as completely as the rock he'd put on her hand did. "Which brings up a slightly more delicate problem."

Her heart raced at the sensual timbre of his voice. Breathless, she asked, "What's that?"

"Our attraction to each other."

"You're delusional." She tried to free her hand, but he held on. "I'm not attracted to you. You're freaking crazy if you think I'll consider having sex with you."

"Who said anything about sex? But as I remember, we were pretty damned good together." Gabe pinned her with his hot gaze. "And you will be my lawful wife. Married couples have sex."

"I get it. I don't owe you anything, right? Except for my body." Her voice betrayed her desire by coming out breathy and low and not at all sounding as pissed off as she'd wanted. She yanked her hand from his and stood away from him.

Gabe stood and stepped toward her. "Come on, Michaela, you can't deny you're attracted to me. We're both consenting adults. I want you, and you want me. I see it in your eyes. Hell, you were sizing me up after you answered the door tonight."

She turned away, headed for the door, but he caught her arm and turned her into his chest. With a thud, she landed against a solid mass of man. The fire he'd started with a look pooled deep and throbbed in her center. She tried to tell herself she was so attracted to Gabe because she hadn't had sex for a long time. And she almost believed it--until he kissed her.

Gabe's lips brushed hers as if he was asking permission. The kiss was gentle but heated at the same time. Against her better judgment, she brought her hands up over the soft cotton of his shirt covering a rock hard chest. He moaned as she wrapped her arms around his neck, pulling him to her. She opened under him, and he deepened the kiss. His hands burned a trail down her back to her butt. She hissed when he squeezed and pulled her against him. His erection pressed into her low belly.

Dear God help her, she wanted him.

"Gabe..." She breathed into his mouth and slid her leg up against his.

He groaned and lifted her onto the counter. The kiss turned into a duel of tongues, and he lifted her blouse to remove it.

She backed out of the kiss and pushed on his chest. With a fuzzy look of confusion, he pulled away.

"Gabe, we have to stop. I can't do this."

Sex with Gabe would prove disastrous to the wall she'd built around her heart.

Swallowing, he helped her off the counter. "I'm sorry." He turned away and squared his shoulders. "You make me crazy, Michaela."

She straightened her shirt and ran her fingers through her mussed hair. The ring on her finger weighed a ton and tangled in the strands. "I think I should go home."

He faced her and nodded, his expression grim. "Yeah. I'll drive you."

# Chapter 9

Micki stared at the orchard where the leaves on the old apple trees were changing to shades of orange and red. In a month she would be married. Her mother shifted in her wheelchair, and Micki focused on helping her into the passenger side of the truck. When she closed the door, the strong morning sun caught the diamond on her ring finger.

For a moment, the way the light splintered and exploded within the massive gem mesmerized her. The damn thing could blind someone.

"It really is a beautiful ring, isn't it?" Her mother's soft voice, coming at her through the open window, jerked her out of the trance. "I don't care what he told you the reason for the wedding is. I think Gabe still has feelings for you. And I know you still love him. But I wonder why he didn't give you Annie's ring?"

She'd wondered the same thing. The ring he'd given to her when they'd been engaged the first time meant the world to Gabe.

"Momma, we've talked about this." Micki grasped the edge of the window frame and fisted her free hand. "The marriage is an act so the judge will give us Jesse. Of course, he got me a huge ring. He's a superstar. The story is that we belong together and decided to get married. But if he really had any feelings for me, he would've given me his mother's ring.... If he still has it." The realization hit her with a strong twist to her heart. Maybe he'd given it to Andrea. She pushed the thoughts from her mind. "You just need to remember not to tell anyone the truth. I still hate Gabe McKenna with a passion, and he hasn't lost any love for me, either."

Momma smiled and patted Micki's hand where it lay on the window edge. "We'd better get going. I can't wait until everyone sees this on my baby's hand."

Micki turned and sighed. She didn't want her mother to tell her friends the truth about the wedding after the morning service, but her total denial that the wedding was, in fact, a farce proved exhausting.

As she folded her mother's wheelchair, Gabe's big Ford pulled up beside her Silverado. When he climbed out of the pickup and headed her way, she didn't like how her heart sped up and her mouth went dry. He was sin on legs dressed in a pair of tan slacks, a navy polo shirt, and his signature tan Stetson.

Leaning in, he kissed her full on the lips. Against her will, she responded to his soft but firm lips, demanding her to kiss him back. As he had Friday night, he overwhelmed her good sense and desire pooled deep within her. The touch didn't last long, and when he pulled away, Micki wanted the kiss to go on.

She immediately stepped away from him and grabbed the folded wheelchair, jerking it toward her with more force than required for the action. This damned lovey-dovey acting was going to drive her crazy, not to mention the way she went up in flames every time he touched her. "I wondered where you were."

"Good morning, sunshine." He took the chair from her hands. "I was on the phone with my manager. Had to get our engagement announcement out." Winking, he hoisted the wheelchair onto the back of the truck. "Sorry I'm late." He leaned down to get a better look at her mother through the window. "How are you this morning?"

Momma returned his smile. "I have to say you surprised me, Gabriel McKenna. About time you came to your senses and married Michaela."

He glanced at Micki, a slight frown pulling at the corner of his lips. She shook her head. "I'll explain later. If we don't get going soon, we'll be late for church."

In that infuriating I'm-in-no-hurry way of his, Gabe leaned against the side of her truck. "I thought we'd talk to Reverend Watson about our wedding. Two of the caterers we spoke to yesterday called back with tentative dates based on their schedules. The soonest either of them could possibly do a small wedding is October thirty-first."

"Halloween?" She snorted. "Well, that's definitely appropriate. That's gonna cost a fortune."

"Yep." She wasn't sure which he was agreeing to. "We have to agree to allow the caterers the right to use our wedding for promotion."

"Hope the food's good. The ceremony's already going to give me indigestion." Micki dug her keys out of her black slacks pocket and ignored his glare. "Isn't the award show that next week?"

"Yeah, November eighth. The timing is lousy, but we can make it work. Just think, we could go to the *CMA*s on our way to our honeymoon."

Fear zipped through her at the wink and fire flashing in his eyes.

"Hopefully Reverend Watson is available that day. If not, we may have to find either another preacher or a justice of the peace to do it. I figured we'd have the service on the ranch." He glanced away and shifted his feet. "Doesn't seem right to get married in the church, considering it's not a real marriage."

Micki hadn't considered where the wedding would take place, but a sudden idea hit her. "I think getting married here is a great idea. Frankie's garden is still pretty in late October. The late roses and chrysanthemums are blooming." She frowned. No one would have tended to the roses since before her sister's death. "Although it might need some cleaning up before the wedding day."

Gabe shrugged and nodded. "Sounds good as any other place. I'll hire a gardener as soon as possible to get it ready."

"The garden is a great place for a wedding," Momma chimed in. "Your wedding color could be that pretty shade of pumpkin orange you like. It would be perfect, considering it's Halloween."

"Not if I ask Lizzie Decker to be my matron of honor, it won't." Cash Nelson's elder sister had a headful of carrot-colored, corkscrew-curly hair.

Her mother pursed her lips. "You're right. That red hair of hers would make her look hideous in orange. What about dark green?"

"Works for me." Gabe looked at Micki with a twinkle in his eyes. "I like green more than orange anyway."

She wanted to deck him. He knew orange was one of her favorite colors, and if it wasn't for Lizzy's hair, she'd love to have it as her wedding color. Maybe she could use orange in her flowers. This whole formal wedding on a rush was a pain in the ass.

"I'd be content with an Elvis impersonator on the Vegas Strip," she muttered.

Laughing, Gabe said, "That would make our marriage look legitimate in Judge Anderson's conservative eyes, but the tabloids would love it."

"Now, Micki, don't be difficult. Just like the last time. If Frankie and I hadn't forced you to buy a dress, you would've gotten married in jeans and a T-shirt." Momma clucked her teeth. "I guess I only have myself to blame for making you into such a tomboy."

"I am what I am. A cowgirl." Micki glanced at her cell phone. They had fifteen minutes to get to the service. She didn't care about colors or about any of the other particulars concerning the wedding. "Gabe, we really gotta go."

He pushed away from the side of her pickup and took her hand. After he led her to the driver's side, he opened her door. Scowling at him when he reached for her again, she grabbed the frame of the truck and hauled herself up into the seat. He closed her door, and she glared out the open window at him. "You know I hate this chivalry stuff. I'm not some Cinderella who needs a man to help me get into my truck, for God's sake. This pretending to actually like you is gonna drive me to drink."

His chuckle was deep and penetrated her senses. "Your stubbornness drives me crazy. Why can't you let someone help you out?" Before she could answer, he leaned through the window and kissed her.

She glared at him and turned the key. "See you later, cupcake."

His laughter followed her down the driveway.

* * * *

After the service, Gabe and Micki waited outside the church until Reverend Watson finished greeting the churchgoers to speak with them. Her mother held an animated conversation with several of her friends, who all stole glances at Gabe and Micki. The ring on her left hand was like a boulder setting on her chest. A big, flashing rock that announced to the world she'd totally lost her mind. Breathing was tough when she spotted someone staring at it, and she wished she could stash it in her pocket. The heat from Gabe's hand resting on the small of her back burned through the thin fabric of her shirt to scorch her skin.

How was it possible to want a man as much as she did Gabe and not even like him? She'd never had many boyfriends and never had casual sex. They'd begun dating when she was seventeen and he was eighteen. Before him, she hadn't been with anyone. After him, she'd only had two boyfriends. Both relationships had burned hot and quickly fizzled, but at least she'd liked those men. She was still friends with both of them.

His gaze snagged hers. "I hoped after we're done here, we can go to Brownwood and do some furniture shopping for the house."

She glanced at her mother. Momma was laughing with a group of women surrounding her. Micki left her alone more than she liked already.

Gabe must have seen her concern and added, "We can bring her with us."

Micki shook her head and looked back at Gabe. "No. I'll talk to Mary. See if she'll watch over Momma for a little while." The women were close friends. Mary loved caring for her mother, although the older woman hated calling her time with Momma anything other than visits. Micki suspected Mary missed her old friend. "But we can't stay out for too long."

"I don't think we'll have to. We'll just furnish the rooms we need." He looked her over, making the tugging pull in her low belly turn into an ache. "Will you need to get a dress?"

"Can't we just get a license and get this thing over with? I don't want to wear a dress."

He smiled and touched the brim of his hat when an elderly couple passed by. Leaning close, his breath tickled her cheek as he said in a low voice, "I don't want it to be too fancy of an event, but if we aren't careful, people will speculate it's a shotgun wedding."

Micki jerked at his words, and her desire evaporated. "The last thing I want is people thinking I'm pregnant. But I do see the irony, don't you? The last time we were engaged, I was pregnant."

Gabe stared at her from under the brim of his hat with deep, dark eyes. "I'm sorry. I didn't mean to bring..."

She swallowed and glanced around the milling neighbors and friends. "I grieved the loss of our baby, Gabe. And I did it alone." She felt a hollow ache as she remembered the baby she'd lost fewer than two weeks before her wedding day seven years ago. Micki met his gaze and shrugged. "Maybe my miscarrying when I did was a godsend."

His eyes narrowed and he stiffened. "How can you think something like that?"

"I didn't plan to tell you I was pregnant until our wedding night--which never happened, because you left me."

Every blasé word she spoke was a stab in her heart. She'd loved her baby, despite losing it a week after discovering she was pregnant. The only person who'd known had been Frankie until the night she miscarried. She'd woken with cramps and bleeding. Gabe found her crying in the bathroom of their small bunkhouse apartment. When she'd explained she miscarried their baby, Gabe had rushed her to the hospital. "You knew how much I was dealing with." Micki forced her voice to remain low to prevent others from overhearing. "Momma fell and broke her hip. I was planning our wedding on a shoestring budget because you refused to take a dime more than your pitiful wage from your dad. I had no money of my own and didn't have anyone to lean on. The last thing I needed after you left was a baby to raise on my own--and I would have. I would've walked through fire to keep Andrea Rose away from my child."

His hand at her back curled, and she felt the strength in his fingers. The shadow of his hat brim made his cold eyes and the hard line of his jaw all the more foreboding. "If you hadn't miscarried, the moment I found out you were pregnant I would've been back. You may have broken off our engagement, but I would have been a father to my baby."

A couple walked past them, grinning at them. She forced a gooey, love-happy smile and leaned into Gabe as if to whisper sweet nothings in his ear. Instead, she said, "And I would have told you the same thing I told my own so-called father: go straight to hell."

He stepped away and his jaw twitched, but before he could unleash the fury she saw brewing in him, the preacher stopped in front of them.

With a huge grin on his round face, Reverend Watson spread his hands. "God bless you both. I hear congratulations are in order for you two. I'm always excited to see true love prevail."

\* \* \* \*

"Why are you doing this?" Cash asked behind her.

"I'll meet you at the pasture." Pasting on a smile, Micki dismissed the two cowboys; then she faced Cash standing in the middle of the driveway.

Waiting until the men were out of earshot, she propped her hands on her hips. She didn't want to lie to Cash, but telling him the truth wasn't an option. He closed the distance between them and stopped only inches from her.

"Micki, don't marry Gabe."

Swallowing her regret in lying, she shook her head. "Gabe and I want to be together. We still love each other."

When the desire for the statement to be true hit her, Micki shifted her feet, hugged herself, and looked out over the pasture behind the barn. She couldn't want this marriage to be real, and she had to remember that it wasn't. Despite all the outward affections she and Gabe had to share in public, he could not be trusted. Not with her heart, anyway.

"I don't buy it." He laid his hand on her upper arm. "You told me just a couple weeks ago you couldn't stand him. If he loved you so much, why was he caught in a lip lock with a stripper?"

"I forgave him for that. He didn't know I still loved him." Every word hurt as she spoke them, but she kept her voice level and her face void of any hint of the ache in her chest.

"Right. Did you forgive him for cheating on you the first time and leaving you?"

"Yes." She about choked on the lie.

"Like hell. You can lie to everyone else, but you can't lie to me." He shook his head in frustration, but then his eyes widened and he stepped back. "That's it! You think if you get married to him, you'll have a better chance at getting Jesse."

She swung her gaze to his. "Look. Gabe and I came to an understanding. That's all I'm going to say. We're getting married and I really don't care what people think the reason for it is. Now if you'll excuse me, I have to finish showing the new ranch hands around, and then Gabe and I have a date with a caterer. See you around, Cash."

She turned and walked to her workhorse, hating the shattered look on Cash's face.

# Chapter 10

Standing next to the fireplace in the ranch house, Gabe twirled the whiskey around in the highball glass and stared at the tabloid in his other hand. A grainy picture of him and Michaela, which had been taken during their shopping trip two weeks ago, was in the corner of the cover page. The byline below it read, "Country hunk Gabe McKenna set to marry pregnant girlfriend."

He tossed the paper onto the end table beside the couch as the night he'd found Michaela sitting on the floor beside the toilet rushed forward in his mind. The front of her T-shirt had been stained crimson from blood.

*"God, Michaela!" He knelt in front of her and pushed her tangled blond hair out of her tear-streaked face. "Are you hurt, baby?"*

*"Oh, Gabe." She sobbed and went into his arms. "I think I lost him."*

*He held her tight, but then lessened his grip, afraid he'd hurt her. "Lost him? Baby, you're bleeding. What's going on?"*

*She pulled away to meet his gaze with red-rimmed eyes. "The baby, Gabe. I'm pregnant. But--but I think I lost him." She hiccupped and hugged him close, burying her face into his neck. "I was scared to tell you. We have so much going on. I loved him so much."*

*He stood, pulling her up with him and swung her into his arms. "C'mon. I'm taking you to the hospital."*

Focused on the memory, he didn't hear Reese enter the living room.

"As your future divorce lawyer, I might suggest you reconsider the wedding altogether if you're already breaking out the whiskey and drinking alone."

Gabe turned away from the fireplace. He tossed back the shot, wincing at the burn as he swallowed the liquor and waited for the heat to spread through him. "Have you ever wondered about the *what ifs* in your life?"

Reese snorted and poured himself a glass of the Jack Daniels from the stocked temporary bar set up in the corner for the reception later. "Hell, who hasn't?"

Gabe glanced at the man dressed in an Armani suit with a white western shirt. Lizard skin cowboy boots and a bolo tie completed Reese's getup.

"Are you coming to your senses?" The lawyer sat down on a plush, overstuffed chair in a red, green, and tan plaid Gabe hated but Michaela loved. "I still think this whole charade is nuts. Even with the pre-nup, the soon-to-be Mrs. McKenna could toast your balls if she wanted to. The pre-nup has no cap on what she could demand from you for child support for Jesse if you do adopt him. Not to mention alimony."

"You already know I don't care about the money. Besides, the trick will be getting her to take the child support I intend to pay for Jesse. She's too damned proud and hates my guts too much to want anything from me." Gabe pointed to the chair Reese sat on. "Case in point. I wanted all top-of-the-line leather for this room. She didn't want me forking out the money since I won't be living here. She would've preferred me not furnishing the house at all."

Gabe begrudgingly admitted the chair went well with the room's colors and with the tan leather couch. He moved away from the fireplace and sat down on the sofa. He remembered how he and Michaela fought over everything, from colors to the style of the furniture he bought for the house; however, the sticking point had always been cost. Gabe had been willing to buy the best and most expensive. Micki wanted something more affordable for her. Since the cheaper furniture was in stock and available for immediate delivery, he ended up compromising.

The excursion to three furniture stores in Brownwood had shown Gabe the stubborn practicality he found so damned infuriating about Michaela and that he'd fallen in love with as a wide-eyed kid some fifteen years ago.

But he wasn't a kid anymore, and he had no intention of falling for Michaela again.

Reese laughed and leaned back into the chair. "I hope you know what you're doing."

"I do. Now, let it go." Gabe picked up the tabloid from the end table. Holding it across the coffee table, he said, "Have you seen this?"

Reese took the paper and read the article. "The old pregnancy angle for the rushed wedding. I like it."

"I don't." Gabe stood and headed for the bar, needing another drink. "It's the last thing I want anyone to think."

Reese moved to stand with Gabe at the bar and took the glass out of his hand before he could drink it. "You've had enough. If the world, and more importantly Judge Anderson, thinks there's a baby, it makes the swiftness of your wedding more realistic."

Gabe glared at his friend. "That might be true, but it also could backfire. The judge could decide that Michaela and I don't love each other and that we married because of the pregnancy."

He picked up the shot of whiskey from the bar where Reese had set it and downed it before the lawyer could take the glass from him again. Gabe turned away and crossed to the mantle, which held photos of Jesse with Sam and Frankie and a few of him and Michaela that Frankie had kept. He picked up one of him and Michaela, taken after her high school graduation.

Would he ever forget the rush of emotions on the night she'd lost the baby? The possibility of fatherhood had scared him shitless when Michaela told him she was pregnant. He hadn't been ready to be a father yet. As he'd held her while she'd shaken with her tears, he'd wished she hadn't lost it.

Michaela had loved the tiny baby. Up until that night, he'd never seen her cry. He sat the frame back on the mantle and faced Reese. "Michaela and I lost a baby."

"I'm sorry. When?"

Gabe tugged on the sleeves of his jacket. "She miscarried about two weeks before the date of our last wedding. She hadn't been very far along, but she loved the baby and it hurt her when she lost it."

*I grieved the loss of our baby, Gabe. And I did it alone.*

"Was that why you called off the wedding?"

Glancing back at the photo, he shook his head. "I didn't call off the wedding. She did." Had she only been marrying him for the baby the last time? She easily agreed to this current craziness for the chance to raise Jesse.

"I thought you were never getting married again?"

Gabe and Reese turned at the sound of the deep voice by the arched door. Gabe smiled and headed for his best friend, and they shook hands. He and country singer Seth Kendall became friends six years ago when Gabe had been Seth's opening act. They had more in common than most people could guess at, which went far beyond them both being from Texas. "Seth, thanks for coming at such short notice," Gabe said.

Seth smiled and cuffed him on the shoulder. "You think I'd miss your wedding? I'm honored you asked me to return the favor and be your best man." Gabe had been Seth's best man last year when he married the mother of his teenage daughter. He then turned and held his hand out to Reese. "Good to see you again, Reese. You still making cheating spouses pay for their stupidity?"

Reese laughed. "You better believe it."

A commotion at the front door had Gabe turning as Jesse burst into the living room.

"Gabe!" His little brother lurched himself into Gabe's open arms. "I can't believe you and Aunt Micki are getting married."

Gabe smiled as he held the boy. "I know. Funny how things worked out. But your aunt and I were together long before you were even born, squirt. So, it shouldn't be too much of a surprise."

"Convenient is what I'd call it."

Gabe looked over Jesse's dark head of curly hair to Lemont standing in the doorway, a smug snicker on his lined face. His eyes as cold as Gabe had ever seen them. He ambled around the room, stuffing his hands into the pockets of his suit jacket and nodding. "I have to say, Gabriel, you surprised me. I had no idea you were behind the corporation that bought this place." He stopped before Gabe and snorted. "Hell, I should've done the same thing; then no one would've known it was me making the bid."

Jesse pressed closer to Gabe. The boy's fear angered him more than the man's words. "Get out, Lemont. Before I call security to throw you off my ranch."

Seth took a step toward Gabe. Leave it to him to have Gabe's back.

He laughed and tipped his white hat. "No need for that. Think how bad tossing the bride's father out would look in the tabloids. I'm here to see my only daughter marry the love of her life, despite my invitation somehow getting lost in the mail. Imagine that." He leaned in and glared at Gabe. "You may think you've won one over me, but I'll prove this so-called marriage is a farce."

Gabe's heart skipped a beat at how easily Lemont figured them out. He gritted his teeth. "I love Michaela. I always have."

The terrible truth in the supposed lie hit him in the chest like a fist.

"I don't care who you are, buddy, but I think my friend asked you to leave." Seth's voice was so low and cold it would have frozen a glacier.

Lemont chuckled again and turned to leave. At the door, he held out his hand. "C'mon, Jesse. We'll take our seats and you'll see your brother and aunt later."

Gabe hated the veiled threat in the tone of the words. "No, I want to visit with my brother. You wouldn't let him be in the wedding, but he's here and I have every intention of talking to him. Now, get out."

Lemont gave Jesse another warning look before leaving.

Jesse looked up at him. "I don't want to live with him, Gabe." The boy wrapped his arm around Gabe's waist and held on tight as a shudder shimmered through him. "He won't allow me to see my friends and started to homeschool me. I don't like the woman he hired to be my teacher. She yells at me and calls me stupid. I'm not dumb. I made the honor roll every year." Jesse paused to catch his breath.

Gabe's anger at Lemont climbed. He should change the subject, but he needed to know exactly how Lemont treated Jesse. "Has he done anything to you?"

"He keeps telling me you and Aunt Micki don't love me." Jesse's blue eyes misted with unshed tears. "He tells me that Daddy and Mommy died because I wasn't a good enough boy."

"Damn," Seth muttered and laid his hand on Gabe's shoulder.

"Dear God." Reese knelt down in front of him. "Jesse, you have to tell the judge what he says to you."

Jesse shook his head. "I can't." The tears let go and ran down his pale cheeks. "Miz Fennel tells me that if I say such things the judge will lock me away because they aren't true. But they are!" He wailed and turned into Gabe, who held him as tightly as Jesse was gripping him. "He's the meanest man I've ever met." Jesse's muffled words impaled Gabe's heart.

Gabe squeezed his baby brother. "I know, buddy. I know."

"Please, Gabe, don't make me go back there."

\* \* \* \*

In the master bedroom, Micki stared at the woman in the mirror and wondered if she suffered from some sort of brain rot. In twenty minutes, she would be getting married in the garden to a man she didn't love.

Despite the desire to keep the farce from getting too big, nearly a hundred wedding guests had descended on the place. Music from the string quartet and chatter from the guests drifted up to her from the yard. Most of the guests were local folks, but Gabe had invited his band members, manager, and a few singers he was close friends with.

Her heart pinched as she remembered the day she, Frankie, and her mother had gone shopping for the gown. Gabe hadn't expected her to get dressed up for their wedding seven years ago. In fact, they'd planned for a small ceremony at the church and a picnic reception behind the bunkhouse. He'd only wanted to spend the rest of his life with her.

Or so she'd believed.

*"You know I'd prefer to get married in my jeans," Micki said when Frankie pulled the strapless, fitted gown off the rack at the expensive bridal shop. Her sister had insisted on buying her a designer gown. "Gabe said he didn't care if I didn't wear a fancy wedding dress."*

*"We know that, Mick." Frankie held the gown in front of Micki. "That's the problem. You want to make Gabe speechless. You want to keep him guessing. And to do that, you need to do the unexpected. I guarantee, if you walk down the aisle wearing this, he won't know what hit him."*

*"Go try it on." Her mother wiped at the mistiness in her eyes. "You deserve something beautiful for the day your dreams come true."*

Micki focused on the reflection of the woman fussing with the tiny buttons up the back of the dress.

"You're so beautiful." Lizzie Decker finished the last button. Cash's eldest sister, Frankie, and Micki had been close friends while in high school. Since Frankie wasn't here to do the honors, Micki had asked Lizzie to be her matron of honor. "Frankie was right about the dress. It's perfect for you. Gabe won't know what hit him." Lizzie picked up a bouquet of white and tangerine roses with a watery gleam to her brown eyes and a dreamy smile on her pink lips. "I still can't believe you saved the dress."

Micki took the roses from Lizzie. "I almost didn't." She turned the bouquet until the pale orange ribbons fell over her hand just right. "I wanted to cut it to shreds." She forced a smile. "I guess it was meant to be that Gabe and I would eventually tie the knot."

Lizzie giggled like a girl half her age. "I can't believe he bought the ranch in secret for you to prove his love. That's so romantic. This whole thing is just so darned amazing. Even after you both wanted little Jesse and went to court and everything, y'all still want to get married." She leaned in and fanned herself with a pudgy hand. "Besides, the man is gorgeous."

"You can't fight love." Micki suddenly wanted to get the day over. Her gaze snagged on the king-sized bed, and she swallowed. Ever since the night he'd kissed her in the kitchen when he'd proposed, she'd been putting him off by agreeing that once they were married she'd sleep with him.

Maybe she wasn't in such a hurry after all. Getting the day over would bring the night sooner, and she wasn't ready for sex with Gabe. The thought of him lying her down on the soft mattress and doing his wicked best to her had her insides melting and aching for his touch.

"Is your momma ready?"

Lizzie's question shattered the fantasy, and Micki turned to her friend. "Señora Hernandez was finishing up with her hair when I left her room to get dressed."

Florencia Hernandez had started working at the ranch on Monday. The middle-aged, Hispanic housekeeper Gabe hired from a Dallas agency was great with Momma and in getting the house ready.

Her hair finished, she stared into the mirror at the daisies Lizzie had woven into her loose curls. She looked like a fairy. Despite her protests about the dress and all the other primping she'd been subjected to, she had to admit she looked amazing. She turned toward Lizzie. "Is Jesse here yet?"

"I don't know."

Micki swallowed hard and nodded. She hoped Lemont wouldn't keep him away to spite her, but she wouldn't be surprised if he refused to let the kid come. After all, he hadn't been invited.

Lizzie picked up her bouquet of orange autumn flowers and roses. "I can't believe you aren't more nervous. I'm shaking in my boots just thinking about all those famous people out there. Plus, Cash said he saw a helicopter flying low overhead earlier." She shook her head of curly red hair. "Can you believe tabloids hire them to get pictures?"

Micki smiled and squeezed the short, chubby woman's clammy hand. "You'll be fine. Take a deep breath. Remember Gabe is famous and just think of where he came from. Those singers out there put their pants on the same way you do. As for the photographers, Gabe hired security to keep them away."

She didn't tell Lizzie about Gabe's plan to sell their wedding photos to *People*. Lizzie was already so nervous she was babbling. The deal was struck last night with the money the magazine will pay for them to go to her mother. To her surprise, *People* was as interested in her, since in the world of professional barrel racing Micki had once been pretty darned famous. Not to mention the daughter of a Texas billionaire. Her marriage to Gabe was truly turning into a celebrity event.

"Well, that's good." Lizzie relaxed her grip on Micki's hand and smiled. "I can't imagine being famous. Must be a royal pain in the keister."

Yes, but not as much as her famous soon-to-be-husband was. Micki laughed and gathered her long, satin skirt into her free hand. "C'mon. I want to get this thing over with so I can get the hell out of this damned dress."

Lizzie giggled again. "And the sooner you can get Gabe out of his tuxedo."

Micki swallowed and shrugged. "I suppose being Mrs. Gabriel McKenna has its perks."

She glanced once more at the stranger in the mirror as they headed out the door and remembered the tearful time that should have been her first wedding day. Instead, she'd sat in her room staring at the dress Frankie and Momma had talked her into letting her sister buy her.

What had possessed her to save the gown? After crying through a box of tissues over Gabe McKenna, she couldn't bring herself to destroy the beautiful dress. She'd taken it off the hanger, wrapped it in white tissue paper, and stowed it away in an old chest with the elegant dress her mother had worn on her wedding day. Over the two relics of broken promises and shattered dreams, she'd vowed to never get married.

She'd never let another man hurt her. The first man had been her father when he'd abandoned her. When Micki was ten years old, she discovered the real reason her father had divorced her mother on one of her rare visits to his Brownwood ranch. Until then, even her mother had led her to believe she'd been the one to leave him. The truth wasn't as sugarcoated. Her father's ruthlessness toward her mother after her diagnosis, simply because she was unable to have another child, made her shiver with anger. As if he'd known he'd look like the asshole that he was, he'd trumped up some nonsense for their divorce hearing that her mother had cheated on him. When Micki was thirteen and Annie McKenna helped Momma sue for custody of her, Lemont had decided he was tired of Micki and called into question her paternity.

Micki gritted her teeth as she descended the stairs, thinking of Lemont. She'd thought Gabe was different from her father when she fell in love with him. She'd been there for him when his mother had died so tragically. Even strained her bond with her sister when she supported Gabe against his father after Frankie and Sam's affair came to light. On their four-year anniversary as a couple, Gabe proposed, promising to love her forever, and she'd foolishly believed him.

Like her father when she'd needed him, Gabe left her to chase his dreams with another woman.

They stopped in the living room where Momma waited. Her mother gasped when she saw Micki. She moved to Momma and hugged her, whispering near her ear, "Don't you start crying. You know this isn't real. I'm doing this for Jesse."

Momma hung on and whispered back, "I'm still giving my beautiful girl away today to a man I wish she could forgive."

As she looked past Momma's shoulder, Micki noticed the photographs on the mantle. Several depicted Jesse at various stages of his young life. In another, she and Gabe were so happy they glowed. She swallowed the memory of how much in love they looked in their first engagement photo.

Sucking in a deep breath, she pulled away from her mother. "I'm sorry, Momma, but I can't do that."

When the wedding coordinator signaled from the French doors, Micki turned away. She had to make this believable for Jesse's sake. For a moment, she filled the empty spaces in her heart with the memory of being in love with Gabe McKenna.

As she walked down the aisle with her mother by her side, her heart broke all over again for what might have been.

# Chapter 11

Gabe stared out the dark window of the master bedroom and lifted a bottle of beer to his lips. Under the window, the side yard was still alight with the lighting set up by the events people. The big white tent where the reception had been held now stood empty. Workers would be back tomorrow to gather up the white folding chairs and take down the tents, leaving behind nothing but crushed grass and a bill to be paid.

As he took another draw on the beer, the image of how Michaela had looked as she stepped out of the living room flashed before him. He'd never seen her look so radiantly beautiful. For the first time since suggesting they pretend to love each other, he feared the danger of this game to his heart.

He couldn't afford to let it be that vulnerable.

After they'd spoken vows neither of them had any intention of keeping and the meal he couldn't remember eating had been served, he took Michaela onto the dance floor. Nate O'Connell, another good friend and fellow singer, had sung a love song, and Gabe had held Michaela close.

Too close. Her scent of summer jasmine had surrounded him. The form-fitting gown had shown off every one of her curves in exquisite fashion, leaving little for him to imagine, and yet hiding her secrets under layers of lace and satin. Her tanned shoulders and upper back had been silky under his touch as he'd moved his hands over them. Her breasts, pushed high in the bodice of the dress, pressed against his chest, and he'd felt the firmness of them even through their clothes. The way her body molded to his had him hard as granite by the song's end.

When she'd looked up at him, the fire burning in her blue eyes and the rapid pulse at her throat left no doubt she wanted him as much as he wanted her. Michaela had licked her lips, and he gave into the temptation and kissed her.

There was no pretending in the passion they'd shared. She'd kissed him back and held on to him as if he were a lifeline. If they had been alone, he'd have swept her off the dance floor, taken her straight to bed, and made long, slow love to her.

Sleeping with his new wife was something he could not do. Michaela was the most passionate woman he'd ever known. He'd been her first lover, and she'd been shy. But when she'd gotten over her inhibitions, sex with her had been explosive.

As much as he wanted her, he wouldn't have her. His heart couldn't take being broken by her a second time. Once they adopted Jesse and became his parents, he'd have ongoing dealings with her for the rest of his life. It would be better for everyone if they became friends and left being lovers in the past.

The door opened, jerking him out of his ponderings. Michaela stepped over the threshold, stopping to stare at him with desire she either couldn't hide or had stopped fighting burning in her eyes. She was still dressed in the white gown. Her long curls had gone limp, and the daisies were falling out. The bottom of the satin skirt was stained from walking in the grass.

He wanted nothing more than to strip her out of the dress and run his fingers through her thick blond hair. He held the half-full beer bottle in a death grip and cleared his throat of the sudden lump. "Is Loretta all squared away?"

She averted her eyes and clasped her hands in front of her. "Yeah."

"That's good."

She licked those luscious lips. Her eyes slid from his to touch his body from his bare shoulders, over his chest, down his black slacks, and to his bare feet. The look was so fiercely sensual he bit back a groan and became so hard there was no hiding the bulge behind his unbuttoned pants. When her eyes settled on his again, she smiled a little lopsidedly. "Lizzie told me she thought you were gorgeous."

Damn, why hadn't he just gone back to his room across the hall? He cleared his throat again, but his voice still came out hoarsely. "And what do you think?"

She moved closer, each step emphasizing the sway of her hips. Did she have a clue how sexy she was? She stopped a few feet away from him. "I told her I hadn't noticed."

"Liar."

Michaela shrugged and took the beer from his hand. She watched him as she put it to her lips and tipped back her head to drain the bottle.

The action had him swallowing. Was she trying to seduce him? Or had she finally admitted to herself she wanted him and was giving in to her wilder side?

She set the bottle on the heavy oak dresser with a thud. "Okay. As much as I hate admitting it. I want you, and I decided you were right. Nothing is stopping us from having sex. So, what do you say?"

He had to get away before he gave into his lust. When she stepped closer, he held her away by catching her upper arms. Her hot, smooth skin burned his hands. "Michaela, I'm thinking that maybe we should keep this deal... uh... sex free."

She moved away and furrowed her brow. "What do you mean?"

He crossed the room, putting some space between them. Running his fingers through his hair, he sucked in a deep breath full of her scent. "I got to thinking, that's all. What if something happens?"

"Like what?"

She crossed her arms under her breasts, pushing the exposed tops upward. He looked away and closed his eyes. *Like maybe I can't afford falling in love with you again.* Instead, he came up with another logical reason. "Maybe we can't afford taking the chance that you'd get pregnant."

"I'm on the pill."

He took another breath and fought for control over every blazing cell of his body that wanted to be buried deep inside her. "You were on the pill the last time, too."

She sighed, the sound so sexy that he ached. "We could use condoms."

He met her eyes, the flame going out of them a little, and he told a boldfaced lie. "I don't have any condoms."

She turned away from him and squared her shoulders. "Then I suppose we shouldn't sleep together."

"Goodnight." He escaped before he gave into what they both wanted.

In the room across the hall, he closed the door and leaned his head back against it. How the hell was he going to survive this craziness?

* * * *

Before the sun was even up, Michaela was in the barn saddling Beau. She needed to forget what had happened last night. Like some sex-crazed hussy, she'd thrown herself at Gabe, and he'd tossed her aside like yesterday's garbage.

She sensed the gelding's eagerness to run the moment she buckled the cinch. The other horses in the barn nickered, and she tossed them some hay before taking Beau out. A stall on the end was empty. Who had taken Sam's stallion out? The answer came to her with a sigh--Gabe. The horse, named Devil's Spawn for good reason, needed to run. She'd exercised the big sorrel, but she hadn't ridden him. To do so didn't seem right since he'd been Sam's horse.

Beau bumped into her with his head, reminding her that he was more than ready to go. She stroked his long face. "Okay, I'm going."

Once they were outside the barn, she mounted him and began his warm-up. When she finished, she brought him into the starting gate and set the timer. She'd been trying for a while now to see if Beau still had his record-setting time of 13.20 seconds in him. Although barrel racing arenas varied, she had her course set up to the distance and configuration of the NFR. As she waited for the buzzer, she leaned over his long neck and whispered in his ear as she stroked his smooth hair, "C'mon, boy. Give me thirteen seconds. I know you can do it."

*  *  *  *

"Whoa." Gabe gently pulled on the reins of his father's horse, bringing him to a stop at the corner of the barn as horse and woman shot out of the frame constructed of two-by-fours in the corral. His heart skipped a beat in awe as Michaela and her big gelding raced at a breakneck speed around the first barrel, then looped the second. Going around the third barrel, Beau leaned over so far, Gabe feared Michaela would pitch right out of the saddle, but the worry was short lived. Horse and rider were too in-tune with each other and worked too well together for that to happen. Beau's thundering hooves grabbed at the dusty ground and straightened up as he came out of the curve, finishing the cloverleaf pattern. He shot like a rocket back to the gate, tripping the timer to stop.

She grabbed her hat and waved it in the air with a whoop. "Yes! That's what I want to see. Thirteen point twenty-five!" Setting the Stetson on her head, she leaned over her mount and patted the horse's sweaty neck. "Good job, boy!"

His heart galloped like a horse. Damn, that time was only 0.5 seconds off her NFR record. "That was some fancy riding."

She turned in the saddle. "You saw it?"

"Yeah. Too bad you're retired. With times like that you'd own the NFR." He rubbed the back of his neck. Despite the chill of the morning air, heat rose in him. Memories of her offering herself to him last night had kept him awake, and the ride through the pastures on the powerful horse had done nothing to alleviate his desire.

Her gaze snagged on his for a moment, and he was certain he recognized the same undeniable need, but she broke the spell when her mount pranced to the side. She steadied Beau and dismounted in a fluid motion that defied the fact the horse was nearly as tall as she. "When do we need to leave for Dallas?"

"By one. Our flight leaves at six p.m." They'd decided the trip to Nashville for the award show would suffice for a honeymoon. The last thing he wanted was to go off to some romantic destination with a woman he desired too much and couldn't have.

She led Beau around the corral one last time as a cool down. "I'll be ready."

Gabe slid out of the saddle and his boots hit the ground with a thud. He patted Devil's Spawn on the shoulder and the horse nipped at his hat. "Hey."

Michaela stopped on the other side of the fence and laughed. "I don't think he likes you much."

Gabe adjusted his hat and glared at her. "We get along just fine." He led the horse into the barn, following Michaela. "I already fed the horses this morning."

She glanced over at him as she unbuckled the cinch of her saddle. "How long have you been up?"

He busied himself with unsaddling Devil's Spawn. "A few hours."

As they cared for their horses, silence rolled between them, building the tension to an almost palpable state. Michaela led Beau out to the fenced-off pasture that was all his own. Gabe followed her lead and led one of the other horses and Devil's Spawn out into another corral of the pasture. Michaela let the last of the horses out, then reached for the rake to clean the stalls at the same time as he grasped it.

They stood boot-to-boot. His hand rested over hers on the smooth wood of the rake handle. He caught his breath, and their gazes locked. As he caressed his fingers over the cotton of her long-sleeve shirt, her muscles tensed under his touch.

Her breath quickened with the advance of his hand to her shoulder, then to the warm skin of her neck. He took her hat off and pulled the band from her ponytail to bury his hand into the golden satin of her long hair. She caressed her free hand over his chest and fisted it in the cotton of his shirt.

Lust boiled through him at the heat in her eyes, and he couldn't stop himself. He pulled her to him as she tugged on his shirtfront. Their lips came together hard. He plunged deep into her open mouth, dueling with her sweet tongue.

She moaned and wrapped both arms around him, knocking off his hat, which fell forgotten to the floor beside the rake. He brought his hands down to her firm ass and pulled her up against him. Not satisfied, he lifted her and she wrapped her legs around him as he pushed her against the barn wall.

Breaking the kiss, she nibbled on his ear, then breathed words as wild as the passion burning between them. "Let's go up to the loft."

\* \* \* \*

Neither of them wasted time scrambling up the ladder. Gabe let Micki go first. She stood on the straw-littered floor of the loft, with bales of fragrant alfalfa and oat grass stacked around her, and waited for Gabe. He pulled her into his arms and kissed her. She yanked open the snaps of his plaid shirt. His chest muscles rippled with the motion and his eyes burned with enough heat to set the hay around them on fire. He laid his shirt on a layer of the bales and reached for her. Her breath left her in a gasp when his mouth sought hers, and he kissed her hard and thoroughly while he unbuttoned her shirt.

She grabbed for the buckle of his jeans and worked to get the stubborn thing open but had to leave her task as he slid her shirt down her arms. Giving up on his belt, she tackled her own, while he did fast work opening his. After pulling his boots off, he shoved the faded denim of his jeans along with his underwear down his legs.

She groaned and sucked in her lower lip at the site of his tanned, naked body. He hadn't changed much in the seven years since the last time they'd made love. The reminder of what they had once had made her doubt the sanity of this, but she'd come too far to stop now. She kicked off her own boots and followed with her jeans.

Standing before him in only her sports bra and cotton panties, she shivered as much in anticipation as from the chill of the autumn morning. Enfolding her in his arms again, he kissed her as he turned her to bring her down on top of the layer of hay bales covered with his shirt. He yanked her bra over her head, then shifted to remove her panties. As he moved over her again, he kissed his way up her trembling body, stopping to suckle and tease her nipples, hardening the sensitive buds to near painful levels. With a loud moan, she tugged on his hair until his face was above hers, while he supported his weight on either side of her head on his elbows. She pulled him down to her and kissed him. A dance of tongues meant to mimic what they both wanted. All the while, her other hand slid along his body to find his hard cock. As she stroked the velvety skin, he hissed in her mouth.

Breathing hard, she broke the kiss. Near his ear, she whispered, "Ride me hard, cowboy."

To emphasize her meaning, she wrapped her legs around him and guided him to her. He didn't need any other encouragement. When he thrust into her, they both moaned.

Gabe paused, and she became accustomed to his size. He stroked her cheek and locked on to her gaze. Something flickered across his amber eyes, and for a beat, she thought she recognized it as the way he'd once looked upon her, with love and tenderness. But then he closed his eyes and tossed back his head. With teeth gritted, he began to move, and then all thought left her as he built her up in blinding light to break apart in a million splinters of purest pleasure.

He groaned and stiffened above her, following her to climax.

* * * *

"Looks like someone already took care of the horses. Hey, wonder whose hat that is? It's a fancy one. Think it's the boss's?"

At the sound of the voice below them in the barn, Gabe pulled himself above Michaela, supporting his weight on his arms. She popped her eyes open and stared at him with her mouth going round.

"Maybe. But whoever let the horses out didn't clean the stalls," said one of the other ranch hands Gabe had hired for the place. "Look here. I found another hat. I think it's Micki's. At least, it's a woman's."

From the soft thuds of footsteps in the breezeway, Gabe imagined the first speaker moving toward the second. "Wonder what happened."

"Don't know. But damn, if I was married to Micki Finn, I sure as hell wouldn't be out here the day after the weddin' doin' barn work."

Gabe smiled at the horrified expression draining Michaela's face of the flush he'd put there only a few moments ago.

"Sure 'nough." Both cowboys chuckled, then the first speaker said, "Hey, what's that? There, hangin' out of the hay loft."

"Looks like a shirt. You don't think...?"

Both Gabe and Micki glanced toward the opening in the loft floor. Her pale blue shirt hung over the edge. Micki closed her eyes and groaned, then slapped her hand over her mouth to stop the sound.

"Uh... I think we found the newlyweds. The stalls can wait." The cowboy, who spoke first, laughed heartily, and a slap sounded as if he'd cuffed the other guy. "C'mon, Jim. Let's get outta here."

The door closed, leaving behind the sound of a bird chirping somewhere in the barn's rafters and his and Micki's hard breathing.

"At least this time we're married." The first time they'd made love had been in this loft. He was eighteen, Michaela seventeen, and he'd just taken her virginity when his dad came into the barn calling for him.

His father must have heard them rushing to get dressed and climbed the ladder to investigate the sounds. Sam had caught Gabe and Micki half-dressed and there was no question about what the two had been up to. Gabe still remembered the lecture he got later about responsibility and possible consequences.

"Oh, God," Michaela groaned again. "Not sure this time is any better."

Gabe couldn't help it. She was too damned cute. He kissed her soundly, and she opened under his questing tongue, running her hands through his hair and over his shoulders. Although he'd pulled out of her, his desire flared, and he wanted her all over again.

He broke the kiss and gazed at her. She stared back at him with an emotion he couldn't guess at. Desire mixed with something old, like the way she'd once looked upon him with love shining in the blue depths of her eyes.

Despite his best intentions, he'd lost his heart to her again weeks ago. He could admit that to himself now, and with that admission a new resolve bloomed.

Micki had once loved him. What happened to cause her to break their engagement the last time, he didn't know; however, unlike when he'd drowned the hurt with his dreams, booze, and the arms of another woman, this time he intended to fight for her.

The gravity of his decision hit him hard. Was he seriously thinking of making this marriage work?

She jerked him out of his thoughts when she moved against him. The last time had burned hot and wild; this time he wanted to make love to her. He kissed down along her neck to nibble at her pulse, beating strong and fast under soft, jasmine-scented skin. She tasted salty and sweet, as intoxicating as any alcoholic drink.

Farther down, he teased and explored her breasts with fingers, lips, and tongue. First one, then the other, bringing moans and mewls from her.

As he moved down to her flat tummy, she fisted her hands in his hair. She shifted to allow him access to her long leg to caress the smooth skin up to the moist, hot place at the apex.

"Gabe!" She arched to meet his fingers as he slid them against her folds and curls. Her breaths came hard and fast as he stroked her and suckled on her hard nipples.

He watched as ecstasy washed over her face and she quaked under him. Leaning over her, gently bringing her down from her high, he whispered, "You are the most beautiful woman."

She opened her eyes, fuzzy from pleasure, and touched his face. "Don't say things like that."

He sensed her withdrawal and refused to let her retreat. She was afraid. Of what, he didn't know--maybe of love? He was determined to show her she could fight that fear and together they'd defeat it. Smiling, he caressed her cheek. "I'll say whatever I want, when it's the truth."

Kissing her, coaxing her to a feverish pitch again, he entered her. Unlike the first time, he rocked slowly into her, letting them both build to an explosion of bliss.

He turned, pulling her on top, and held her. As their breathing slowed, he stroked her back for a long time. Neither of them spoke. He was afraid of breaking whatever spell they were under.

Michaela was the first to move. She shifted off him to sit next to him on the edge of the hay bales. "I need to go inside to make sure Mrs. Hernandez has everything ready for Momma for while we're away."

She found her clothes and started getting dressed.

He sighed and sat up, then reached for his own clothes. The magic moment was over. "Okay."

As she stepped onto the ladder, she looked back at him. "Just so you know. I'm not sure we should do this again. Sex. I mean. I don't want something to happen."

Her words stabbed his heart as hard as if she'd used a pitchfork. What was she so afraid of happening? "Yeah," he said, despite his question, and swallowed the lump in his throat. "You're probably right."

As Michaela hurried down the ladder, he prayed he hadn't made the biggest mistake of his life by making love to his wife.

# Chapter 12

Micki avoided Gabe until they had to leave for the airport. The events in the barn still rattled her. She'd needed the hot, wild sex the first time to release the pent-up desire and frustration. Their second coming together had been anything but raw and stirred too many emotions. Gabe's gaze and the gentle way he'd touched her had reminded her of when they'd first fallen in love.

The unthinkable had happened; she wanted this marriage to be real. Was she being foolish for entertaining such an idea? She believed Gabe had loved her before, but he'd abandoned her as soon as he was given a chance at Nashville.

"We'll be at the airport in fifteen minutes," Gabe said from her side.

Nodding, she watched the traffic zip by on the highway from the backseat. Jake, one of the cowboys hired on at the ranch, was driving the BMW to the Dallas-Fort Worth airport.

Gabe shifted on the seat beside her. "I hope we can avoid the paparazzi, but I wouldn't bet on it."

She looked at his profile. He was dressed in jeans and a long-sleeve T-shirt with a guitar logo on it. His unruly dark hair curled around his ears as he scribbled on a tablet. He scrunched up his face in concentration, reminding her of Jesse when he tried to figure out a math problem.

She was kidding herself. They were only in this for Jesse and to think otherwise would turn out disastrous to her heart.

As Jake parked the car next to the curb to drop them off, Micki spotted two men near the door with professional cameras, watching the parking cars.

She jumped when Gabe took her hand and squeezed it. "Looks like word got out that we were headed for our honeymoon."

Jake looked over his shoulder from the driver's seat. "You want me to drop you off somewhere else, boss?"

"No, this is good." He held Micki's gaze. "You ready?"

*No!* "Yeah." She reached for the door, but he grabbed her hand.

Shaking his head, he let go and shoved his notebook into a leather bag. "Let me play the part of a gentleman, okay?"

She ignored him and opened the door. Grunting something that sounded like "Figures she wouldn't listen," he got out of the car and came around to her side. He challenged her with his smile and with the twinkle in his dark eyes as he held out his hand. Taking a deep breath, she put her hand in his and savored the buzz she got when he touched her.

Cliff, another ranch hand who rode shotgun, retrieved their bags from the trunk. Jake pulled away from the curb and headed for the parking lot where Cliff would meet him later for the three-hour trip back to Bluebonnet Creek.

As the taillights of the dark gray luxury sedan disappeared into the traffic, she wished she could go home with them.

Gabe wrapped his arm around her waist, pulling her against his side. She wanted to move away, but his hot breath on her cheek stopped her.

"Smile. Like it or not, we'll be on the cover of every tabloid out there, so get your lovey-dovey on." His low, deep voice flowed through her ear like water, flooding her senses with memories from this morning in the barn.

She forced a smile. "Freakin' wonderful. I should've bargained for hazard pay when I agreed to marry you."

"Get used to it, Mrs. McKenna." He grinned and kissed her full on the lips, just as the paparazzi flashed their cameras. She shivered, not sure what frightened her more: the heat of his kiss as he pressed her into him, the husky way he said her name, or the thought of such an intimate act being splashed in the tabloids.

* * * *

The first-class flight to Nashville was uneventful, but Micki came off the airplane feeling like she'd been bounced around the entire hour and forty minutes. She'd never flown in first class before nor with a celebrity. Sure, she was known in the rodeo world, but even that notoriety was small compared to what she experienced as Gabe's wife.

The flight attendants, after several moments of being starstruck by him, had catered to him--and by extension to her, which she found surprising. She'd been given a fluffy pillow before she asked for one. The women brought her snacks, and although alcohol flowed freely, they brought her a diet Coke when she'd asked, then continued to keep them coming. She'd been treated like a queen, and that she'd enjoyed the attention scared her as much as the gentle way Gabe had touched her. For a long time into the flight, he'd held her hand. Then, as they disembarked their plane, he rested his hand on her back.

She was in a daze as Gabe guided her through the airport. A tall, redheaded woman waved and rushed toward them. She was dressed in a stylish jade pantsuit and carried an iPad and a large designer handbag. As Micki stood by forcing a smile, Gabe greeted the woman with a quick hug, sending an unexpected jolt of jealousy surging through Micki.

The woman smiled and moved forward. Before Micki knew what happened, she was wrapped up in a hug.

"Glad someone finally married this guy," she said and stepped back. Micki's shock must have shown on her expression because the lady blushed and shook her head, sending red curls bouncing on her shoulders. "Sorry, I was so thrilled to hear about Gabe's wedding. Maybe it will keep him out of trouble..." She glanced sideways at Gabe. "Making my job easier."

Gabe folded his arm around Micki's shoulder and chuckled. "Michaela, I'd like you to meet my assistant, Trish Russell."

She recognized the name from their rushed invitations and smiled. Trish was married to the son of Gabe's manager. "Nice to meet you, Trish. I don't envy you. Keeping him out of trouble must be a fulltime job all in itself."

"Hey!" Gabe narrowed his eyes at her but couldn't mask his amusement. "Don't worry, Trish is well paid for what she does."

Laughing, Trish motioned for them to start moving. People were noticing them and staring. "That's debatable."

"How's little Bella feeling?" Gabe took Micki's hand as they walked toward the baggage claim. For her benefit, he added, "Bella is Trish's two-year-old holy terror she calls a daughter. She's the reason she couldn't come to the wedding."

Trish beamed. "She's feeling better. Thanks for asking." She looked at Micki. "I'm truly sorry I couldn't come, but Bella is almost never sick and this is the first time she's had strep throat. I just couldn't leave her here with my mother while I went to Texas."

"Of course not. We understand." Micki didn't know this woman, but she already liked her. "You were exactly where you should've been."

*Besides, the wedding wasn't real anyway.*

The sting to her heart at the reminder hurt more than it should have.

Forty minutes later, Trish turned the luxury SUV through a wrought iron gate that looked like it should have belonged to a plantation on a wide tree-lined street. Micki had heard of gated communities, but she'd never seen one, except on TV. Although night had fallen, street lights lit up enough of the Georgian mansions peeping though hedgerows and behind other gates for her to get a feeling of wealth beyond what she was accustomed to. The only mansion she'd ever seen that could compare was her father's rambling monstrosity.

Trish turned down another street bordering a lake. Silver light reflected off the ripples in a peaceful ballet. Across the water, lights lit up a large classical pillared building. The huge fountain in front glowed in an array of changing colorful lights dancing through the spray. By the faint moonlight and the overflow of street light, she got an impression of rolling knolls and trees beyond the expensive vehicles parked in neat rows behind the building.

"This place is beautiful. I can't imagine what it looks like in the light of day." Micki swallowed and rubbed her palms on her jeans.

Gabe leaned toward her as if to look out her window. "That's the country club and golf course behind it. I like to watch the sun come up over the green.

Dear God, Gabe lived *here*?

On the other side of the street, the homes were a little less grand, but no less impressive as the mansions they'd passed.

Although keeping with the southern plantation theme with frontal columns, the modern design of the insides spilled out of the glowing large glass windows.

Trish slowed the car and pulled into the drive of the fifth house on the street.

* * * *

Gabe exhaled a breath he'd been holding in as Trish parked her SUV in the driveway. He didn't see any prying eyes of tabloid scum anywhere in sight. One more benefit of paying the price for a gated community.

He glanced at Michaela and fought to keep the snicker off his face. With her very kissable lips shaped in an O, she stared out the window at his two-story home as if she'd never seen a house before. As she let out a low whistle, she turned wide glowing eyes to him. "Trying to compensate for your deficiencies much?"

He opened the door and chuckled. "You know better."

"I know nothing. Except this place is freaking huge." She pushed on her door and climbed out.

"You two sound like an old married couple." Laughing, Trish stepped up beside Michaela and put her arm around her waist. "This place is big, but it's not excessive." She led Michaela toward the front door. "My sister-in-law manages a rock star who has a freaking bowling alley and an Olympic-sized pool *inside* his house. He also has twenty-five bedrooms and lives alone. Now, that's excessive."

Trish opened the door and headed in to turn on the lights. As if unsure she wanted to enter his house, Michaela hesitated a moment. When she glanced over her shoulder at him, he smiled.

She flicked her gaze over the darkened street behind him, then entered. Her sharp intake of air as she paused in the entry caused him to shake his head and chuckle. "Michaela, for Christ's sake, stop that already."

He sat their bags on the polished marble tile of the foyer, and she snapped narrowed eyes at him.

"I'm rich. Get over it." Anger flashed in her gaze, and he couldn't help himself. He caught her around the waist and pulled her to him. As her eyes grew wide with surprise, he captured her lips in a kiss meant to let her know he wasn't going to let her get much sleep that night, despite whatever craziness he'd agreed to this morning in the barn. She fought him at first; then she fisted her fingers into his shirt. The low moan escaping her had him responding to her, and he held her closer.

Trish's throat clearing reminded him they weren't alone. "Hey, lovebirds, what do you say we discuss your schedule for the week, and then I'll get out of here?"

When he pulled away, he couldn't get enough air in his lungs and her scent filled every bit of breath he did manage. Michaela's dilated pupils were unfocused and full of the same desire he'd seen in the barn this morning.

He swallowed down the need for her and forced his gaze to his assistant. "Good idea."

Trish raised a coppery brow at the raspy response but didn't say anything. As she tapped a finger on her iPad, he took Michaela's hand and led her into the living room. They sat on the couch.

Without looking away from the tablet, Trish said, "Gabe, you are due in rehearsals at eight a.m. You're scheduled as an opening act along with Seth Kendall, Nate O'Connell, and Logan Cartwright, and you all are to sing your collaboration. Seth said he and Nate talked to you at the wedding about the song."

"Yeah, we talked about it. We've only sang the song twice live together so we decided to do something fun." The song had been a number-one single earlier that year from Logan Cartwright's second album. The rowdy anthem to pickup trucks, hot women, and beer had won the award for Best Musical Event in one of the early award presentations last week. The first award of many for him, he hoped. "We'll work out the bugs during rehearsals."

Micki looked up at him. "I'd love to meet Logan. He and I are second cousins, but I don't know him. Momma moved away from Colton when she was eighteen, after her parents were killed in a car accident."

Trish glanced up from her iPad. "It always amazes me how small the biggest state in the continental USA is. I swear everyone is related down there in Texas."

"Not everyone is related, but I know what you mean." With a chuckle, he wrapped his arm around Michaela's shoulders. She sat rigid beside him and tapped her foot as if she were getting ready to run. He had no intentions of letting her escape. When she turned a confused gaze at him, he smiled and pulled her close to him. She didn't relax much, but the fidgeting stopped. "I'll make sure you meet him." Then he turned his attention back to Trish. "Where's my solo performance happening in the show, and when's that rehearsal scheduled?"

Trish consulted her iPad again. "You'll go on after the Male Vocalist is announced. Gary said that's a great spot." She looked up and smiled. "Especially if you win the category. Your rehearsal is at four p.m. tomorrow and again Thursday at one p.m. You, Seth, Nate, and Logan also rehearse again at eight a.m. that morning."

"Damn, can't you or Gary get the *CMA*s to schedule the rehearsals closer together?"

"Sorry, Gabe, but that's what we got. Gary also wanted me to tell you that he set up an interview with Robin Roberts for her *CMA* special, which will be taped Wednesday at ten a.m." Trish glanced at Michaela. "She'd like to get the two of you on camera, but Gary was noncommittal, since he didn't know how you'd react."

When Michaela shifted in his arms, he glanced into her worried face. He didn't have to read her mind to imagine what she was thinking. "You don't have to do that if you don't want to."

She took a deep breath and shrugged before looking at Trish. "Sure. I'll do it. But I think it prudent to have the questions beforehand." She met his gaze again. "We don't need any surprises in the interview. Also, our family, including his brother--my nephew--are off limits. We'll talk about us and about his career. Hell, I'll even answer questions about my time as a barrel racer. But everything else is personal and off limits."

He smiled because he never worried about interviews. Usually, he evaded any questions he didn't want to answer, but her way of thinking was much better and could work very well to their advantage. "Great idea."

She shrugged against his side. "Great business sense. But I was hoping to see a little of Nashville while here. Guess that will have to wait until the next time."

*Next time?* He stroked her cheek, not for the lie they were living, but because he wanted to feel her soft skin and watch her eyes dilate with desire. She didn't disappoint him and even gave a little shiver in answer to his touch. "I'm sorry. I hoped to show you around town a bit before the show Sunday night."

"You have to work. That's okay." She looked around the room but quickly turned her gaze to his again. "I'm sure I can find something to do around here." The sensation of her warm breast pressed against the side of his chest had him sucking in a breath.

"Don't worry about Mrs. McKenna." Both he and Michaela turned to Trish as she sat on the chair across from them and smiled. "I think I can find something that will keep her busy."

Michaela looked from Trish to him then back again. "Actually, I was wondering..."

"Yes?"

She moved out of his embrace and crossed her arms. "Where will I be sitting?"

Trish consulted her iPad again. "Gary has you seated beside Seth and his wife on your left in the second row. You and Gabe are sitting on the end by the center aisle."

He glanced at Michaela. She was getting that panicky look in her eyes again. "You met Abby at our wedding. She's a nurse from north Texas."

She closed her eyes for a second. "I remember. I liked her. Her daughter is a singer, too, right?"

Nodding, Trish glanced at her iPad. "Yes. She's next to her dad. I put you next to Abby. I figured you girls have something in common. If nothing else you're both from Texas and not in the business." She smiled and pushed her red hair from her eyes. "She and Seth haven't been married all that long either."

Micki groaned and the panicky roundness of her eyes worsened. "Wait. I liked Abby, and Seth, too, but their crazy relationship is in the tabloids almost as much as Gabe is. If I'm sitting beside them, wouldn't that make me a better target for the cameras?"

Trish nodded and her smile widened as if the situation was perfect. Gabe had to agree with Michaela. The other couple's relationship had been a tabloid favorite when Seth announced he was the father of Abby's teenage daughter a little over a year ago. The whole show would be a media orgy of juicy gossip and rumors. Unlike Michaela, he saw this as an advantage, but he couldn't explain how to use it in front of Trish.

"You're bound to be a favorite of the TV cameras for sure," Trish said.

Michaela's mouth fell open. "Jesus, save me." Putting some distance between them on the leather couch, she looked at him and narrowed her eyes. "What if I don't go? Isn't the interview enough? At least it can be controlled. I know they'll swing those cameras on me at the most awkward moments. What if I yawn during your performance?"

Gabe chuckled and shrugged. Michaela had always hated this sort of stuff. Every year she'd won the NFR, she would sneak out of the arena before she could be interviewed by the ESPN reporter covering the barrel racing event. "Wouldn't that make for some interesting speculation in the tabloids? But I think the more *glaring* news would be if you weren't there to yawn at me shaking my ass around on stage."

Closing her eyes, she took a breath deep enough to move her shoulders up and slowly down. She'd gotten his hidden point. The last thing they needed was bad press. As long as they played their parts, anything the media caught on camera could only help their case. She opened her eyes and turned to Trish. "I suppose I'll need some fancy sparkly nightgown pretending to be a dress for this dog and pony show."

"Yes. Of course." Trish furrowed her brow as though perplexed by Michaela's question. "You don't have an evening gown?"

"Nope." Michaela laughed and leaned back. "I honestly didn't think about it. I guess I'd better go shopping."

"Understandable. You just got married and crammed all of that planning into a few weeks' time. Don't worry. I know just the place to find what you'll need to knock the socks off the red carpet commentators." Trish tucked her iPad into her bag, getting ready to leave. "I'll pick you up at nine tomorrow morning."

When she stood, he and Michaela followed to their feet. Michaela nodded, but a shadow creased her forehead. "Okay."

He saw Trish to the door while Michaela paced around the outside of the room like a caged bull. When he returned to the living room, she stopped her trek and wrung her hands together. "Dear God, how am I going to afford a fancy dress? I should have thought of it. I could have found *something* in Brownwood when Lizzy and I went shopping for her dress for the wedding."

Gabe pulled his wallet from his pocket and removed a credit card. He held it out between two fingers. "Here." When her face grew a stormy red, he shook his head and waved the card. "Don't say it. I know what you're thinking. Damn it, Michaela, you're my wife."

"Don't remind me." She spun away without taking the credit card. "I think all this pretending to be something we aren't has really clouded your brain." She turned back to him. Something fleeting sparked in her eyes, but before he could name the emotion, it was gone and replaced with anger. "We are only married for Jesse."

He tossed the card onto the end table in front of her. "I know why we're married. For that reason, I would like you showing up at one of the biggest nights of my career in something amazing." As he took a step toward her, his own anger boiled to the surface. He'd been a fool to think they might actually have a chance. "I meant what I said. Every news outlet interested in country music--from the network to radio stations to tabloids and magazines--will be focused on us. We have to prove to the world that we can provide the perfect family for Jesse and that our marriage is full of love, even though we both know that will never be true."

Gabe turned and headed up the stairs to the loft. At the landing above, he peered down at her blond ponytail. "You can sleep in the guestroom on the right. Just make sure you're up and the bed made before Trish shows up in the morning. She said nine, but she'll be here by eight, if I know my assistant."

"Don't worry about appearances. I know my role in this game." She picked up his credit card and faced him, meeting his gaze with cold eyes. "I've already made a deal with the devil and I will follow through. I want Jesse as much as you do. I'll show up at the show in something *amazing*, but I will pay you back every penny I spend if it takes me a lifetime to do so. I want nothing from you."

He turned away, his heart aching with love he'd never be able to share with Michaela, and entered his room, closing the door behind him.

# Chapter 13

Micki pulled on the brass handle of the door of the boutique with sweaty hands. Despite the chill the cold rain pelting the sidewalk sent through her, she sweated under her denim jacket. The place looked like something out of a movie, with front windows filled with manikins displaying dresses she could only imagine celebrities wearing. Dear Lord, was she actually married to one? Taking a deep breath of air lightly scented with the sweet spiciness of pumpkin and cinnamon, she stepped into the store.

To her right stood a manikin dressed in a silvery sequined gown. A slit up the side of the shimmery, fitted skirt showed off the model's leg up to only inches from the hip. The strapless bodice, if it could be justified with the name, showed more flesh than it covered.

"May I help you?"

She turned toward the sales woman frowning at her. Where was Trish? How long did it take to park a car? She fisted her clammy hands. "Ah... I'm looking for a dress." Although she'd never be caught dead in the thing, she couldn't help but ask, "How much is this one?"

"That is a one-of-a-kind by a new designer named Vincent D'Angelo. He's designed for some of the hottest actresses in Hollywood."

Impatient with the woman's haughty tone, she pointed at the dress. "How much?"

"Ten thousand dollars."

"Holy shit!" She gasped and stared at the woman. "You've got to be kidding. For *that*?"

The woman pointedly looked over Micki's scuffed boots, faded jeans, and worn jacket, before narrowing her eyes on her makeup-free face. "That dress wouldn't suit you anyway."

"You've got that right."

"Miss, this is an exclusive boutique. Maybe you are in the wrong type of shop."

Micki easily translated the woman's condescending glare and tone to mean she belonged in Walmart. She almost turned on her heels and walked out as the dress shop scene from the Julia Roberts's movie *Pretty Woman* flashed into her mind. She considered pulling out Gabe's black credit card to prove she had the money to pay for anything she wanted, but she had more pride than that.

The door opened behind her, and she let relief flood her as Trish stepped inside. "I'm sorry, Micki. I couldn't find a parking space anywhere." She shifted her bag onto her shoulder and closed her dripping umbrella, then smiled at the clerk. "Hello, I'm Trish Russell and this is Micki. Gabe McKenna's wife. We need something glamorous for the *CMA*s."

Micki didn't hide her smile at the way the woman's eyes widened with surprise.

She blinked and smiled with warmth that rang untrue. "I'm sorry for my reaction, Mrs. McKenna. We get a lot of tourists who wander in here hoping to see someone famous. Welcome to Tolberts. If we don't have what you're looking for, no one else will either." Turning on her sky-high stilettos, she stalked toward a rack of sparkly dresses. "Please, follow me."

"Micki?"

She turned at the sound of her name. The woman handed the clerk behind her a long pale yellow gown. Over the rack, a sign marked it as maternity and listed several designer names. Micki smiled as she recognized the wife of country star Seth Kendall. "Abby, it's nice to see you again. Trish said we're sitting next to each other at the show."

Abby pushed her long dark brown hair out of her face, then rested a hand on her rounded belly. The couple's second child was due in less than two months, and if Micki believed the tabloid rumors, the baby was supposed to be a boy. "Yes. I'm so glad. Seth and I have been married for a year, but I don't come to Nashville much and don't know many people. It's nice to meet someone who is as culture shocked as I am."

Micki laughed and glanced around. "I couldn't agree more. I'm not looking forward to finding a dress."

Abby looked at the clerk holding the gown she'd chosen. "Please check if you have that one in my size and hold it with the other one I chose. I'll try them on later."

"Let me know when you're ready, Mrs. Kendall." The woman smiled and headed toward the back of the store.

"Thank you." Turning toward Micki, Abby took her hand. "I hate dress shopping and put it off as long as I can. C'mon. Let's find something wonderful for you. Some of the most famous singers and their wives shop here."

Trish chuckled and shook her head. "You both know that list includes y'all."

"Don't remind me." Micki let Abby lead her toward a rack of gowns with a famous designer name over it. "I don't dress up much."

With a laugh, Abby stopped in front of a manikin showcasing another over-the-top scrap of sequins and silk. "Neither do I. Especially now that nothing fits. But even if I wasn't as big as a buffalo, I'm much more comfortable in scrubs or jeans. Of course, I don't wear scrubs now that I quit my nursing job and stay home to manage our ranch." With her hair lying over one shoulder, Abby looked very much like a Native American maiden. She regarded Micki with deep honey-brown eyes. "You were gorgeous on your wedding day."

"Thank you."

Trish and the sales lady who'd greeted Micki circled the rows and manikins. Trish stopped in front of one of the models beside another rack full of dresses.

"I think you should try this on, Micki." She pointed to a long navy dress with a waistline embellished with clear rhinestones that sparkled like diamonds.

"This dress would be perfect on you, Mrs. McKenna." The sales lady pasted on her fake smile. "I'll have to go in the back to find your size. You're a size two?" Now, she was just sucking up.

"No, I'm an eight." Micki drifted toward Trish and the manikin like a skittish horse toward a person holding a carrot. She wasn't sure about the gown, but she liked the subdued color and the old Hollywood look of it.

Abby followed. "I agree. That blue is such a complimentary color for you."

Micki brushed the organza overlay of the skirt with a trembling hand. It was one of the most beautiful dresses she'd ever seen, and excitement filled her. Gabe wanted her to look good, and as she let the soft silk of the gown soothe her fingers, a need to impress him filled her, regardless of how much it would cost her.

She looked up and smiled. "It is a beautiful dress."

The sales woman returned from the back of the store with the gown in Micki's size draped over her arms. "Mrs. McKenna, I'll show you to the dressing room."

* * * *

"Michaela?" Gabe's muffled voice echoed from the living room below. "We have to go."

She sucked in a deep breath and took one last look at her reflection in the mirrored closet door of the dressing room inside Gabe's master suite. Earlier that day, Abby had taken her to have her hair and nails done, as if they somehow became undone since the day before her wedding a week ago. She had to admit she loved the sleek, classic look of the updo the hairdresser had twisted her usually messy locks into. The dress fit perfectly and reminded her of something Elizabeth Taylor may have worn in her heyday.

She took a deep breath and rested her hand on the cinched waist. As she filled her lungs with air, the off-the-shoulder bodice lifted, revealing a little more cleavage. The neckline dipped low but not far enough to make her self-conscious. A diamond pendant that had belonged to Frankie hung at her neck, and simple diamond studs, belonging to her mother, glinted at her ears. She'd worn them on her wedding day and was thankful for the impulse she had to pack them for the trip to Nashville. As on her wedding day, stinging nerves battered her insides. With a touch to the rhinestone leaf design at the waist of the dress, she prayed she'd survive the night, then dropped her hand. Time to face the lions.

"Coming." She picked up a rhinestone-covered clutch that Trish insisted she carry and stepped into the ridiculously high shoes Abby had helped her pick out. As she headed through Gabe's bedroom, she glanced at the king-sized bed and closed her eyes. Was she crazy to wish things could have been different between them?

She picked up the layers of the skirt in the hand she also held her purse with and applied a death grip on the handrail as she maneuvered down the stairs. So intent on not tripping over either her dress or her high heels, she paid no attention to Gabe until he whistled low in his throat.

Stopping mid-flight, she looked at him as he stared at her with a fire in his eyes that scorched her despite the distance between them. She forced her eyes to the stairs and bit the inside of her cheek to keep a pleased smile from forming on her lips. Not wanting him to see how his appreciation affected her, she continued her hesitant journey down the curved staircase. "You startled me and are damned lucky I didn't fall and break my fool neck." She stepped off the last stair, let go of her skirt, and took a good look at the country music hunk that was her husband. "Oh, I see it's perfectly okay for you to wear jeans and boots, but I have to dress up like some damn princess."

He set his hat on his head and grinned. She would never let him know how hot he looked in the tight black jeans and light blue western shirt open at the neck. A western-styled black leather jacket, boots, and a black Stetson completed his red carpet look. Nor would she let him know how dressing up somehow transformed her into feeling like Cinderella ready for the ball. But she knew at the end of the night she'd turn back into a cowgirl, and he'd still be the man who had broken her heart. He'd never be her prince.

Her hand trembled at his touch as he wrapped his around it. "You look amazing."

His gruff voice set her heart free at a full gallop, and she shivered when he kissed her fingers.

"Isn't that what you wanted?" Did that husky sound belong to her?

"I never doubted that you would. I am honored to stand beside you tonight." The openness of his gaze stopped her breath.

He leaned forward as if to kiss her, and she wanted it, but she broke the trance she was under by taking a step back. "We better leave."

"I have a gift for you before we go." He picked up a long, white fur coat off the couch.

"What's that?" She hadn't seen it there before she'd gone upstairs to dress.

He held out the coat. "It's November in Tennessee. You forgot to get a coat."

As beautiful as it was, revulsion flooded her. How many poor exotic animals gave up their lives for a coat? By no stretch of the imagination was she a tree hugger. She worked on a ranch that raised beef and she wore plenty of leather made from cattle, but killing some defenseless animal for its skin alone went too far. "I can't wear it."

He laughed and lifted the coat for her to put on. "It's not real, Michaela. The coat is faux white mink. I wouldn't buy you a coat made from the fur of an animal that's only raised for the purpose of being skinned to make coats. I'm not that heartless."

She smoothed her hand over the silkiness of the coat. "I hope no one thinks it's real."

"They won't. Not many people wear real fur anymore." He shook his head and chuckled. "Now the thing is to get a fake coat that looks more real than anyone else's, not to compare whose dead animal is more exotic and expensive." As he helped her into the coat, he leaned over to whisper into her ear from behind. "I can't wait to show you off. I wasn't exaggerating about tonight being the most important night of my career, and I'm glad you are here beside me to share it with me."

She turned and met his gaze, not sure which heated her more: the intensity of his eyes or the coat. "I'm glad I'm here, too. Thank you for the coat."

He feathered his fingers over her cheek to her lips. Before he could kiss her, the door opened and Trish bustled in. "Gabe, we've got to leave now."

Grinning, he winked at Micki and took her hand. "C'mon, Mrs. McKenna, time to show the world how much we love each other."

She swallowed hard and forced a smile. Inside her heart, she found it harder to distinguish between what was an act and what was fact.

\* \* \* \*

"Gabe, you're on in ninety seconds."

Gabe looked over his shoulder at the stage director. "Thanks, Natalie."

His heart still raced from being named Male Vocalist, but it also thumped heavy in his chest for a different reason now. Despite his always getting nervous at award show performances, tonight was different. His stomach churned and his skin was clammy. He wasn't only singing on national TV and to his peers; he was singing to the woman he loved, which scared him to death.

With a deep breath, he picked up his guitar and headed to the stage. As the hostess announced him, he took his place in front of his band.

Joel watched him with a pucker in his forehead. "You're sweating. You okay, man?"

His bass player had always been too observant.

"Yep." When the panel concealing them from the audience split and opened behind him, he turned into the blinding lights of the Bridgestone Arena. Despite the glare, he knew exactly where Michaela was in the crowd and looked in her direction. He swallowed and strummed his pick over the strings of his guitar. "This is for my beautiful wife."

He took another deep breath, hoping to calm the jitters, and played the intro of the ballad he'd written on their wedding night after leaving Michaela and going to his own room across the hall. As his backup singer, Jessica, joined in with the mournful sound of a fiddle, the song poured out of him. On their way to Nashville, he'd changed some of the verse he'd written that night. He'd made it a love song that apologized for all that he'd done wrong. As he belted out the story of a romance gone wrong and the joy of finding love again in lyric and rhyme, his heart ached with the painful truth. He wished he could see Michaela's face as he asked for a second chance and that he'd always love only one woman--her.

When the song ended and the audience applauded, he bowed and waited for the panel to close again, anxious to get back to his seat. As the show went to a commercial break, he handed his guitar, wireless mike, and earpieces to a waiting stagehand, then hurried for his seat.

Seth grinned and cuffed him on the shoulder as they passed in the aisle. He was the next multiple award nominee to sing. "That, my friend, was a great song."

He supposed if anyone understood the joy of forgiveness and rekindled love, it was Seth. "Thanks." Gabe took his seat beside Michaela. She watched him with open curiosity. What was she thinking? His heart raced as he took her trembling hand. "Did you like the song?"

She swallowed and chewed on her bottom lip. "When…When did you write it?"

His heart sank a little at her avoidance of answering by asking another question. "On our wedding night."

The surprise in her widened eyes gave him hope. Maybe she could forgive him and give them a chance.

The announcer came over the PA system to welcome them back to the *CMA*s, and Gabe kissed Michaela with the depth of his true feelings.

* * * *

Micki watched the rest of the show in a daze. What the hell did Gabe mean by singing a song about regrets, forgiveness, and love? Did he mean any of it? Or was it just part of the act of them pretending to be in love?

She didn't have any answers, but a budding hope that he did love her filled her.

Could she ever forgive him?

She hated to admit that for them to ever have any future, she had to let go of the past. Did she have the strength to forgive him--and as importantly--trust him again?

He shifted in his seat as if anxious and drummed his fingers on his thigh. She glanced at him and took his hand. He gave her a small smile and gripped her fingers. His hand was cold, and she wasn't sure if it was from his nerves or the cool temperature of the Bridgestone Arena, where only a makeshift floor covered the Nashville Predators' icy home. What had him so rattled?

During a commercial break, Emily Kendall moved past Micki and Gabe and the reason for his case of the jitters dawned on her. Emily was one of the presenters for the Entertainer of the Year award. Gabe had seemed to be nominated for every award except the band awards and Female Vocalist. He'd won three categories so far. Besides Single of the Year and Male Vocalist awards tonight, Gabe, Seth, Nate O'Connell, and her cousin Logan Cartwright had won the Best Vocal Event last week with the song they'd opened the show with.

After the commercial break, which seemed to be when the sets were changed and people shifted to the stage and back to the audience, the hosts announced the last set of presenters--two of country music's fastest rising stars. Emily Kendall, who was quickly becoming a teen country-pop sensation, and the ex-divorce lawyer who melted hearts with his love songs, Logan Cartwright, entered the stage from a center break in the panels that acted like curtains. He was tall and handsome, wearing the same outfit as most of the male singers--jeans and a western-style shirt. Emily was dressed in a super short, low-cut, slinky dress with large cut out patterns revealing provocative areas of her skin under thin, gauzy black mesh. The mess of a dress was nothing like the elegant, conservative gown she'd worn only moments earlier.

"What the hell is she wearing?" Seth's low grumble was hard not to overhear.

Sitting beside Micki, Abby gasped. "I have no idea. She wasn't supposed to change for this."

Micki supposed she would be a little upset, too, if her seventeen-year-old daughter wore something more suitable for a strip joint than a formal event. She glanced over at the Kendalls as they whispered to each other. Thank God Jesse had no interest in singing.

Gabe squeezed her hand and she brought her attention to him. He took a deep breath and closed his eyes for a moment. Was he praying? How badly did he want this award?

She shook her head and focused on the stage. Logan Cartwright and Emily took turns announcing the nominees. Micki's heart beat faster as Gabe and then Seth were listed while clips from their recent music videos played on the large screens on either side of the stage.

Logan grinned at the audience as Emily fumbled with the envelope, seemingly having trouble getting the seal to break. "Shouldn't there be a rule about conflict of interest considering we all know you want your daddy to win?"

As a sputtering of laughter at the ex-lawyer's joke drifted through the audience, Emily broke the seal and looked at Logan with a bright, red-lipped smile. She showed him the name inside the card and together they said, "Gabe McKenna!"

Gabe leaned over his long legs as he let out a breath he must have been holding. His face beamed with so much joy, Micki couldn't help but be swept up in it. He pulled her to her feet and hugged her so tightly she couldn't breathe, then kissed her on the lips. As he headed up the aisle, several other singers congratulated him by shaking his hand or patting him on the shoulder while the crowd applauded and whistled.

When he reached the stage, he accepted the crystal statue from Emily and took his place behind the microphone. Micki joined in the wild clapping. Gabe lived for this. She'd never wanted him to go to Nashville and become famous, but as she sat there and watched him stare down at his award, she knew if he hadn't taken the chance he had all those years ago, he would have withered and died inside. Performing was part of his soul.

With the thought, she shivered. Was she beginning to forgive him?

He let out a whoop and looked out at the audience, but like when he'd sung, he seemed to be looking right at her. "Wow! I think I thanked everyone in the business the other times I was up here. So this time, I want to thank my fans for getting me here. I also want to thank the most beautiful woman in the world for marrying me last weekend and making tonight all the more sweeter for being by my side."

Micki gasped at the intensity of his words.

"I want the world to know this is for my wife and little brother. I love you." As he spoke, he held the award above his head in one hand.

The depth of the emotion in his deep voice shook Micki to her bones. Was he professing his love to her, only to Jesse, or was he just talking to his fans?

# Chapter 14

The drive back to Gabe's house was excruciating for Micki. She was pulled in a thousand different directions--wanting the trip to take forever, but she couldn't wait for it to be over. Trish had been surprised when Gabe asked for his keys and asked her to make excuses for him at the after-show parties. She'd smiled knowingly and agreed as she handed over the keys to his SUV. Gabe had posed for a few pictures with his four awards for the media backstage. Afterward, leaving his awards in the care of Gary and Trish to get delivered to his home, Gabe took Micki's hand and left the arena.

The soft music playing on the radio filled the charged air around them with seductive promise. Micki folded and refolded her hands in her lap, not sure what to say to break the tension between them. She took a deep breath, hoping to relieve the anticipation, and looked out the side window as the lights of downtown Nashville flew by them from the freeway.

"You held your own tonight."

His low voice rumbled through her. "Thanks. I liked the song." She let out a breath and looked at his profile.

He met her gaze for a moment before turning back to the road. "I meant what I said in the song. I'm sorry, Michaela. For everything that I've done to you."

She looked down at her hands. Was he expecting her to forgive him? Could she forgive him? "Gabe, what do you want from me?"

"A chance."

His husky words hit her with a force she hadn't anticipated, and small cracks started in the wall she'd built around her heart. Hadn't this been what she'd wanted?

He glanced at her again when she didn't reply. "I'm not going to rush you. But I want you to know that I want a future with you."

What could she say to that? Another crack in the wall. Could she even admit to herself how much his declaration meant to her or how much she wanted the same things? "You hurt me and I don't know if I can ever forgive you. But I--" She took a deep breath and let it out. "I don't want to throw away the chance we might have a future together either."

He winced as if her words pained him, but when he looked at her, he gave her a lopsided smile. "That's all I can ask."

They were quiet for the rest of the trip back to Gabe's home, but the desire beating through her thrummed. By the hot glance he gave her when he pulled off the highway and stopped at the light at the end of the ramp, he wanted her as much as she wanted him.

Ten minutes later, he stopped the SUV in front of his garage and got out. She met him in front of the vehicle. He shook his head at her. "You just can't let me be a gentleman, can you?"

She took his hand. The contact sent tingles through her and all she could think about was his hands touching her. Her lower belly clenched at the thought of how those talented fingers would play over her body. "Nope." Was that raspy voice hers? "I have more creative ideas on how you can show me how gentlemanly you are. Or aren't."

Even in the dim glow of the streetlight, she saw his eyes darken with undeniable lust. "That's a challenge I can't pass up." He twisted the key in the lock of his door and opened it, then turned to her and swung her into his arms.

She called out and laughed as she put her arms around his neck. "What are you doing?"

"I didn't get to do this on our wedding night."

Her heart raced at the promise of passion in his eyes. "What's that?"

"Carry you over the threshold. Isn't that what a groom does to ensure a life of good luck with his bride?" He stepped through the door before she had a chance to protest that she wasn't sure if they had a future together.

Without setting her down, he shut the door, then turned on the light and hit the code on the pad beside the door to disable the security alarm. She removed his hat and tossed it onto a table near the door. With hands that trembled from both desire and fear of what her heart was telling her, she threaded her fingers into his thick black hair and leaned in until her lips touched his. "There's something else we didn't do our wedding night."

She settled her lips over his mouth, and without hesitation, he opened up to let her tongue slide against his. He tasted of the glass of champagne he had drunk after the show and of sweet, hot desire, an intoxicating mix that had her panting by the time he broke the kiss.

Without words, he carried her across the room and up the stairs, taking them two at a time. His strength only served to turn her on more. By the time they reached his room, she was feverish with need. As he switched on the bedside lamp, he set her down on her feet. She was glad he held her because her rubbery legs were useless. He attacked her mouth with lusty licks and nips while shrugging out of his jacket, then helped her out of her coat. Kissing him, she slipped her hands over his shoulders to the top snap of his shirt. With deliberate slowness, she undid each of the buttons. When she pushed the shirt off his shoulders, her nails grazed over his bare skin, causing him to hiss into her mouth; then he delved his tongue into her mouth. She sucked on the hot flesh. Gasping, he pulled away. He spun her around and undid the zipper of her dress.

She couldn't get enough air as he pressed hot, wet kisses to her neck, shoulder, and spine as he peeled the dress off her, then pulled the pins from her hair to allow it to fall around her shoulders. He turned her to face him again, and the gown slid to the floor to pool around her feet, leaving her standing before him in her skimpy silk underwear and sky-high heels. She shivered as the heat of his gaze burnt her exposed skin.

"You're so beautiful." Taking her into his arms again, he lifted her away from the forgotten gown and laid her on the king-sized bed. After a lingering touch to her face, he stepped back and toed off his boots.

When he undid his belt, desire tumbled through her, making her insides tighten. A moan slipped past her lips as he gripped his jeans to push them off his hips. He stopped the slow progress before he exposed himself completely to her and raised a brow. A cocky, satisfied grin lifted his full, wet lips. "Like what you see?"

"If singing ever fails you, you could always take up being a striptease." The words were heavy with lust. She did a little teasing of her own by caressing a hand over her breast and belly to the edge of her panties and pushed the lace over her hip to show the top of her mound. "But two can play that game."

He chuckled low and deep, which only made the thumping in her core worse; then he sobered and pushed his jeans and underwear off. She'd seen him nude the other day in the barn, but somehow tonight the impact of seeing him in all of his glory had more of a profound effect on her. He climbed on the bed and leaned over her, and his mouth came down onto hers. Wrapping her arms around him, she pulled him to her and held on as their tongues tangled and danced.

She gasped for air when he pulled away to rain nips and kisses down her neck to her breasts. He shifted to kneel between her legs and flicked open the clasp of her bra to expose her breasts. Her nipples instantly hardened when he brushed the rough pads of his thumbs over them as he cupped her breasts.

He leaned over her and whispered in her ear, "Tell me what you want."

As he brushed over her nipples again, she bowed her back under him and moaned. "Make love to me."

Without a word, he took her right nipple into his mouth and sucked it hard. She groaned and fisted her fingers in his hair. He caressed his hand down her belly to the edge of her panties; then he suckled and teased her other breast. She sucked in a breath as he slipped his hand under the lacy band of her panties. Lights danced behind her closed eyes when he slid his fingers through her curls to encircle her clitoris.

She arched off the bed and let out a long moan as he teased her. By the time he shifted over her and helped her out of her panties, she was a trembling mess. Too close to the edge to stop, but not close enough to fall over it. "Gabe... I want you... inside."

He kissed her belly and grinned that infernal cocky smile. "Not yet, sweetheart." He lifted her legs over his shoulder and turned his head to kiss her ankle above the strap of her high heel. "These shoes are so sexy." When his gaze found hers again, it was hot enough to burn her to a crisp, and he rested her legs over his shoulders, opening her to him. "I've been fantasizing about this for weeks."

She fisted her hands into the bedding when he brushed over her sensitive bud with a hot, wet lick. With her breathing hard and fast, she rode the waves of pleasure he caused with each swipe of his tongue; then when she thought she was at the top of the pinnacle, he sucked in her flesh and the world splintered. She cried out and quaked under and around him.

He brought her down and moved to lay over her. She opened her eyes to his as her rapid, thumping heart sputtered over a beat at the emotional fire she saw in the golden depths of his gaze. Unable to name the feeling she saw there, she fought to keep the wall around her heart from cracking to the breaking point.

As he settled between her legs and slowly thrust into her, he leaned over to her ear and whispered in a low, deep, vibrating timbre, "I love you."

The wall crumbled, and she held on as he took her to a place she'd only ever been in his arms. "Damn you... I didn't want this... to happen... I love you, too."

He groaned deep in his chest as he kissed her; then he started moving in a slow, deliberate motion, rotating his hips with each thrust. With her legs over his shoulders, he was so deep, filling her with unexpected pleasure. Soon, she was soaring again, clenching around him, and he shifted into a relentless rhythm. He hissed between his teeth, arched his back, and shuddered as her body shivered around him when her orgasm crashed into her.

With a growl that could have been her name, he pushed into her so deep it would have been painful if she didn't relish the feeling, and he stilled as he emptied into her.

Breathing hard, he fell to his side and pulled her over him to lie on his chest. He held her as their hearts thundered and contented sleep overtook her.

* * * *

Gabe shuffled through the semi-darkness into the kitchen. The morning had dawned gray and rainy. A perfect day for staying in bed and making love to the woman he loved.

He stifled a yawn as he pulled a water bottle out of the fridge and closed the stainless steel door of the extra-large refrigerator. Like most of the appliances in the massive gourmet kitchen, they were way too flashy for the kind of cooking he did. He didn't need a six-burner stove to heat stuff in the microwave or have take-out delivered.

As he sipped the water, he leaned against the ultra-modern, polished concrete countertop of the L-shaped island. The kitchen was a cook's wet dream. Remembering Michaela's reaction to the luxury amenities of his Nashville home brought a smile to his face. He wanted her to feel comfortable here--in their Nashville home. As much as he wanted to spend most of his time on the ranch, he couldn't leave Music City completely. He'd have to maintain a place here, and he wanted Michaela and Jesse to share it with him.

She'd liked his kitchen and had spent a lot of time in here over the past week, making them supper nearly every night. She even invited Seth, Abby, and their daughter, Emily, over for dinner Thursday night. He loved that she'd taken a liking to his best friend and his family. After the Kendalls left, he told her their dinner party had been the first time his dining room table had ever been used. The memory of the way her incredulity had slacked her jaw and widened her eyes when he told her brought a smile to his face. Damn, he'd known she was a fair cook from their past together, but his cowgirl surprised him. Like a fine wine, she definitely improved with age.

In more than just her cooking skills. Last night had been some of the best sex he'd ever had.

He took another draw on the water. Sex always made him thirsty and last night he'd outdone himself. After Michaela had slept for an hour or so, she'd awakened him with butterfly kisses over his chest. Just the memory of her going down on him had him wanting her again, despite them making love three times over the course of the night. Their last round had been slow and gentle, and after her third orgasm, he'd exploded deep inside her. She'd kissed him and told him again that she loved him before drifting off to sleep. Though exhausted, he'd watched her for a long time, until he had to get a drink. She'd wrung him dry.

God, she told him she loved him. Her admission sent a shiver through him and had his heart singing of the possible future with the woman still soundly asleep in his rumpled bed.

The ringing of the doorbell jerked him out of his daydream of a life with Michaela.

"What the fuck?" He tossed the empty water bottle into the trash compactor and headed out to the door to murder whoever thought it wise to show up at his house at six a.m. Throwing opened the door, he didn't care he was wearing a pair of gym shorts and nothing else. "Gary, this had better be--"

But it wasn't Gary on the other side of the door. Lydia Greenhow stood on the porch, holding a bundle covered in a pink blanket. That's right; she'd said she had a baby when he'd seen her in Cheyenne. But what was she doing here? She ran her gaze over his body and an appreciative smile touched her red-painted lips. The sight made him wish for a full set of clothes.

"You need to leave before I call the cops." He made to shut the door, but she stepped through before he had the chance.

"Where's the wifey?" When he didn't justify the question with an answer, she looked around his great room with widened eyes, then clucked her tongue. "So, this is how the other half lives? Wow…"

He crossed his arms over his bare chest and glared at her. She had some awesome balls to show up at his home. How the hell did she find his address? As far as he knew, he paid Gary a handsome fee to keep such personal information from making it into the public Internet cesspool. "How did you find my address? Screw that. How the hell did you get on the property?"

She shrugged, shifted the baby in her arms, and walked into the living room. "A friend of a friend. You know."

He didn't know, but he would talk to the community management about this invasion.

Stopping at the leather couch, she touched the arm and smiled at him. "Nice. I knew you'd have good taste."

Except when it came to picking up annoying groupies. God, what had he seen in her? Dressed as she was this morning in a short black leather miniskirt, a short, fake fur jacket over a low-cut, tight shirt, and high-heeled boots, she looked more like a hooker than a dancer. "What do you want?"

She sat on the couch and faced him, making herself at home, which pissed him off all the more. The baby made a mewling sound as if she was waking up. "I got to thinking after we met in Cheyenne and news came out that you married your pregnant girlfriend--"

"My wife is not pregnant." He cut her off, hating the tabloid rumor still making rounds. "You need to leave, or I'll throw you out."

When her smile turned calculating and she shifted the bundle in her arms to face him, the baby looked up at him with dark brown eyes. Lydia pulled the pink blanket away from her head, revealing a tuft of brown hair. As the only possible reason for her to show up on his doorstep with a baby dawned on him, his heart fell into his stomach. "I don't think you'll do that after you meet your daughter." She nuzzled the baby's dark hair but never took those gleaming, triumphant blue eyes from his. "Natasha, meet your very rich daddy."

# Chapter 15

The sound of the doorbell awakened Micki from a sound sleep. Gabe's side of the bed was empty. The sheets held his residual heat, and she stretched into it, relishing the memories the slide of the soft, warm sheets on her naked body conjured. She ached in places she hadn't in years. Damn, she'd forgotten what sex with Gabe was like.

Gabe's lovemaking wasn't all she recalled. Her heart beat faster as his words of love rushed over her. He wanted a future with her, and she admitted she loved him. Had she forgiven him? Maybe she had enough to believe they could build a life together.

She had to finally admit she'd missed him. This past week had been interesting and fun. After the first day, she made herself at home in his house. She loved the layout and clean design of the place, and she could see herself and Jesse living here at least a few weeks out of the year. Home would always be the Lazy M, but she liked what she'd seen of Nashville.

What would life with him be like? Last night had been a taste of his fame. She didn't like being in the limelight. The red carpet was a nightmare of gargantuan proportions, but Gabe moved them through the reporters, photographers, and fashion commentators' nosy questions as quickly as humanly possible. If she hadn't been so grateful, she may have believed he was embarrassed of her, but she knew that wasn't the case. He respected her dislike of such invasions of her privacy.

She had to pee but didn't want to get up. Curling around Gabe's pillow, she buried her face into the soft down, closed her eyes, and breathed in his scent. She'd forgotten how much she loved his spicy sandalwood fragrance. The idea of waking up every morning with him sent a tingle through her.

When she heard voices downstairs, she glanced at Gabe's phone where it was docked in a charging station, which was also an alarm clock, on his bedside table. Twenty minutes after six. Who would show up this early? Hopefully whoever it was would soon leave so Gabe could come back to bed.

Back home on the ranch, she never slept in this late. Although he'd worn her out, she wanted another round of lovemaking with him the moment he returned. She could think of a few things she'd like to do to her very sexy husband.

"I don't fucking believe you." Gabe's raised voice startled her out of her morning after fantasy.

She sat up and listened. Who was he talking to? Gary? Trish? They were the only logical conclusions.

"Fine, don't believe me, but I can make things really interesting for you and that new wife of yours," said a female voice Micki didn't recognize. "I wonder what the press would make of my story."

When someone brought up the press that usually was a sign whatever they were saying wasn't good. God, that was the last thing she and Gabe wanted.

Micki got out of bed and grabbed her old, terrycloth robe from a rack of hooks inside Gabe's massive closet. As she headed out of the room, she tied the belt and finger combed her hair. She hoped she wasn't spotted on the mezzanine overlooking the great room.

The cry of a baby brought her up short and froze her to the corner of the bedroom in the hallway. She stared over the wrought iron railing at the edge of the mezzanine and held her breath. A woman dressed in a super short black miniskirt, fur jacket, and high-heeled boots held a crying baby wrapped in a pink blanket. She stood next to the couch, bouncing the child as she held her to her shoulder and cooed to soothe her.

Micki recognized the blonde immediately from the tabloid and Internet articles she'd read featuring the stripper with Gabe. He must have seen Micki move as she covered her mouth at the top of the stairs, or otherwise sensed her, because he looked up at her. His face was stained red and his eyes dangerously dark. Lydia Greenhow followed the movement of his gaze and turned to glare in her direction.

Lydia's lips twisted into a smug smile. "Well, don't you look like you've been ridden hard and put away wet? I do know how that feels. Imagine my shock sixteen months ago when I discovered I was pregnant a few weeks after the best sex I'd ever had."

Gabe's face contorted into a frightful sneer, and he grabbed the woman's free arm. "I want you to get the fuck out. Now."

Like in a dream, Micki descended the stairs. Her heart clinched painfully in her chest. Dear God, was that baby really Gabe's? The little girl's big brown eyes, red-rimmed from her tears, stared at Micki over her mother's shoulder. Her chubby cheeks were wet and splotched with pink. She looked healthy as she sucked on her thumb. Micki's heart ached at the thought of Gabe having a baby with another woman. Although she was jealous, mostly sorrow filled her.

She knew how it felt to be rejected by her father.

He propelled Lydia toward the door. In the entry, she jerked out of his grip and glanced at Micki. "I don't have anywhere to go. My mother tossed me out on my ass and I used all the money I had to get to Nashville."

"Do I look like I care?" Gabe clenched his fists. "I don't believe for a moment that baby is mine. I know I wasn't the only man you fucked, and just because the timing might be right doesn't make it so. My guess is you're broke and decided to see how much you can get from me."

"Gabe." Micki rested a shaking hand on his arm. "You can't send her and a baby out into the cold."

He glanced at her and some of the anger drained from his face. After he took a deep breath, he ran his hand into his already mussed hair. "Okay." He went over to the table by the door and pulled out a drawer. When he turned, he held a business card out to Lydia. "Take this to the Motel 6 by the interstate and give it to the front desk. Tell them to call the number on the back to arrange for payment."

Lydia narrowed her eyes on the card. "Right. Like the clerk would believe me."

"I'm calling to let them know you're on your way."

Lydia took the card and glanced at it. "You know, you haven't heard the last of me."

She reached for the door, but Gabe stepped in front of her and glared down at her. "Later today my lawyer will call you. He will arrange to take you to the hospital."

Micki was as puzzled as Lydia looked.

"Before I give you a cent more, I want a paternity test." Then he smiled, but the sight caused Micki to shiver. "If the kid is mine, you will sign her over to me and my wife."

"I will do no such thing." Lydia's face drained of color and she held the baby closer to her.

He ignored her. "Then I'll pay you a million dollars to get the hell out of my life. If by some chance any of this gets into the press before the bank transfer, the money stays right where it is. Understood?"

Micki shuddered at the coldness, not only Gabe's expression, but in his tone. A horrible thought occurred to her as she remembered his words to her after church on the day they announced their engagement.

*"If you hadn't miscarried, the moment I found out you were pregnant I would've been back. You may have broken off our engagement, but I would have been a father to my baby."*

She stared at Gabe, fear and anger tumbling through her, freezing her blood. Would he have treated her this way if she hadn't miscarried their baby?

Lydia looked as afraid as Micki felt at that moment, but she shrugged the shoulder not supporting her baby and pasted on a wan smile that never reached her eyes. "Fine, but if you want me to be quiet, you'd better make it two million, and I'll need fifty grand of it now."

He snorted and shook his head. "I'll pay for your hotel and make sure you don't go hungry, but I won't give you a dime until I know for sure the kid is mine. Trust me, if you tell your tale to the press and the baby is mine, you get nothing and I'll fight you for the baby." Reaching behind him, he opened the door and moved out of Lydia's path. "The choice is yours, but I think I know what it will be. Now get out."

Gabe closed the door with a bang that made Micki jump. "Fuck! Like I need this bullshit." He stabbed all of his fingers into his hair and gave the dark mess a tug.

Micki wrapped her arms around herself and shivered. In a way, she understood Gabe's behavior toward the baby until he learned her paternity, but his coldness toward the baby made her angry. He didn't even seem to acknowledge the little girl.

"Is this how you would've treated me if I hadn't lost our baby?" She couldn't believe she asked the question.

He let go of his hair and turned to face her. "What are you talking about?"

She shook her head and moved toward the kitchen. "Nothing. Go make the phone call to the hotel before Lydia gets there."

Several moments later, Gabe's footsteps brushed along the Italian tile floor as he entered the kitchen. She stared out the French doors at the rain splashing off the pool cover as she sipped a cup of coffee she'd brewed with his Keurig. When he stopped behind her, she took a deep breath and turned. He was barefoot and still dressed only in a pair of loose shorts. Dark curls outlined his toned pectorals and defined his six-pack. With his hair mussed and the dark beard stubble clinging to his jaw, he was gorgeous.

"Michaela, I'm so sorry about this morning." He rubbed a hand over the back of his neck and his gaze slid from hers. "Hell, I'm sorry about ever setting eyes on her."

He moved toward her and reached for her, but she sidestepped away from him. She met his furrowed gaze and set the mostly full cup of coffee on the bar. "I can't say I'm happy about this. Damn, you having a child with her will make our case for Jesse all the more complicated."

"I've already called Reese. He's working on making this go away."

His words sliced through her. "Go away? Gabe, that baby could be yours."

"Yes, she could be. But she could as easily not be." He headed toward the coffee maker. After disposing of her used K-cup, he popped in a fresh one. A moment later, the sound of steam escaping and the pungent scent of coffee filled the air. "She's a gold digger. And the last thing I want is for her to damage our chances to adopt Jesse."

She thought about the young man she'd fallen in love with, before fame and fortune jaded him. "Gabe, you would have thrown her out of here into an icy rain without even caring if she had a place to stay if I hadn't stepped in. That scares me."

He took a deep breath and looked down at the floor. "I wasn't thinking." He took a step toward her and reached for her again. This time she let him touch her. He held her shoulders. His golden-brown eyes filling with--*fear*? "Michaela, I was afraid of what her having my kid would do regarding Jesse and of what you'd do when you found out. I can't lose you. Not now that we're together."

He enveloped her into his hug, but she didn't embrace him back. She had to untangle her emotions. What kind of complication would this would bring to their adoption case? How many more women were out there who would show up on his doorstep claiming their kid belonged to Gabe? But the feeling clogging her heart the most was the fear that if things didn't work out between them, he would simply take Jesse away from her.

She had no illusions about their marriage. He'd told her once before he'd loved her but left with another woman to make his dreams come true. It was only a matter of time before he abandoned her again. Only this time, Jesse was also at stake, not just her heart.

She backed away and shook her head, her sinuses burning with the bitter tears she refused to let fall. "No. Just because we had sex and said things we didn't mean doesn't erase our deal. We adopt Jesse and get a divorce."

"Michaela?"

Before the first treacherous tear could roll down her cheek at the pained rasp of his voice, she turned away. "I think I should be getting back to Texas. I've been away from Momma long enough. Besides, she has an appointment next week with the neurologist to discuss the facial surgery, and I don't want to miss it."

She was halfway up the stairs when he said, "I'll book a flight."

With a nod, she hurried to Gabe's bedroom. Once inside, she took a deep breath and banished the moisture from her eyes. Tears never solved anything, and they sure as hell weren't going to ever fix her and Gabe.

The only thing that would do that was to get away from him.

\* \* \* \*

Later that night, Gabe entered his empty house after leaving Reese's office. How could a day that had started out so promising end up so damned shitty?

After Michaela left that morning, he'd gone with Reese to an appointment the lawyer had set up with Gabe's personal physician at his clinic. Trish arrived with Lydia and the baby a few moments later. In the lab, the physician took a cheek swab from both Gabe and the baby, then reassured them they'd have the DNA results back in a few days. They'd left the clinic and headed to Reese's posh office, where Lydia oohed and ahhed over the richness of the lawyer's space and the fantastic view of Nashville from the thirtieth floor.

Despite the hours they'd spent together, first at the clinic, then at Reese's office going over the terms of the contract Lydia signed, Gabe felt no more connected to the baby than he had when he'd first seen her. Sure, the timing of Lydia's pregnancy was perfectly in line with the time they'd spent together in Vegas sixteen months ago, but wouldn't he have sensed something if the baby was his?

He pulled his cell phone from his pocket and dialed the one person who might have an answer. Twenty minutes later, Gabe answered his door to let Seth Kendall in.

Seth moved into the living room and removed his trademark black Stetson. When he turned to Gabe, he narrowed his eyes on him. "Where's Micki?"

Gabe snorted and poured them each a glass of Gentleman Jack. Seth took his whiskey and sat on one of the leather chairs opposite the couch.

He dropped onto his couch and stared into his glass of amber liquid. Had Michaela lied about loving him? If she loved him, why did she still want the divorce after they adopt Jesse? The thought of letting her go again ripped his heart in two. "She went back to Texas this morning."

Seth swirled the whiskey in his glass with a contemplative furrow in his brow. "I've been wondering something, and I think I've kept my trap shut long enough." When Seth's bright green gaze caught his, Gabe knew his friend figured out the reason for the rushed marriage. "You and Micki got married, hoping you could adopt your brother. At first I thought maybe she was pregnant, but I didn't think so after I saw you two together at the wedding. Something seemed off."

"I guess our plan is pretty transparent, but yeah, we got married for Jesse. Our plan was"--remembering Micki's words that morning, he winced and corrected himself--"is to get divorced once the adoption goes through." Gabe tossed back half of the fine Tennessee whiskey.

"You fell in love with her." Seth leaned back into his chair and let out his breath.

"Yeah, well, she never felt the same as I did. I should have known better." Gabe finished off his whiskey and went to the bar to get more. He returned with the bottle of Jack Daniels and sat down. "But my fucked up marriage isn't why I called you."

Seth watched him. "You said you wanted to pick my brain. I thought you wanted some songwriting help, but I figured out the moment you opened the door that probably wasn't why you called. Out with it."

Gabe swallowed some more of the smooth whiskey, letting its heat melt his trepidation away. Was he afraid that little girl might be his or that she might not be? "That stripper I screwed in Las Vegas, Lydia Greenhow, showed up here this morning with a seven-month-old baby girl she is claiming belongs to me."

Seth widened his eyes and let out a whistle between his teeth. "Holy shit."

Gabe let out a chuckle. "Yep."

"Is that why Micki left?"

Gabe wasn't sure if he even understood why she'd left. "In a way. She was mad because, when Lydia showed up here, I didn't believe her. Damn it, Seth, I don't want to believe her. The whole time all I could think of is how this will screw up my chances to get Jesse away from Lemont Finn. I said some things that probably made me sound like a pure heartless bastard. I told her I wanted the kid tested, and if she turned out to be mine, I wanted her to sign the baby over to me. In exchange, I'd pay her off. Which only made me madder because the bitch agreed to those terms without blinking an eyelid. In fact, she demanded more money."

He remembered Michaela's question and signed. "I think Micki thought I would have done the same thing to her if she hadn't lost our baby before our breakup. But she's different than Lydia. Michaela would never have given up her baby for money."

"You were in shock. I know, when I got the news I was going to be a father the first time, I was in denial. It was the last thing I wanted." Seth set his glass on the coffee table, which Gabe noticed was still full; then his friend leaned over his legs and folded his hands. "Getting the news that you're a father or gonna be one isn't easy. It's a hell of a responsibility, but if I could have done things differently, I would have."

"Leaving Abby was the hardest thing I've ever done, and the stupidest." With a wince as if the memories still caused him pain, Seth looked up at him. "I wasted fourteen years that I'll never get back with my daughter. While I was off getting rich and famous, she was being raised by a sadistic bastard. Now she's her own person. I've always loved her, but not knowing her as a little kid still hurts."

Seth shook his head of curling strawberry-blond hair. "The only advice I can give you is to fight for that baby if she turns out to be yours. But you can't exclude Lydia from her life. To do that would be the same thing Abby and her ex did to me."

Gabe knew in his heart Seth was right, but he didn't want to be tied to an immoral stripper for the rest of his life. What kind of strain would that put on his and Michaela's marriage? Hell, did they even have a chance at a future? Then an even more terrifying thought occurred to him: If their marriage did fall apart, he'd already agreed she'd keep Jesse, but who would help him care for his daughter? Lydia? God, he hoped not.

He pictured the dark-haired, brown-eyed baby and tried to feel a connection, to see some semblance of recognition. But he saw none. The little girl didn't look much like Lydia, but he sure as hell couldn't see himself in her either.

Gabe emptied his glass and asked the question for which he'd called his friend. "Wouldn't I know if the kid was mine? I mean, shouldn't I be able to recognize some part of me in her?"

Seth took a deep breath and leaned back in his chair. "That's a tough question. I don't know. I've always known Emily was my daughter, so when I met her for the first time..." He paused and shrugged as if remembering, his eyes taking on a faraway glaze as he stared toward the coffee table. "She answered the door and smiled. I still get chills when I remember the first time I laid eyes on my little girl."

Gabe smiled at the emotion his friend conjured but lost the smile as he thought of his reaction this morning. If the baby did turn out to be his, how would he ever live with his memories of how he treated her?

"Yes, I instantly recognized her as my daughter, but I was also expecting to see her that afternoon." Seth quirked his lips up into a one-sided grin. "Who knows if I would've recognized her if she'd shown up on my doorstep and I hadn't known she even existed. I'd like to think I would have, but..." He shrugged, picked up the glass of whiskey he'd sat on the table, and drained it. "I can't say that I would have."

# Chapter 16

"What the hell do you mean the lab lost the samples?" Gabe gripped his iPhone so tight his hand hurt. "I paid you to get those results rushed through."

His doctor sputtered on the other line. "I'm sorry, Gabe. These things happen. I'll have to take another sample from you and the baby, and I'll take responsibility for the tests."

Gabe stared out the French doors at the cold November morning sun reflecting off the glass-topped table setting on the patio by the pool. "Fine. I'll call Reese to get in touch with Miss Greenhow."

He hung up the phone and it instantly started vibrating again. As soon as the call connected, Michaela's worried voice sounded in his ear. "Have you seen the latest report on TMZ?"

"No." The doorbell rang, and dread caused his heart to sink. He headed for the front door while he told her about the lost DNA samples.

"That's the least of our worries. TMZ is reporting the news that you have a daughter and that you don't want her."

"Fuck!" Gabe stabbed the fingers of his free hand into his hair and fisted it. "When did the report come out?"

"I don't know. This morning, maybe." Micki's voice quivered, and she cleared it. "I think it would be best if I distance myself from you. I don't want this to hurt my chances to get Jesse."

Fear of a different sort coursed through him, causing his heart to clench. "What are you saying?"

"I'm contacting a lawyer from Dallas who might be able to help me get Jesse."

He sighed as the person on the other side of the door gave up ringing the doorbell and resorted to pounding and shouting. Gary. He should have known if Michaela had seen the report, so had his manager. Gabe's heart shattered. Maybe Michaela did have a better chance of getting Jesse on her own now. "What's the lawyer's name?"

She was silent for so long, he thought she'd hung up. When she spoke, her voice sounded watery, and for a moment, he wondered if she was fighting back tears. "Lance Cartwright. He's my second cousin, so I thought he'd be willing to help. I got the idea after seeing our mutual cousin at the *CMA*s."

Logan Cartwright hadn't always been a singer. His first profession had been being a successful divorce lawyer in a law partnership with his first cousin. How long had she been planning to leave him? Gabe closed his eyes and rode out the searing burn in his chest. He'd been a fool to fall in love with her again. "He's as good--if not better than--Reese. Whatever you want, I'll agree to. Our prenup gives you the ranch and money to take care of things. Maybe--" He had to swallow the sudden bitter lump in his throat. "Maybe it's for the best."

He hung up the call and opened his door. To his surprise, Gary wasn't the only one on his doorstep.

A grim Reese stood beside his furious manager. "We have a problem. Lydia Greenhow checked out of her hotel this morning and vanished."

* * * *

The morning after the news broke, Micki told her mother about her plan to contact their cousin's law firm in Dallas. Feeling as if her entire world was exploding around her, she sat on the couch in the family room where she'd found her mother watching TV and looked down at her folded hands in her lap. "I think filing for divorce would be my best option. I need to distance myself from this mess of Gabe's before I'm dragged in."

Momma narrowed her eyes on her when she finished her plan. "And you think filing for divorce two weeks after getting married will make this all go away?" She didn't give Micki a chance to respond. "You can't run from this, Micki. In fact, you should be doing the complete opposite. You and Gabe need to present a united front. You said you married Gabe for Jesse, but if you leave him now, how do you think that will make you look in the eyes of the judge?"

Micki swallowed and closed her eyes. "I don't know. But what chance do I have to get him if Gabe is entangled in this mess with that stripper?"

"Damn it, Michaela Jo!"

Her mother's use of her full name had Micki looking up at her with surprise. Momma hadn't called her by that name since she was a little girl.

"You're a fool if you think I don't know what you're really doing." Momma rolled her wheelchair closer to the couch and rested her arthritic hands on top of Micki's. "Micki, I know you love him. You're afraid he'll leave you again. But what if he doesn't? I heard that song he sang to you at the award show. God, girl, the man has it so damn bad for you it made my heart ache." She gently squeezed Micki's hands and sat back in her wheelchair with a wince. But whether it came from her disease or from the memory, Micki didn't know. "If your father had loved me half as much as Gabe McKenna does you, I--I..."

When a tear slid down Momma's cheek, Micki took her mother's hands and shook her head. She hated the pain her father's betrayal still caused her mother. "Shhh... I won't call Lance. You're probably right. Filing for divorce would be a stupid move."

But how could she stand with Gabe? He was bound to break her heart like her father had her mother's. After all, he hadn't discouraged her when she brought up getting divorced yesterday. Could she stay and risk even more of her heart?

* * * *

Micki stared out the master bedroom window. The day dawned cold and breezy, but the bright sun belied the weather forecast of rainstorms later that day. She prayed for torrential downpours. Maybe then the cars and vans parked along the county road outside the front gate would go away--at least for a little while

Ten days of hell.

That was the prison she and her mother found themselves in. Sure, they were living in the ranch house and had plenty of food and comfort, but outside the front gate was a horde of reporters and paparazzi. Not all of them were tabloid hacks either; a few of them were from the local TV stations, which justified prying into their private lives as local special interest stories.

Gabe was still in Nashville where he dealt with the brunt of the reporters. Every time she booted up the Internet, his face flashed on the screen in some story posted by the tabloids on the newsfeed of her search engine. Some of the reports even speculated that they were splitting up. In another story, her mother's illness and the scheduled surgery were mentioned as the causes of her coming abruptly back to Texas following the CMA awards.

Gabe had hired a private investigator to find the stripper, but so far he was coming up with nothing.

She turned away from the bedroom window and headed downstairs. As she walked into the kitchen, Florencia Hernandez was watching the small TV sitting in the corner of the counter while she made breakfast for them.

*Sara Walter Ellwood*

The tall, middle-aged Hispanic woman Gabe had hired to be the family's housekeeper was also a registered nurse, whom Micki discovered had worked in a Dallas hospice until burnout forced her to change careers about five years ago. Her husband had died a year ago, leaving her with two kids in college. Micki liked the quiet, unassuming woman, who spoke flawless English and preferred to go by the nickname Flo.

As Micki slid onto a barstool at the breakfast island, she took one of Flo's whole grain blueberry muffins from a plate. She picked a piece off the golden brown top and popped it into her mouth. Her stomach churned as if it were going to eat itself.

On the TV, a pretty blond special interest reporter from one of the local stations stood in front of the gate of the Lazy M. In the distant background, the white two-story house stood surrounded by trees and pastures enclosed with white rail fencing. The wind picked up and the trees and winter grass in the fields swayed behind the reporter. If the house wasn't the one she was currently living in, she may not have recognized it.

The wind tossed the reporter's hair into her face. "The drama coming from the latest scandal involving country superstar Gabe McKenna is heating up." Micki's heart skipped a beat as the reporter's face flashed away and a photo of Gabe and her from the red carpet at the *CMA*s popped onto the screen. "A source within the McKenna camp reported that his new bride was devastated by the news that Gabe and Las Vegas stripper Lydia Greenhow have a daughter together. The newlyweds have separated." Another picture flashed on screen; this one was from over a year and half ago and featured a candid shot of Gabe with Lydia at a Las Vegas club. Micki swallowed against the bile rising into her throat at thought of Gabe and the stripper together. "The source also told us Lydia is in hiding out of fear of Gabe, who threatened to take her baby away and bribed her with a monetary payout if she signed custody papers giving the seven-month-old to the country star. We were able to verify this report from public documents filed at Davidson County Tennessee on November tenth."

Micki had enough and got up to leave the kitchen, but the reporter's next words stopped her. "As we reported before, Gabe and his wife are in the middle of a strange custody battle with her estranged father, Texas billionaire Lemont Finn, over Gabe's ten-year-old brother, who is also Michaela McKenna's nephew." The reporter smiled and brushed her long, wind-blown hair out of her face. "Confused yet? I know we are as today we got information that Michaela Finn McKenna may not be who she says she is. A source in the Lemont Finn camp has brought to our attention that the businessman is again raising the question about his daughter's paternity. The first time was twenty-eight years ago when he filed for divorce from former barrel racing champion Loretta Cartwright Finn. It is yet unclear what Mr. Finn wishes to achieve from this most recent accusation since the man Loretta Finn had been accused of having an affair with died over eight years ago."

Flo violently whipped pancake batter and shook her head. "I can't believe they won't let you and your mother alone."

The queasy feeling amplified, turning the muffin in her stomach to stone, and the bile rose a little farther into her throat. Damn, what did those old rumors have to do with anything? None of them were even true. Her mother had never cheated on her father. On the screen, an old photograph of Momma from her mother's barrel racing days and the rodeo cowboy her father had accused her of sleeping with replaced the reporter's face. In the faded picture, Loretta smiled up at bull rider Jock Blackwell, a much older man she'd known from her hometown of Colton, Texas, as she presented him with a huge buckle at some rodeo.

"Why are they dragging my acquaintance with Jock Blackwell into this mess?" At her mother's pained voice, Micki turned away from the TV. She'd been so engrossed in the report she hadn't heard Momma coming into the kitchen. Momma stopped her motorized wheelchair by the edge of the island and fisted her hands in her lap. "The man is dead and gone."

Micki was wondering the same thing when a thought came to her. "Momma. I think Lemont is worried." She slid off the barstool and bent to kiss her mother's forehead. "I think it's time Gabe and I share a holiday together."

Momma had been right. If they wanted to show the world their relationship was strong and could weather any storm, the last thing they needed was to be apart right now. She needed Gabe to come home.

Lemont was worried about something. Early in this mess with Lydia and the baby, the *source* from his camp had released to the tabloids his belief that Micki and Gabe had married solely for the hope of their union persuading the judge to give them custody. Micki had felt the blood leave her face when she'd read it, but the ironic thing had been the reporter totally discredited the rumor by offering her version of the truth: Either Micki was pregnant and they married out of obligation, or, according to the author of the article, it was more likely Gabe and Micki had rekindled their old flame. The reporter's proof had been to embed a video of the love song he'd sung to her at the *CMA*s into the report.

With the truth being discredited, why else drag in the old rumor her father couldn't prove now any more than he had been able to during his and her mother's divorce, unless he wanted the judge to have the idea that Micki may not be Jesse's aunt when the custody case was revisited in a few weeks?

She was halfway up the stairs to call Gabe when the queasiness she'd felt since waking up that morning turned into full-fledged nausea. Hurrying into the master bedroom, she made it to the bathroom just in time before she vomited up the meager contents of her stomach.

Damn, the last thing she needed now was to catch the stomach virus going around.

Putting up with Gabe over Thanksgiving and in Las Vegas when they went to the NFR was going to be hard enough.

She turned from the toilet to the sink and splashed cool water onto her face. As she wiped it away with a plush towel, she met her gaze in the mirror. "Time to get the lovey-dovey on."

# Chapter 17

She and Gabe calculated and planned everything. From the time he flew into Dallas to her meeting him at the airport Wednesday afternoon. Waiting for him outside the security zone, she frowned as a man whistled at her and wished she hadn't taken her mother's suggestion to dress sexy.

Paparazzi were in the crowd, which she and Gabe had wanted, but she hated the short dress she wore. Although she didn't like spending his money, her mother talked her into buying a designer dress. Now she stood in the crowded airport with people staring at her in a flirty, cotton dress that cost more than it was worth, a denim jacket, and her red Tony Lamas. She fought the urge to fidget as she watched Gabe approach. He stopped in front of her and set his bags on the floor. In the next beat, he caught her up in his embrace and kissed her.

She'd known it was coming, but the intensity of the kiss took her breath away. Wrapping her arms around him, she held on, kissing him back with the same urgency, and hated that none of her actions were part of the charade. She'd missed him and wanted him.

When he pulled away, his amber-brown eyes glowed hot in the bright florescent light of the airport. "Damn, I've missed you."

Cameras flashed around them and she had an insane thought. She leaned in and whispered into his ear, "Please put me down. As short as this dress is, my butt is probably sticking out."

He let her slide down against him and grinned. "I definitely don't want that cute ass of yours in the news. No one better see it but me."

Excitement shivered through her at his implication. But she pushed the desire and trepidation of having sex with her husband away as the two ranch hands, who'd come with her, moved in to take his bags. Gabe shook their hands, then wrapped his arm around her waist to steer her out of the airport.

Once they were in the back of the same deep-blue BMW that had driven them to the airport after their wedding, Micki took a deep breath and tried to relax, but all she got was a nose full of Gabe's delicious, spicy scent. How could she still want him after everything that had happened?

He watched her for a few moments, then furrowed his brow. "How've you been holding up?"

She met his concerned gaze and shrugged. "Okay. I guess. Any word about Lydia?"

With a shake of his head, he glanced out the side window. "No. The PI hasn't been able to find her."

"Do you think the idea of giving up the baby scared her?" She'd asked him this question last week, but he hadn't answered her.

He looked back at her. "I'm beginning to wonder if she ran after we did the paternity test because she knew how it would turn out. I've been thinking hard about the coincidence of it all. The lab lost the samples and she disappeared. Then the TMZ report came out all at the same time. It's too calculated not to have been planned."

She gasped at the idea. "But by who?"

He snorted and shook his head. "Who has the most to gain by all of this?"

"You think Lemont is behind it?" Her father was a heartless bastard and had a long reach, but what Gabe suggested seemed too farfetched even for Lemont.

With a shrug, he ran his hand through his hair. "I don't know. But I don't believe for a moment that baby is mine. Because I can't prove it and can't find the woman feeding the reporters with stories that make me sound like a kidnapper, I'm beginning to wonder if he didn't put her up to this sham."

\* \* \* \*

Gabe didn't expect Micki to invite him into her bed, but that night as they stood in the hallway and said "Goodnight," he felt a pang of regret when she didn't ask him to stay in her room. Sleep didn't come easily. He stayed up trying to figure out what he could do to change Michaela's mind about wanting a divorce.

By the time the cold, gray, and rainy morning of Thanksgiving dawned, he'd decided he had to lay everything out on the line. If he wanted her, he had to let her in on his secrets; then maybe she could face hers.

He made his bed, putting the room back as he'd found it. Flo wasn't in on their deception and he wanted to keep it that way. Not that he didn't trust her, but the fewer people who knew the truth about why he and

Michaela married the better. After using the bathroom down the hall, he headed to the master bedroom. Sounds of an occasional clang from the kitchen drifted up the stairs. Flo must be preparing the turkey and fixing breakfast. Delicious spicy aromas filled the air with the promise of pumpkin pie and cranberry muffins. His stomach growled.

Before his hunger derailed him, he knocked on Micki's door, then opened it to slip into the room. From the bathroom, the shower turned on and her less-than-perfect singing voice greeted him. A smile tugged at his lips and his heart warmed when he recognized the song. He couldn't help but sing along. "Heaven Tonight" was his second hit song, and he'd written it when they'd started dating as teenagers.

With a grimace as she sang the chorus completely off key, he headed to the bathroom. He stripped off his pajama pants and entered the steamy room. Behind the frosted glass of the shower door, Michaela's provocative, silhouetted movements as she washed her body sent a jolt through him, causing his semi-hard cock to stiffen to full attention.

He took a deep, moist breath filled with the sweet fragrance of summer jasmine, then opened the sliding door of the shower, singing the words of the song that she now hummed.

She whirled around at his intrusion, her mouth open and her eyes wide. Foamy bubbles dappled her skin in enticing areas, making him want her even more.

"Gabe!" She let out a breath. "Damn you. You scared me to death."

He suspected she was more embarrassed that he'd caught her singing his love song in the shower than scared. With a snort, he reached over to turn the heat down a bit. She loved the water temperature set at scalding. Wrapping his other arm around her slick body, he chuckled and pulled her to him. "Were you expecting someone else?"

She pushed at his chest without force. "No. But I wasn't expecting you. What are you doing?"

He nuzzled her neck and sucked on her wet earlobe. She rewarded him with a shudder despite the heat of the water raining down on them. In her ear, he whispered, "Water conservation."

Before she had a chance to retort, he brought his mouth to hers and kissed her. She fisted her hands where they lay on his chest and opened her mouth under his. As she snaked her arms around his neck, she moaned. She held him to her as their tongues plunged, tasted, and danced. He pressed her back against the sandy-colored tile of the shower wall and moved his hand down her side to the hot, moist folds of her sex. With a groan, she slid her leg up and along his outer thigh to hook it on his hip in blatant invitation. As she sucked on his tongue, he palmed her and teased her clitoris.

She broke the kiss and panted. Lolling her head back, she closed her eyes. "Oh, Gabe. I've missed you."

His heart skipped a beat at her beauty. He wanted to be inside her. Now.

Moving his hands under her firm little butt, he lifted her against the wall. She wrapped her legs around his hips as he thrust into her. When she cried out, he paused to allow her to get accustomed to him.

"God, you're so tight and hot," he rasped into her neck. "I want you so bad I can't think straight."

She answered with a loud moan that may have been his name, then held on to his shoulders and used the slickness of the wall and their bodies to move with him. He hit deeper and deeper with each thrust until he couldn't hold back much longer. "Michaela, baby, come for me."

"Yes... Gabe..." She clenched around him as her orgasm quaked through her.

"Michaela..." He tensed his body as he thrust into her one last time, the burn of white-hot pleasure turning him inside out as he emptied into her. "I love you."

He held her for several moments as their breathing returned to normal. As he let her legs slide down to the floor, he kissed her tenderly.

She grinned up at him. "Water conservation, huh?"

With a smile he knew was cocky, he shrugged, then picked up the bar of soap and relished the way her eyes darkened with desire as he lathered it over his body. She shook her head as if to clear it and faced away from him to wet her hair. He squirted a small amount of her shampoo into his hand, caught up her damp hair, and worked the soap into the silky strands.

"Emm..." She leaned back against him as he caressed her sculp. "I love when you wash my hair."

He leaned over her shoulder to kiss her neck. "I love washing your hair." He turned her around. As the water sprayed over her, rinsing out the suds, he tilted her face with his thumbs under her chin to force her to look at him. When she met his gaze, he said, "I want to wash you for as long as we live, Michaela."

"No, you don't. Once we've adopted Jesse, you'll want out of this marriage." She shook her head and tried to back out of his grasp, but he held her.

"When will you stop running from your feelings? I know you love me. When will you let yourself believe that I love you? Yes, I made a horrible mistake when I left with Andrea. I didn't know your ultimatum was out of fear, not out of lack of love for me or your disbelief in my dreams. I know your father hurt you by leaving, and his lack of love is what you're afraid of. I'm not Lemont. I may have left you once, but I was so wrong." She closed her eyes, and he rubbed his thumb over her cheek. "Michaela, I'm sorry I didn't come back. But I'm here now, and I will never leave you again. Even if this mess I've found myself in ends up costing us Jesse--"

"Don't say that." She opened her eyes and gripped his forearms. "We will get him, Gabe. We have to."

He took a deep breath of the steamy air scented with Jasmine. "Then we will." He made sure the soap was out of her hair and kissed her gently on the lips. "C'mon, let's get out of here before we use all the hot water and turn into prunes."

* * * *

Micki wrapped a fluffy towel around herself. She couldn't look at Gabe, as doing so would only complicate her sudden desire to never let him go. Could she believe him? Did he truly love her?

A sudden sensation of hunger made her nauseous. She put her hand over her belly and flinched. "I hope I didn't give you this virus I have."

He stopped rubbing a towel over his hair and looked at her. "What virus?"

She turned toward the sink and squirted some leave-in conditioner into her hand. As she worked it into the ends of her hair, she shrugged and met his gaze through his reflection in the mirror. "A stomach bug. Nothing to worry about. I think the stress I've been under hasn't helped either."

How could she feel so comfortable with him? Although they'd been married for nearly a month, they hadn't acted much like a married couple. But this morning felt so normal, like they'd always been together. Was he right? Was she sabotaging their love by comparing Gabe with her father? Gabe was nothing like Lemont; so, why did she expect him to do the same things?

"I'm sorry about all this. I never should have been with her." He came up behind her, wrapped his arms around her, and buried his face into her neck. "But I was at a low point in my life when I met Lydia. I was missing you so bad and needed to forget." He turned her around and held her face as he searched her gaze with eyes so fierce her heart raced. "I've never stopped loving you, Michaela. I met Lydia on what should have been our wedding anniversary. I know that sounds perverse, but... God, I'm sorry."

The thought that he'd hook up with someone else on a day she usually spent riding the range alone hurt, but how could she truly judge him? Hadn't the few times she'd had sex since their breakup happened during that same week of July when they should have been celebrating their wedding anniversary? She feathered her fingers into his wet hair. "I forgive you. To be honest. I've done the same thing once or twice."

His eyes narrowed and she felt his body go stiff.

*So, he's jealous. Good.* She didn't elaborate about her past flings and was glad he didn't ask her to. "But we do need to figure out what to do about this mess. The adoption hearing is right after Christmas."

"I think as long as we stay together and show the world we are united we should be okay. I'm not the first celebrity to be accused of fathering a child." He found his razor in the top drawer of his side of the double-bowl vanity. As he lathered his face with shaving cream, he rinsed the blade in the sink and started to shave. "Next week I'm heading to Vegas for the show I have scheduled to do there during the NFR. I'd like you to be by my side as we'd planned."

She was having a hard time concentrating on anything but how damned sexy he was standing at the sink shaving with nothing but a towel wrapped around his waist. To distract herself from watching him, she stood at her side of the vanity and applied her moisturizer. "I planned to be there. I'm having lunch with some of my barrel racing friends." She glanced at him again. His muscles and sinews moved under his broad shoulder as he stroked the razor over the dark growth on his jaw. She wanted him.

Now and forever.

"Gabe, I do love you. I've always loved you." She set the lotion bottle on the counter and took a step toward him. "You were right about me being afraid of your leaving to chase your dreams all those years ago."

He wiped his face and turned toward her.

"I've always believed in you. You are so talented. It's not that I didn't want you to sing. I didn't want you to go to Nashville because I truly believed you would decide you didn't want me." Her sinuses burned. She sniffed and wiped at the offending moisture in her eyes. "So, I pushed you away. I still am afraid you'll get tired of me."

She leaned against the countertop and took a deep breath. Was she ready to truly commit to him? He could still leave, which scared her, and her stomach turned over at the emptiness the thought caused her. She laid her hand over her belly and met his gaze again.

"I will never tire of you." He brushed his warm fingers over her face. "You don't have to be afraid."

"It's hard not to be. But it's also too hard to fight my feelings. I want a life with you. I may not like some aspects of your fame, but I know how important it is to you."

"Michaela." He cupped her face between his big hands and stared so intently into her eyes, she got the impression he was trying to show her his soul. "I'd give it all up if you asked me to."

His declaration sent a jolt straight to her heart. Could she believe him? "Gabe. I'd never ask you to do that. I know how much you love singing and performing."

"I do. But I'm not twenty-four any more with something to prove with nothing but the clothes on my back." His voice rumbled through her and sent a chill up her spine. "I've proven myself, and I have more money than I'll ever spend. But it cost me the most important thing in my life, and I will never choose it over you again."

He swung her up into his arms and kissed her with a blazing passion that set her on fire. She wrapped her arms around him as he carried her out to the bed where he laid her down and made the sweetest love to her.

Two hours later, they entered the kitchen with Gabe holding her from behind. He'd found her ticklish spots and teased her relentlessly.

"Gabe!" she squealed between peals of giggles as she struggled to escape him. "Stop!"

He stilled in tickling her and held her close from behind. In her ear, he whispered, "I love to hear you laugh. You're so beautiful, I can't believe you're all mine. I'll love you forever."

She turned her face to look over her shoulder at him. "Be patient with me. That's all I can ask. I love you, too."

He kissed her hard on the lips, but the soft chuckles coming from the doorway of the laundry room had them stepping apart. Flo wiped her hands on a dishtowel and watched them with humor glinting in her dark eyes. "Good morning, Mr. and Mrs. McKenna. I'll get you your breakfasts."

Micki cleared her throat and adjusted her blouse that Gabe's tickling had set askew. "Thank you, Flo."

"We were wondering if you two were planning on spending the whole day in bed." At the kitchen table, Momma leaned away from the newspaper she was reading. Her face brightened with a wide grin. "It's good to see you both finally came to your senses."

# Chapter 18

A week later, Micki stood in the wings of the stage at the MGM in Las Vegas watching her husband do what he loved to do. He'd told her earlier that the Garden Arena had sold out at nearly 17,000 people. She'd agreed to go out onto the stage with him for his last song, since most of the people in the audience were in Sin City for the NFR and she had been a rodeo champion. No one had beaten her times since she and Beau set the record two years ago; she was something of a legend, though she hated the idea. Now, the reality of going out on stage with him before all those people made her queasy stomach churn.

Taking a deep breath, she concentrated on settling the twisting snakes in her belly. She started doubting she had a stomach virus two days after Thanksgiving when she realized she'd missed her period. She was two weeks overdue, which for someone who could have set her watch to her monthly cycle only meant one thing. Damn, why had she thought about *that now*? Closing her eyes she focused on Gabe's voice. First, she had to get through this; then she'd worry about a possible pregnancy. She could do this.

Gabe finished his crowd pleasing, bad-boy song, "One Night Rodeo." As the crowd cheered, a stagehand approached her. "Mrs. McKenna. It's time."

"Thanks." She pasted on a smile, stepped out from the shadows, and waved at the crowd. Her focus settled on Gabe's smiling face, and she made it across the stage without mishap; then he wrapped his arm around her waist and pulled her close.

He moved his wireless microphone away from his mouth and whispered close to her ear, "You okay?"

She nodded and glanced at the crowd but couldn't see much except for the bright lights. As she fought the urge to squint, she fixed her smile firmly on her face, measured her breathing, and calmed her skittish nerves. How could Gabe be so comfortable out here? Hell, why on earth did he want to do this?

Micki wasn't sure she'd ever understand his need to sing in front of people, but she accepted singing gave him the same thrill barrel racing had her for so many years. She missed riding and probably always would. Gabe had mentioned that she could go back to the rodeo, but she hadn't made any decisions. She still managed the ranch, and her mother still needed her despite Flo's excellent care. Besides, once they adopted Jesse and if she were pregnant, she'd have a lot to keep her busy.

Gabe jolted her out of her thoughts. "I'd like for you to meet my beautiful and amazing wife, Micki Finn McKenna. Two-time barrel racing champion and holder of the fastest time in the history of the NFR!"

The crowd cheered, and she focused her scattered mind on how wrong his calling her Micki sounded. She'd asked him to introduce her by her rodeo name. No one but Gabe called her Michaela and that's how she wanted to keep it. Years ago, she'd asked him why he always used her given name, knowing it bothered her that he did. At the time he'd laughed and simply told her it was her name. But last night after they'd made love she asked him again.

*He stroked her back as she curled up next to him, resting her head on his shoulder. "I know you don't like it because Lemont gave you the name, but I call you Michaela because I love your name. It sounds beautiful, and I think it fits you better than Micki. Michaela is a strong name, and you are one of the strongest people I know." She shifted to meet his gaze, and his glorious smile didn't fail to dazzle her as it always had. He kissed her softly and feathered her hair off her face. "But mostly I call you Michaela because I'm the only one who ever does, and it's... Well, as odd as this sounds, think of it like a nickname or an endearment."*

After his admission, Micki never wanted anyone else to ever call her by her given name. He made a name she'd long hated seem special. If she was honest with herself, she'd always loved that he called her by her given name because he made it sound beautiful.

Gabe forced her attention back into the moment when he indicated that she should take a seat on a stool she hadn't noticed before. She stiffly sat and forced her attention on steady, calming breaths to slow her racing heart and still her churning stomach. Maybe she'd been wrong to agree to Gabe's crazy idea of bringing her on stage.

"As many of you know, Micki and I were high school sweethearts." He winked at her and smiled as his fans responded by applause and whistles. As he turned back to them, he reached for his guitar, which rested in a stand next to him. He sat on the stool beside her with the guitar in his lap. "Every love song I've ever penned has been about my one true love."

A new sensation competed with the other ones Micki was trying to calm down. Her sinuses burned with a prickling of tears. Did he really mean this? She knew songs like "Heaven Tonight" had been about her, but all the rest?

He smiled at her. "This song has never been recorded, but I wrote it a long time ago. It's called 'Chasin' Dreams.' " He started strumming his guitar, and the band joined in with a melody she'd never heard before. Gabe started singing about wanting to be famous and chasing his dreams, but what caused Micki to finally leave all her doubt behind was when he sang about giving it all up to be with her. Her love was all he ever wanted or needed.

The first tear rolled down her cheek and she quickly brushed it away. Had she been the one who screwed things up the last time? If she'd just trusted Gabe, their pasts would have been so different. She'd never make that mistake again.

*"I'll go on chasin' my dreams, baby,*
*But you're the song in my heart."*

She sniffed as he finished the last words of the song.

Not caring about the thousands of people watching them or that whatever she said would be picked up on his microphone, she leaned forward and smiled. "I love you."

He shifted his guitar and leaned toward her. Before their lips met, he said, "Forever and always."

\* \* \* \*

Gabe woke up the next morning to an empty bed. Michaela's side was still warm. He glanced at the time on his phone and grinned. Last night had gone better than he'd ever thought it could have. After the show, an ESPN reporter asked them for an impromptu interview. Gabe had been ready to refuse, but Micki agreed. Together they answered the reporter's questions about their relationship, and for the first time, they were honest. They weren't pretending anymore. Although their time on stage had been planned, he never expected her to publicly admit that she loved him as she had.

Sounds coming from the bathroom of the luxury suite had him getting out of bed. He went to the door when he heard the retching noise again. Once there, he leaned in and listened as his concern for Michaela had his heart beating faster. She was throwing up--again.

"Michaela, are you okay?"

The toilet flushed; then the water turned on at the sink.

"The door's open." Her words were raspy, making him more worried than he'd been in a long time.

He entered to find her staring at a rectangular package on the vanity top. As he wrapped his arms around her from behind, he sucked in a breath. "Michaela?"

She met his gaze in the mirror. "I don't think I have a virus."

Gabe got his surprise under control, and a warm tingling thumbed through him--excitement. "You haven't taken the test yet?"

She shook her head and turned in his embrace. "From what I've been reading about the onset of morning sickness, I must have gotten pregnant the very first time we made love. Gabe, I'm sorry. I know the last thing you probably want right now is for me to be pregnant."

He kissed her softly and hoped his excitement shined through his smile and eyes. "Let's not put the horse before the cart. Take the test." Next to her ear, he whispered, "And I'm praying it's positive. I can't wait to start a family with you."

She pulled away and her gaze turned watery. "I want to have a family with you, too."

"Not that it matters, but you said you were on the pill." He'd heard contraceptives could cause miscarriage when taken during early pregnancy. The thought sent an icy chill through him as he remembered when she'd lost their first child. "I hope you stopped taking it."

"Yes, but I stopped about a week after I missed my period. I should have guessed what it was before then, but with everything going on, I didn't notice that I missed my cycle. I hadn't been sick at all the first time I was pregnant." She searched his gaze. "Maybe my being sick is a good thing. It means my hormones are right. But you're right; let's not jump to conclusions." Looking over her shoulder, she picked up the pregnancy test, then took a deep breath and grinned up at him. "Okay. Let me pee on this and we'll go from there."

His cellphone buzzed. Who wanted a piece of him *now*? He pointed over his shoulder with his thumb. "I'll let you do your thing while I answer the phone."

He hurried to the bedside table where his phone lay. His heart skipped a beat when he read the caller ID. He connected the call, and without preamble, asked, "Daniels, have you found her?"

"Yeah, boss," replied, with a heavy Southern accent, the PI he'd hired to search for Lydia after her disappearing act in Nashville. "She's renting a place here in Vegas on North Wallace Drive." Daniels gave him the address. "She's not alone. Joel Horner is with her."

He must have misheard. "That's my bass guitarist. Are you sure?"

"As sure as the grass is green and the sky is blue." The roar of an engine sounded over the phone. He pulled on a pair of jeans and reached for a T-shirt. "What's going on?"

"Damn idiot," Daniels mumbled. "I'm watching the house from across the street and one of those jacked-up pickups just went by. Are you coming to pay the woman a visit?"

"Yeah. Keep me--"

"Shit!"

Gabe stilled at Daniels's surprised oath. "What?"

"You ain't gonna fuckin' believe who just showed up."

Gabe pulled his shirt over his head and spit out, "Who?"

"Your father-in-law. Lemont Finn."

Gabe let out a breath and watched as the bathroom door opened. Michaela held the pregnancy test up as if it were a trophy and grinned from ear to ear. He met her gaze. If Lemont could be tied to Lydia they would have every advantage regarding Jesse's adoption. She lost the smile and lowered the test as she headed across the large room to him.

He touched her face and said into the phone, "Thanks. Stay where you are and keep me posted. I'm on my way."

"Who was that?" She searched his face.

"The PI. He found Lydia." Before she questioned him, he grinned and prayed she had the answer he suddenly wanted to hear. "Well, you gonna keep me in the dark? Or am I going to be a daddy?"

She wrapped her arms around his neck and laughed. "We are going to be one confusing family once we adopt Jesse." Then she leaned up to kiss him. "Yes, you're going to be a daddy."

He let out a whoop as joy hit him square in the chest and made it difficult to breathe. After picking her up, he spun her around and kissed her hard. When he set her on her feet again, he told her about his phone call with the PI.

"Lemont? Was Daniels sure?" Michaela's excitement shone in her eyes. "God, Gabe, if we can prove he's involved with her, we will have everything we need to swing the judge in our favor."

He hugged her close and grinned. "That's my idea. Now, I have to go."

She backed out of his arms and headed for the closet. "You aren't going anywhere without me."

He didn't like the idea of Michaela going with him, but he knew better than trying to stop her. Resigned, he sat on the edge of the bed as she got dressed. "Okay, but hurry. I don't want her to bolt before we have a chance to talk to her."

\* \* \* \*

Gabe and Micki parked their rented BMW down the street from the squat, single-story that looked as if it were weighed down by years of neglect. Most of the buildings in this part of Las Vegas were modest, single-family homes tucked in on small lots. The house at the address they'd been given had a flat roof and cracked, sandy-colored stucco. It was a small dwelling with a splotchy thatch of dying yard in front. An older model Chevy Cavalier was parked in the carport and a late model BMW Joel had rented sat in the driveway. Parked on the street was a sporty Lexus, which had to belong to her father. The front of the sad house contained only one window with a slashed screen over it and a door that might have been painted bright red at one time but now was a dull orange-brown.

She took a deep breath. "What connection do you think Joel has with Lydia?"

He shrugged and pulled the key from the ignition. "I think he's the kid's father. And I think he's in on this plot. Remember the party in Cheyenne?"

"How can I forget?" She met his gaze, but she couldn't see his eyes. The brim of his hat shadowed the top half of his face.

His jaw clenched as he turned to look out the windshield again. "Joel set that party up. Lydia said she was there visiting her mother. Daniels found out her mother lives in Dallas and has no connection to Wyoming. But Joel's family owns a restaurant in downtown Cheyenne. I think she was there with his family."

She couldn't keep the surprise out of her expression. "You think he'd betray you like that? He's your friend."

"Joel is my employee. Nothing more. He and I have had our share of disagreements on music. He still thinks he's a hard rock musician. I keep him in the band because he's one of the best in the business. But, yes, the thought that he'd betray me makes sick to my stomach." Opening his door, he glanced back at her. "Now I want to know what he and Lemont were scheming with Lydia."

The PI stepped out from behind a privacy fence next door. Dressed in the uniform of a public works employee, he held out his hand to Gabe, who shook it. Daniels smiled at Micki with a nod of his head.

"Is Lemont still in there?" She rested her hand over her upset stomach. Not eating this morning hadn't done her any favors.

"Yes. I think your bass player has a gun." Daniels turned to Gabe. "I'm not so sure you should barge in there."

Gabe turned toward her. "I want you to go sit in the car and call the police. I don't honestly think Joel would shoot someone, but I'm not taking the risk with you."

She shook her head as fear and anger warred with each other inside her. "I don't think either of us should go in there. Not if someone has a gun. But I'm not staying out here while you risk your fool head. If you go in, so do I."

"Fine. But stay behind me." Gabe hurried to the corner of the house and crouched under the open window. A dark curtain hid the inside of the room. Gabe stepped up onto the stoop to open the door when a gunshot rang out. Gabe wrapped Micki in his arms, crouched next to the window, and leaned over her. A second later, a woman's shrill scream sent a shiver through Micki, and several dogs barked at the disturbance on the sunny December morning.

"I'm calling the police," whispered Daniels, who crouched beside Gabe. "Get the hell out of here." He pulled out his cell phone, then hurried around the corner of the house and disappeared.

"Joel!" Lydia's hysterical voice caused Micki to shiver despite the warm desert air. "Oh God, you shot him?"

Micki's heart skipped a beat. Had Joel shot her father? What if he was dead? She glanced at Gabe, who, by the furrow in his brow, must have been thinking the same thing. She waited for the sting of grief at the thought of her father's demise, but nothing happened. The only emotion she felt was a strange sense of hope, which made her feel guilty.

But the feeling was short-lived as her father's voice cut through the tension. "The fucking idiot."

"You shot him!" Lydia all but screamed. "Joel? Oh... Oh, God... I think he's dead. Call an ambulance."

"He is dead. I shoot to kill. He shouldn't have been so stupid to pull a gun on me." Lemont's cold tone held a dangerous edge. "Now that the kid doesn't have a father, you are going to do exactly what I tell you to do. Let Gabe find you and agree to the paternity test. I will make sure Gabe is ruled the father."

That Lemont could kill a man in cold blood made Micki want to throw up.

"Why... are you doing... this to me?" Lydia's voice shook with sobs.

Lemont's cold laugh chilled Micki to the marrow. "Because you are a greedy slut just like your mother."

*Lemont knew Lydia's mother?*

"I don't want the money anymore," Lydia wailed over the sound of a police siren coming down one of the parallel streets. "I won't let you take my baby."

How much more did they need to prove Lemont Finn was the last person on Earth who should be raising a child?

The sound of boot heels pacing on a hard floor drew closer, then stopped at the window. The curtain pulled back as if he were looking outside. Had he heard the siren? Micki held her breath as she and Gabe huddled close to the side of the house. They both let out a breath when Lemont spoke again, and, by the sound of it, he faced away from the window. "Why did you willingly go along with this plan when I found out you made me a grandfather?"

*Grandfather?* Shock from the implication numbed Micki to the core.

Was Lydia her sister?

*Dear God!*

Mick was so stuck on the revelation she almost missed his next comment. "You wanted my money then just like your mother did when she showed up on my doorstep twenty-seven years ago with you."

"I had no choice!" Lydia's hysteria made her words shrill.

Gabe must have understood the implication, too. He pulled Micki even closer to him and kissed her temple.

Her brain seized with the information, Lydia must have been a baby twenty-seven years ago. The thought made Micki shudder. Had Lydia's mother done the same thing to Lemont as the stripper had tried to do to Gabe?

"Everyone has a choice, my darling girl." Lemont's deep voice shattered her thoughts. "After the test proved you were my spawn, I offered your mother fifty thousand dollars to take you and leave me alone, or she could take me to court. That I'd never have allowed, and she knew it. I killed one wife for threatening me and destroyed another when she tricked me into marrying her, thinking she'd sponge off me when her disease crippled her. Instead, I denied her one penny of my money. Your mother was smart to take the cash. I didn't want another worthless girl and I sure as hell didn't want one from a whore I paid to fuck."

The accident that killed Frankie's mother had long been considered suspicious. Police had ruled it a suicide; now she knew the truth. All of it. Her father was a sick monster. He thought Momma had tricked him into marrying her? He'd pursued her when he discovered she was part of the prestigious Cartwright family from Colton, Texas. Not the other way around.

The burn in Micki's sinuses was fast and fierce. There was no holding back the tears. She buried her face into Gabe's strong, warm chest and cried.

"My mother may have been a prostitute, but you are one sick sadistic son of a bitch." Lydia's voice quivered.

"Put the gun down, Lydia. I don't want to shoot you, too."

Micki looked up into Gabe's face. Lydia must have picked up Joel's gun. They had to stop Lemont. He'd kill Lydia. Gabe squeezed her upper arms and let her go. She wanted to go after him, but fear and a crippling sickness she figured had nothing to do with her pregnancy froze her to the spot between the window and the door.

Two police officers, followed by Daniels, ran around the side of the house. The cops glanced first at Gabe, who'd flattened himself against the house again, then at her before taking up positions on either side of the door. Daniels crouched under the window beside her.

"There's something you don't know about me, Daddy dearest." Inside the house, Lydia's voice shook, but the hysteria was gone, and dangerous determination replaced it. "After my mother met you she taught herself how to shoot; then she taught me when I was old enough. She swore she'd never let another man treat her like you did. You nearly killed her when you raped and beat her because she didn't want to play your sick games."

The officers pulled their guns and braced to break down the door. Down the street more sirens broke through the mid-morning neighborhood. Micki then noticed the people huddled across the street.

Inside the house, Lydia went on, "I'm not going to play your sick games either."

When a second gunshot shattered the day, the officers crashed through the door, at the same time Micki's vision blurred. She had a feeling of falling.

"Michaela!"

Nothing but blackness.

* * * *

Gabe paced the waiting room floor of the emergency department. He ignored the stares of the people sitting in the vinyl-covered chairs and was grateful the hospital's security held the throng of reporters out at the door.

"Mr. McKenna?"

He stopped and spun toward the feminine voice. His heart pounded so hard in his chest it hurt. "Yes?"

"I'm Doctor Cassidy." The young doctor, dressed in green scrubs and a white lab coat, held out her hand and smiled.

He shook her hand, surprised by the strength in the petite woman's grip. "Is my wife okay?"

She glanced at the room full of other waiting patients and family members and motioned for him to come with her. Once they were out of earshot of the waiting room, she said, "Yes. You can see her."

"Thank you." He closed his eyes and let out a breath.

The doctor led him to the room where Michaela had been taken after being brought to the hospital. Those tense moments back at the house flashed through his head and made his heart ache with the same bone-crushing fear that had frozen his blood when he'd watched Micki fall to the ground. His first thought had been that she'd been shot. The EMT on the scene assured him she'd only fainted.

He entered her room and rushed to the bed. She had an IV attached to her arm and an oxygen cannula at her nose. When she held her hand out to him, he took it and squeezed. "God, Michaela, I thought…"

"I'm fine." She gave him a wan smile.

He glanced at the doctor, who fiddled with a knob on the IV tubing. "What's going on?"

The doctor looked at him, then at Michaela with a wide smile. "You were in shock and dehydrated, but you'll be okay."

"The baby?" Michaela's voice quivered as she laid a hand over her lower belly. He rested his free hand over hers.

"The baby is fine." The doctor picked up a computer tablet and swiped the screen, then typed on it. When she looked up, she said, "Your labs are just starting to come back and show a perfect HCG level for as far along as Mr. McKenna said you are. We can do a sonogram, but I think the shock of what happened this morning is what caused the fainting spell, and it had nothing to do with the pregnancy."

"Thank God." Relief made Gabe's knees so weak he had to sit down on the stool by her bed.

"I'll let you alone now." Dr. Cassidy picked up a call button and clipped it to Micki's pillow. "Just push this if you need anything."

Michaela nodded. "Thanks, Doctor." Once the doctor closed the door behind her, Michaela turned to Gabe. "What happened at the house?"

"Lydia shot Lemont." When she widened her eyes, he added, "In the shoulder. He's also in this hospital somewhere. He's in police custody.

They're waiting for us to make a statement as witnesses to him shooting Joel."

"How're Lydia and the baby?"

"Lydia is shook up. The police took her in for questioning." He caressed his fingers over her cool cheek. "The baby wasn't in the house. She was staying with one of Lydia's friends."

"Gabe, she's my sister."

He hated the pain in her voice. "Yeah, but you don't have to think of her as such."

She shook her head and a tear rolled down her cheek. "But how can I not think of her as my sister? Gabe, I know this might sound weird, but I want to get to know her. That baby might not be your daughter, but she is my niece, and I want to be her aunt. Lemont threw all of us out like garbage--me, Lydia, Frankie." Her eyes turned fierce as she stared up at him. "I hate that man. Makes me wish my mother had screwed around on him and he hadn't fathered me."

"Michaela, Lemont Finn has never been a father to you. It takes more than biology to make a man a father." Gabe shifted to sit on her bed and wrapped his arm under her shoulders to pull her into an embrace.

"I know," she whispered and snuggled close to him. "At least, I know you'll never be like him."

"No." He kissed the top of her head and rested his hand on her belly. "I love this little guy, and you already know how I feel about Jesse."

She met his gaze and smiled. "You need to call Reese. There's no way in hell Lemont can keep him now."

He matched her grin. "Already done. He'll be waiting at the Lazy M when we get home."

# Chapter 19

Micki carried the plate of still-warm chocolate chip cookies to the living room. At the archway, she paused and leaned against the doorframe to watch her husband and nephew sitting on the floor by the massive, decorated Douglas fir. Their dark curly heads bent close as they fiddled with the ancient Lionel train engine. "Flo just gave me this plate of cookies for Santa."

Gabe glanced over his shoulder at her and smiled, while Jesse narrowed his eyes on her.

"I don't believe in Santa Claus."

Gabe ruffled the boy's hair. "Since when?"

Jesse shrugged and looked down at the train car in his hand. "Since last year. If he was real, I shoulda got what I wanted. Besides, I'm not a baby."

Micki set the plate of cookies on the coffee table and knelt on the other side of Jesse. She wrapped an arm around him and caught Gabe's gaze for a brief moment before focusing totally on her nephew. "No one ever said you were a baby, Jesse. So, you don't believe in Santa anymore. Fine." He turned his blue eyes to hers. She hated that the wide-eyed innocence was gone from them. Losing his parents had dulled it, but the mental abuse her father inflicted afterward completely snuffed it out.

Her heart ached at the stories Jesse had related to the judge last week. Lemont locked him in his closet as long as a day and denied food for such things as mentioning her and Gabe's names. He told Jesse he was the reason his parents were dead. The boy had been denied friends, and Lemont was in the process of enrolling him in a boarding school in England.

Lemont got what was coming to him. The police arrested him for the murder of Joel Horner and for a whole slew of other charges. Now, she and Gabe needed to repair the damage living three months under Lemont

Finn's roof had done to the little boy they both loved enough to slay their own dragons to protect.

Gabe squeezed her hand where it rested on Jesse's shoulder. "You know, our dad was about your age when he got this train set for Christmas."

Jesse loved hearing Gabe's tales about their father. Micki had a feeling the stories were doing Gabe as much good as they were Jesse. Although Gabe hated what his father had done to his mother when he'd cheated on her with Frankie, he still loved the man. When she and Gabe were younger, she'd envied his relationship with Sam. Having a loving father was something she'd never known.

She rested her hand on her belly. But her children would know. Gabe was already proving to be a good father figure for Jesse.

"He told me that." Jesse set the car on the track, which ran in a large circle under the tree. "He also told me that Santa brought it for him."

Gabe turned the knob on the control box, and the ten-car toy train chugged along the metal track. "Santa did." At the boy's dubious expression, Gabe shrugged and rubbed his chin. "I don't just have Dad's word. I have Grandpa's word."

"Grandpa?"

Gabe nodded and smiled. "Yep, Dad's dad. He passed away when I was just a little older than you. You're named after him, in fact. And that man never told a lie." He winked at Micki, then continued his story. "You see, when Dad was little there was a time when the McKennas were about broke. They almost lost the ranch, even. There was no money for Christmas presents, but Dad wrote a letter to Santa asking for a train set and a pony for his baby sister, our aunt Susan."

"Aunt Susan always gives me money for my birthday."

Gabe chuckled and nodded. "Yeah, she still gives me money, too. Wish she'd stop that. She needs it more than me."

Jesse's eyes widened; then he crawled around the track to fix the engine where it derailed. "You think she'd give me your share?"

Micki hid her laugh behind her hand and shook her head. "I don't think so, squirt."

"Oh, I don't know. Tell you what, next time she sends me money I'll give it to you, how about that?" Gabe pulled Micki into his lap and wrapped his arms around her.

"Okay!" Jesse had to fix the engine again.

"Why don't you tell us what Santa didn't bring you?" Micki knew Frankie and Sam had given Jesse whatever he'd wanted for Christmas.

The train set right on the track again, Jesse folded his hands in front of him and studied Gabe and Micki. "Here's the thing. Santa can't bring me what I wanted for Christmas because he can't bring babies."

Micki's heart skipped a beat. "What do you mean?"

He shrugged one of his shoulders in nonchalance, but Micki saw the disappointment in his eyes as he looked back at the train. "I wanted a little brother." He glanced at Gabe and quickly added, "Not that you aren't a great brother, Gabe. But I really wanted someone to be a big brother to. I wouldn't even mind a little sister." He wrinkled his nose. "Although girls stink." Then he covered his mouth. "Sorry, Aunt Micki!"

Chuckling, Gabe met her gaze as she looked over her shoulder at him. They'd talked about telling the family about the pregnancy. She'd been to the doctor last week and everything was exactly the way it should be. Gabe tightened his grip on her and turned back to his brother, or, as in the eyes of the Texas courts, their adopted son. "Well, see, Santa is going to make your wish come true this year."

Jesse furrowed his brow and narrowed his eyes at them. "How?"

Leaning over, Micki smiled and took her nephew into her arms. He settled against her chest. As she rested her chin on his shoulder, she said, "I'm going to have a baby."

"A baby?" Jesse turned around so fast that he pulled Micki with him. If Gabe hadn't had her wrapped up so tight, she would have plunged face first into the rambling train and probably the Christmas tree, too.

Gabe nodded against the side of her face. "Yeah, buddy. I guess he'd really be your nephew... or cousin, depending on how you want to look at it, but I think it would be so much better if you think of our baby as your little brother."

Micki rested her hand over her T-shirt and still-flat belly.

Jesse's gaze followed the motion and his brows pinched into a deep grove as if he didn't believe them. "When will he come out?"

Micki laughed and poked Gabe in the ribs. He was as bad as his ten-year-old bother when it came to insisting she was carrying a boy. "He or *she* will be born in July. So you have some time to help us come up with a name."

The boy who'd lived through too much at such a young age gave her a smile that belied his age. "I know the perfect names. We should name him after Daddy." He added as an afterthought, "Or her after Momma if it's a girl."

Micki glanced over her shoulder at Gabe. He'd be the last person who'd name a child after her sister. Leaning over, he ruffled Jesse's hair again. "Tell you what, we'll think about this some more when we get closer to meeting the little fella. Okay?"

Jesse nodded and studied them both. "I'm glad y'all got married. Momma said she wished that someday you would."

Micki's heart clenched a little with pain at the mention of her sister. She'd love to name her daughter after Frankie, at least in part--maybe Anna Frances after Gabe's mother, too. They had plenty of time to think about it. She stood up and held out her hand to him. "Your momma was a smart lady."

"Yeah." He watched the train as it disappeared behind the tree stand. "She was."

"You know, just in case Santa is real, you'd better be getting to bed soon." Gabe met Micki's gaze and smiled.

Jesse frowned but didn't argue. Instead, he stood up and looked at Gabe. "You don't lie either, Gabe. So maybe I'm wrong about Santa." He hugged his big brother. "Good night, Gabe. You're the best."

He hurried past them and out of the room as Gabe watched him. "Having him in my life almost makes up for what Dad and Frankie did to my mom." Turning his gaze to her, she was surprised to see a mistiness clouding his golden-brown eyes. "I wouldn't have him if they hadn't been together."

She rested her hand on his shoulder and gave it a squeeze. "Fate has the way of one screwed-up comedian when it comes to life."

"You got that right." He snorted and squeezed her hand on his shoulder. "You know, that sounds like a great line for a song."

"Just don't give me credit if you write it." She headed for the door. "I'm going to tuck Jesse in. I'll be back."

Twenty minutes later, she entered the living room again. Gabe had turned off all the lights, except the Christmas tree lights, and was seated on the couch in front of the warm blaze in the fireplace. He grinned at her as she settled in the crook of his arm and snuggled up next to him.

"What time are Lydia and the baby supposed to show up tomorrow?"

She shrugged against him. *Yeah, Fate had one sick sense of humor for making her and Lydia Greenhow sisters.* "She said before dinner. I'm still not sure about this. She's one messed up girl. And it's a little weird finding out you have a sister that you didn't know about."

He kissed her temple and rested his chin on her head. "Why did you invite her here for Christmas dinner?"

"Because she is my sister and because I want to get to know Natasha. I'm her aunt. They're Jesse's family." She moved so that she could meet his gaze. "Gabe, does having her around bother you? I mean you and her were... ah... together once."

"Does it bother you?" He feathered his fingers over her face.

"Not as much as before." She wrapped her arms around his neck and shifted her body so that she could straddle his thighs. "But let's not talk about any of that." She kissed him hard on the lips.

When he broke the kiss, he held out a small black velvet box. *What the devil?* She narrowed her eyes on him. "What did you do?"

He shrugged and opened the box. Lying on the satin inside was a simple platinum engagement ring. "Um..." She wiggled her left hand and the indecent sparkler dominating her ring finger. "I think we burnt that bridge. I'm yours for better and for worse."

"That you are." Gabe took the ring out of the box. "But I want you to have my mother's ring back. It belongs to you."

She glanced at the beautiful diamond he'd put on her finger when he proposed to her after they'd lost Jesse's custody case. As obnoxious as the seven-carat diamond was, she had grown to love the ring. She wouldn't ever part with it. Meeting his expectant gaze, she held out her right hand. "I would love to wear your mother's ring, but I'm not giving up on mine."

He slipped the ring on her right ring finger and grinned. "I wouldn't have it any other way, Mrs. McKenna." Then he stood, shifting her into a bridal carry. "Now, I'm taking you to bed. I know what I want Santa to bring me."

She giggled as he carried her through the room and up the stairs. "And what's that?"

"You." His smile turned deliciously wicked, and she shivered as he whispered in her ear, "I want to make love to you until neither of us can move."

# Meet the Author

Although Sara Walter Ellwood has long ago left the farm for the glamour of the big town, she draws on her experiences growing up on a small hobby farm in West Central Pennsylvania to write her contemporary westerns. She's been married to her college sweetheart for over 20 years, and they have two teenagers and one very spoiled rescue cat named Penny. She longs to visit the places she writes about and jokes she's a cowgirl at heart stuck in Pennsylvania suburbia. Sara Walter Ellwood also writes paranormal romantic suspense under the pen name Cera duBois.

Please visit her at
www.facebook.com/sarawalterellwood.ceradubois

http://www.twitter.com/sara_w_ellwood
http://www.sarawalterellwood.com/blog/
https://plus.google.com/u/0/102888788054405451480/posts

http://www.goodreads.com/author/show/6869635.Sara_Walter_Ellwood

Be sure not to miss Sara Walter Ellwood's sequel to Heartsong

Heartland
Read on for a special sneak peek of the next book in the Singing to the
Heart series!

Learn more about Sara Walter Ellwood at
http://www.kensingtonbooks.com/author.aspx/29486

# Chapter 1

Emily Kendall was tired of life-changing events. She'd had enough. But God or whatever fate controlled the universe wasn't done fucking with her life. "Are you sure? Hell, it's been weeks since I've even seen my husband, let alone had sex. Maybe the test was wrong."

She'd heard many life-changing words in her twenty-two years of life. The first had come when she was only fourteen and discovered superstar country singer Seth Kendall was her biological father. A few weeks after that revelation, the man she'd grown up loving as her father had shot her real dad and planned to kidnap her to sell into sex slavery.

Since then, a lot had happened. She'd become famous. Most people would even argue she was more famous than her dad, who helped her get her first record deal when she was barely fifteen. She broke sales records set by some of the best singers in the business, won countless awards, and sponsored everything from acne creams to jeans.

When she was three months shy of turning twenty, she'd met the British pop star Fabian McPhee. They'd collaborated on a TV special for the CMT network. He was fifteen years older than she was, mega famous, and super sexy. A month later while she was on tour in Australia, he'd asked her out to a nightclub.

That night had been full of firsts. Fabian introduced her to what would become her drugs of choice--cocaine and gin. Then, she'd lost her virginity to him. She'd thought she was in love. He was like no one she'd ever known. Despite her parents' outrage over their tabloid-crazed, whirlwind relationship, only two months after that first date they were married by Fabian's drummer, who happened to be an ordained minister from some online course he'd taken.

The medical director of the facility sitting across the wide, gleaming oak desk leaned forward and clasped his hands. "Your blood test isn't wrong. You are pregnant."

"Fuck." She was on a birth control shot, but she'd forgotten to get it. The last time she'd seen Fabian had been about six weeks ago. They'd had sex, but she thought he'd used a condom. She couldn't remember much of the event, like most of their two years of married life together. They'd split up ten months ago, but neither of them had gotten around to filing for divorce or could resist an occasional tumble in the sack or getting high together.

Not able to sit still any longer, she stood to pace the length of the posh office and folded her arms tightly around herself. She'd only been here for three days and already wanted to get the hell out of the medical facility. "How far along am I?"

Dr. Barton slid his finger over the screen of the computer tablet on his desk. "According to the history you gave the nurse who checked you in and your hCG level…" When she furrowed her brows trying to remember what the letters stood for, he clarified, "Pregnancy hormone. You would have to be six weeks."

She closed her eyes and took a deep breath. Her skin was too tight and hot. A coating of sweat caused her fingers to stick together, and she wiped her shaky hands on her jeans. Turning toward the window, she stared out at the woodland park surrounding the Fernwood Rehabilitation Center. In the past three years, she'd checked into the facility's drug and alcohol program to sober up three times, and each admission had been against her will. She didn't belong here because she wasn't an addict. So what if she went a little too far this last time and was booed off stage? The venue, if the college auditorium could justify that name, sucked anyway.

This news was the very last thing she needed to hear. She turned and vigorously rubbed her arms, really needing a hit right now. The desire for a line of coke brought to mind another issue. She remembered when her mother had been pregnant with her brother five years ago she wouldn't even take Tylenol for her headaches. Did she honestly want to know the answer to what all the coke she'd snorted could have done to her baby if her mother had been afraid to take something as harmless as over-the-counter pain pills? But she had to know if she'd harmed her child. "Do you know if the baby is okay?"

Dr. Barton stood to come around his desk. He leaned his backside on the heavy oak edge and folded his hands before him. "I don't know. Emily, there is a chance your baby will be born with problems. You are an addict." He held up his hand when she started to protest. "No, I'm not listening to your rationalizations. You've got to stop the drugs."

"I can quit. I have before."

He took a deep breath that made his shoulders rise, then fall. "And yet here you are again. Why were you admitted this time?"

She needed to get the hell away. "My manager has gotten a little too big for her pants." Maybe she should fire Trish Russell for talking her into even thinking about this place again. Trish had been her manager for three years, ever since she was promoted by her father-in-law and took Emily on as one of her first clients. She considered Trish one of her few true friends, but, sometimes, the older woman was a pain in the ass.

She spun on her heels, which made her lose her balance as dizziness whipped her world out of control. Grabbing the back of the chair to keep from falling over, she tossed over her shoulder, "I think we're done here."

"Emily, I'll let you go as soon as you tell me why you are here."

She stopped halfway to the door. If she didn't answer him, he'd only follow her. Letting out a long breath, she stared at the white-painted ceiling. "I'm here because I was too high to sing."

The past five shows were a blur. Nothing fun or amazing about any of them. No fans waiting for her to autograph their T-shirts. But then again, when was the last time she took time to talk to her fans after a show? When was the last time she did anything special for her fans? Once upon a time, she'd put on massive productions in front of stadiums full to bursting with screaming, adoring fans.

Her last tour hadn't even sold out to rundown opera houses and college auditoriums. In the early days, she'd arrange spontaneous private showings for more fans than had showed up for her current tour. She'd simply leave a date, time, and place on Twitter and a hundred or so of her fans would show up for a show. When had she last sent one of her own Tweets? She knew Kelly, her assistant, did all of her social media crap for her these days.

"I'm here because my record label said if I don't sober up, they're cutting me."

"They aren't happy with you?"

She shrugged and started pacing again. The cagy feeling was getting worse. "No. My last album is six months past due its production deadline. But I can't help that all the songs suck."

"Why do they suck?"

Turning, she met the doctor's steady gaze. She wanted to tell Dr. Barton that her label and her manager had sabotaged her by giving her shit songs, but she couldn't say that. Were the songs bad? Her father's old friend, pop superstar Amanda Lang, had written four of them and had given them to Emily as a gift, despite three other singers wanting them. The other two songs she'd recorded were from an award-winning songwriter, and they, too, had been sought after by the best in the business.

She blinked when the realization hit her. The songs weren't the problem nor were the studio musicians playing on the record. She was. "I don't want to talk about my career. I want to talk about my baby. Is there any way we can determine if it's okay?" As she laid her trembling hand on her belly, she silently prayed to a God she doubted would listen to anything she asked of Him. *Please let my baby be okay.*

Dr. Barton looked down at his hands, then went back to his big leather chair and sat. "I'd like you to meet with a colleague of mine. Doctor Marcella Summers is an OB/Gynecologist who specializes in babies born to addicted mothers. She'd be the person who might know the answer to your question."

She faced the wide windows again, but the early summer day and the forested mountains surrounding the center weren't what she saw. "Okay."

How was she going to handle a baby? Hell, she could barely take care of herself. What if it had a major problem from all the crap she'd put into her body?

She closed her eyes and fisted her hand over her belly. Dear God, what would Fabian say about the baby? He'd warned her when they got married he didn't want any kids. Would he blame the pregnancy on her as he had so many other things over the past two years?

"Emily, I don't know an addict who easily admits they are one." Dr. Barton broke into a tirade of questions, bombarding her. "By your own admission, you use cocaine at least four times a week, but most weeks you use it every day."

She glanced over her shoulder at him. He swiped his finger over his tablet, the paused to read more of her medical record. "In August twenty-eighteen, your father admitted you to Fernwood when he found you passed out on your tour bus. According to your blood toxin levels, you were only a snort of coke away from overdosing; then in June of last year, you were admitted after falling off stage and breaking your arm. Again, your blood work showed dangerous amounts of cocaine and alcohol."

Although she snickered at the memory, the humor was short lived, and she sobered. That had been her last stadium show. Tabloid and entertainment reporters hounded her after her release from Fernwood. Fabian's own career also took a nosedive when he was arrested for drunk driving and resisting arrest. The two of them and their antics had been a favorite topic in even mainstream news since then.

He cleared his throat and folded his hands in front of him. "Your blood results weren't as toxic this time, but if you don't make an honest attempt to get clean and stay clean, not only will you jeopardize your child, you're going to end up dead."

The truth smacked her hard in the gut. She was an addict. Up until now, she never believed she was one. She used coke and drank gin because she liked them, not because she couldn't live without them. But the reality was she used drugs to deal with life and all of its shit.

Would she have become so screwed up if she'd never met Fabian McPhee? Or had she been destined to a life of drug use due to her messed up childhood and sudden super stardom? Who knew? But in that moment, she hated the man who first introduced her to drugs and destroyed so much of her life. Her country music career was dead, and the fans she'd garnered when she put out a total pop album a year and half ago at Fabian's insistence had abandoned her. She hadn't spoken to or seen her parents, except from a distance at award shows, since her marriage. Since severing her ties with her mom and dad, she hadn't seen her four-year-old brother. Now, she was responsible for developing a tiny baby who may very well end up paying for her lousy judgment.

She turned and met the doctor's patient brown eyes. The man had to be a saint to manage the care of spoiled brat idiots like her. "Okay, Dr. Barton. I'm an addict. I use coke because I can't deal with life." She squared her shoulders and let out a breath. "There, I admitted it. Set up the appointment with the OB. But there's something else I'd like you to do." One of the conditions of admission into Fernwood was no contact with the outside world except for approved visitors on an extremely short list. "I want to file for divorce before I tell Fabian about the baby."

The doctor's surprise registered in the slightest widening of his eyes. "If that is want you want."

Emily couldn't help the snort as she sat in the chair in front of the desk again. "Oh, don't be coy, Dr. Barton. I know you've been hoping I'd ditch Fabian McPhee since the first time my father dragged my sorry ass into this place a year and a half ago." She looked at her hands as a rare moment of clarity blasted away the rosy sheen she'd painted over her life with her husband. "My counselor is right. Fabian and I do have a crazy love type of relationship. He might not beat me, but he has made me dependant on him by making me an addict."

For the first time in years, she felt relief flood over her. She smiled and met the doctor's eyes again. "For my baby and for me, I have to get away from him."

Emily laid a t-shirt in her suitcase and turned at the knock on the doorframe. She smiled at the willowy woman as she entered the room. "I'm glad to see you. I'm ready to get out of here."

The eight weeks she'd been a resident of the rehab had been the longest time she'd ever stayed, but once she finally faced her demons and committed herself, she didn't want to leave until she was free of her addiction.

Trish tucked her medium-length bright red hair behind her ear and glided into the room. "Paul isn't happy about postponing your record," she said, referring to the CEO of Midland Records. "But I convinced him that you needed a break to get completely sober and to stay that way."

Emily laid another T-shirt in the case. Her reason for being at Fernwood was no secret, but the only person outside of her doctors who knew about her pregnancy was Trish. After telling her, Emily asked her to convince her record company to push her production deadline to sometime in the future. "He doesn't suspect anything, does he?"

Trish sat on the overstuffed chair in the corner of the modest room. "No. I made a convincing case about your wanting to finally quit the drugs. He's not happy, but he's also glad."

Emily moved the suitcase off to the side and sat on the edge of the bed, facing Trish. "Has Fabian signed the divorce papers?"

"Yes. Reese is filing them today, in fact." Reese Goodwin was a family friend and a Nashville divorce lawyer. "Your divorce should be final by the end of the month."

She closed her eyes and took a deep breath full of relief. Although she hadn't demanded anything of Fabian, she feared he'd delay signing the papers to end their ill-fated marriage. "Thank God."

Trish leaned back in the chair and folded her hands in her lap. "When are you going to tell him about the baby?"

With a shrug, Emily stood, opened a dresser drawer, and pulled out a stack of bras. As she set them in her bag, she said, "I'll set up a meeting with him sometime before I go home to Texas."

She planned to get out of Nashville before she started showing. At almost four months pregnant, she knew she was on borrowed time.

"How do you think he'll take the news?"

Emily went back to the drawer and took out a stack of panties. "Hopefully, he won't take the news well and will leave me and my baby the hell alone."

She swallowed at the thought of her baby never knowing her father like she hadn't known Seth, but Fabian wasn't a good man. Despite being nearly forty years old, he still partied too hard and didn't take much seriously. He'd wasted most of his own fortune and a large portion of hers on fast cars, drugs, and lavish parties.

"He didn't fight about selling the penthouse and the mansion?" Three months after they were married, Fabian talked her into moving out of her downtown craftsmen home she bought on her eighteenth birthday and into buying a twenty-million-dollar estate outside of Nashville. The place was too big and flashy and put a considerable dent into her savings. He'd convinced her by arguing that as two successful entertainers, they were expected to live in such extravagance. Besides, he swore he'd pay his share of the cost. Instead, he conned her into buying a penthouse in Manhattan. He spent a lot of time there, but she hated New York and preferred to live in Nashville.

"He wants the penthouse." Trish pulled her iPad out of her purse. The woman never went anywhere without the thing. "But he's okay with selling the Nashville property and letting you keep the money from the sale if he can keep the penthouse."

"I'm glad he wants the penthouse so badly." Emily closed her suitcase and smiled as she turned to face Trish with her hand over the slight swell of her belly. "Because then I have a bargaining chip to keep him away from us."